the Sperm engine

Stephen Greco

the sperm engine

Stephen Greco

Green Candy Press

The Sperm Engine
by Stephen Greco
ISBN 1-931160-11-2

Published by Green Candy Press
www.greencandypress.com

Cover and interior design: Ian Phillips

Some proper names and details have been changed in the
following autobiographical essays to protect the privacy of
living individuals.

"The Last Blow Job" first appeared in *Flesh and the Word 3*; "Field
of Vision" previously appeared in *Obsessed: A Flesh and the Word
Collection of Gay Erotic Memoirs*; "Good with Words" first
appeared in *Advocate Men*; and *The Penguin Book Of Gay Short
Stories*; "Simon's Chair," "My Favorite Porn Star," and "The Sperm
Engine" previously appeared in *Afterwords: Real Sex from Gay
Men's Diaries*.

Printed in Canada by Transcontinental Printing Inc.
Massively Distributed by P.G.W.

TO KJ

Acknowledgments

For their advice and support I am indebted to Alan Brown, Victor Bumbalo, Deborah Gimelson, Max Harrold, Scott Heim, Andrew Holleran, David Leavitt, Michael Lowenthal, Mark Mitchell, David Mossler, Tim Myers, Felice Picano, Angela Rizzuti, and Donnie Russo. Thanks, also, to my parents and to my sister and her family.

Fondly I acknowledge the editorial guidance of the late Robert Ferro, Michael Grumley, Barry Laine, Boyd McDonald, Robert McQueen, John Preston, and George Stambolian,

Special thanks to my publisher, Andrew McBeth.

Contents

How I Met My Boyfriend
(The Real Story)

A few weeks ago my boyfriend, KJ, and I attended a small dinner party given by our friends Federico, an interior designer, and his wife, Renata. I call them "friends"—and I do hope we get to know them better as time goes on—but Federico is really only a colleague of KJ's, and this was the first time we'd all done anything together socially. They know KJ and I are gay, of course, and probably assume that like a lot of the gay men they know we are amusing and respectable. And KJ and I are that—sort of.

There were six of us in all. The other couple, a man and a woman, both artists, aren't married but live together with children. Dinner took place in the large apartment that Federico and Renata have just bought (and with massive good taste decorated) in a newly renovated warehouse in the Dumbo section of Brooklyn, on the East River, between the Brooklyn and Manhattan Bridges. Over coffee Renata told us the story of meeting Federico through a client of his. She thought Federico arrogant at first, then ran into him again a year later, only to discover he'd been secretly smitten with her. We all agreed the story was charming and then—I knew where this was going—the other couple told how they had met. It was at an artist colony.

"And you boys?" Renata asked sweetly. "How did you meet?"

I bumped knees with KJ under the table.

"At an outdoor party," I said. "We ... liked each other immediately."

"Oh, that's nice," Renata purred. "Some people do just know."

Dumbo is just down the hill from Brooklyn Heights, where KJ and I live. He was silent as we walked home. "Look, there's Squibb Park," I said, pointing to a large building that abuts the park, two blocks away. "Maybe I should have just pointed out their window!"

I was trying to be chipper, but KJ was irritated. I had lied about how we met. In the elevator, going down, he had complained that this was especially unnecessary in the case of Federico and Renata, who are so worldly. I knew he was right, but I had been afraid they might not understand the, shall we say, special context of KJ's and my meeting. Given that everyone has different ideas of amusing and respectable, I never know what to say until I know people better.

Here's how KJ and I really met:

One night, eleven years ago, I was out walking, looking for sex, on the Promenade. That's the quarter-mile-long pedestrian walkway cantilevered out over the two-level expressway that Robert Moses built in the '50s at the edge of Brooklyn Heights. With spectacular views of lower Manhattan, across the East River, the harbor, and the Statue of Liberty, as well as of the Brooklyn Bridge, the Promenade is popular with strollers and sightseers during the day. By night, until midnight or 1 A.M., it's used mainly by heterosexual couples sitting quietly, talking or making out. After that, until dawn, the Promenade and the streets nearby become places where men prowl for hook-ups with each other. These are gay men and straight men, and those who describe themselves—at least for a season or two, until experience renders the word obsolete—as "in between." In fact, I've often seen guys show up there in their cars at 2 A.M., alone, after having dropped off the nice Bay Ridge girls they were sitting there with, parked, an hour before, when the gay foot traffic would have been just picking up and probably hard to miss, between kisses. Men meet out there and either go home to have sex or do it in a nearby alleyway, on a dark stoop, or between parked cars. (Vans make the best shadows!) The area has been this way, more or less, depending on mayors and health crises, for as long as I have lived in the Heights—the last twenty-six years.

It was a warm August night around three. After making my usual south-to-north sweep of the Promenade itself I decided to look in on Squibb Park, a small, cyclone-fenced cul-de-sac of a playground just beyond the north end of the Promenade. Built as an afterthought on an artificial terrace of land fifteen feet below side-walk level and set into the slope where the expressway dives under a land bridge then ramps into Brooklyn, the park can be a danger-ous no-man's-land. There's only one way in and out of it, a foot ramp leading down from the sidewalk, which means that a gang of kids or even one crazy guy can trap and attack a lone cruiser in the park, as always happened once or twice a summer before the rela-tive peace of the Giuliani years. The lighting there is dim, which means that on a night when nobody attacks, the playground can be great for sex. At times when a critical mass of men converges, it turns into the largest, open-air backroom in the world.

I stood at the top of the park, at a parapet overlooking it. There were twenty or so guys inside, walking, sitting, standing—enough to make it safe to go in—so I walked down the ramp. I was wearing one of my "I'm easy" cruising outfits: an old pair of baggy, combat-green, button-fly chinos, from which most of the buttons had fallen off, no underwear, and a brown leather flight jacket, open, with no shirt. Inside the park, there was slow move-ment in the shadows around the periphery, on or near the benches: men getting blown, men lurking nearby hoping to join in or be next. Right in the middle of things, out in the open, were two guys: one standing, the other kneeling in front of him, sucking cock. I joined them and, receiving no signal to back off, smiled my approval and whispered, "Yeahhh ...." While scanning peri-odically for signs of danger or opportunity, I watched the balding head of the cocksucker piston in and out greedily on the other guy's cock. I took out my cock and started playing with it—I was very in need of head myself. Then the guy pulled the head off his cock and pushed it onto mine. The mouth was awesome, all alive and responsive. *This cocksucker's technique is fantastic*, I remember thinking: effortless deep throat with no gag, a real hunger for cock and/or cum that I could sense with my whole body. Definitely one of the best ever. Instantly the cocksucker responded to the *interest* (and probably the size and shape) of my cock, groaning in delight and kinda scooting over toward me on his knees so he could get better traction.

The other guy, either finished, bored, or perturbed, just zipped up after a second and walked away. For a moment I felt guilty. Then I went right on receiving one of the most spectacular blow jobs I would receive all summer outdoors. After I shot, I put my wet cock back in my pants, said a brief good-night, and started up the ramp. I made a mental note of what the cocksucker looked like, hoping to see him again: short, on the heavy side, but adorably handsome, with a big, sparkly smile. At the top of the ramp I turned back to see that he'd followed me up, so we talked for a minute.

For a balding guy, he's awfully young, I thought. Maybe early twenties.

"That was awesome," I said, stroking the short curls on the back of his head.

"Sure was," he said brightly.

"I hope we can do it again soon."

"You live 'round here?"

"A few blocks away."

"Me too."

"So I'm sure we'll see each other again."

We had nothing to write with. He told me his number and I told him mine. He headed home and I stayed out for another hour. When I got in, there was already a message on my machine, saying "Thanks again" and repeating the number. I called early the next evening. He came over and we started a sexual friendship that lasted as such for four years—while he continued to see his then-girlfriend, then broke up with her, then came out, joined a gym, shaved his head, changed careers, and started seeing me socially as well as sexually—until we realized we were in love.

Yup, that was KJ, the man whose family I will visit this Christmas and who will visit mine, the man with whom I've cuddled nieces and nephews, shopped for bedding and appliances, shared medical and financial concerns; the man whose eyes I want to look into forever. I'm perfectly happy that we met the way we did, but I know there are people, even sophisticated and liberal friends of mine, who are uncomfortable hearing about recreational gay sex. Even if they don't consciously think of it as a sin or a crime, they can still remain bound by the unconscious belief that it's dirty or dangerous. AIDS didn't help matters. The possibility of finding everlasting love in a dark alleyway doesn't ring true for a lot of people—possibly because they're not used to hearing from those of us who have met this way.

But how to talk about it? This is a real issue for KJ and me, because we socialize in so many different circles. I have sometimes found myself, after speaking too enthusiastically in straight company about late-night life on the Promenade, being shown the caution that's applied to people who get drunk at other people's houses and bump into artwork. Not that this is a gay-straight issue. I've also met gay men who exercise the same caution. I've always stereotyped them—ridiculously, considering how willingly I act like them in other company—as uptight faint-of-hearts, unwilling to challenge that habit of keeping certain cruising practices private or even secret. They—maybe all of us—suck in and peddle "respectably" coded behavior and speech like addicts.

Respectability has its dangers. When I met KJ I had been a widower for four years. I had been looking for the next boyfriend in all the wrong places—lunches, dinners, parties. Friends set me up with guys they'd describe as "a really great catch." During those years I dated most of New York's most eligible gay bachelors—handsome, successful, independent, available men who worked as book editors, lawyers, entrepreneurs, choreographers, producers, models. I had a lot of pleasant conversations and, now and then, some sex that was pleasant though never mind-blowing. But on the so-called respectable route I met no one as comfortable with his body and its needs as my late boyfriend had been. I began to worry that my first relationship was some kind of fluke. I wondered, sadly,

if I should cross "mind-blowing sex" off my list of marriage require-
ments, as I suppose untold billions of people have done since the
dawn of mass media (which is only when word of mind-blowing sex
began reaching vast numbers of people who would probably never
have it). Thank God I had always cruised outdoors, even by agreement with my first boyfriend, during the entire fifteen years we
were together! Thank God I continued doing so while he was dying,
and afterward!

Thank God for KJ! One of the things I love most about him—
perhaps the thing that made me fall *in love* with him—was his
faith in sex. It's a major blessing. Instead of fearing and hiding his
erotic needs, he followed them like a beacon into a happier and more
fulfilled stage of his life. Now I'm trying to use KJ's example as my
own little beacon. It wasn't shame per se that kept me from sharing our story with Federico and Renata, KJ suggested. It was my
fear that providing my idea of a "full context" for our story—the
larger narrative of American gay sexual practice since World War
II, real estate development on the Brooklyn waterfront, Robert
Moses and the inadvertent development of male sexual space in
New York, Eros and civilization—would bore people. That rang a
bell: I know I tend to overexplain. What KJ recommended is that
the next time, instead of telling the wrong story, I should just bash
off and tell the right one, in a way that's entertaining and not
pedantic—pedantry being held in lower esteem than public cocksucking by almost everyone.

I got my chance to do this a few nights later, at a party given by
KJ's friend Julia, a gutsy, fun-loving socialite originally from Tulsa,
and her rich, slightly annoying industrialist/art collector husband,
Milton. In their Sutton Place penthouse, with a spectacular view of
the East River, there were twelve of us. It wasn't such a surprise
when the subject of how people met came up, since it has often
been reported in the gossip columns that Julia is a former beauty
queen who swept Milton off his feet at a two-day-long "caravan"
party given by a media mogul in Morocco. With relish, Milton

repeated the whole story—how Julia appeared in his private tent one night in a caftan specially made by Lacroix, how a guitarist played behind a latticework screen while the two of them made love on silk pillows. "She was just an Oklahoma oil girl," he said, glowing with obvious affection and possibly amused that in the years following the party in Morocco vast amounts of money and a talent for joining the right boards had secured Julia a place among New York society wives.

Other stories were told. One couple met in Cannes, as journalists covering the film festival; another, skiing in Kashmir.

Milton didn't exactly ask me how KJ and I had met. He demanded to know, in an aggressive manner that reminded me why I don't like him very much. KJ beamed me a hopeful look.

"Let me start," I said, "by quoting Foucault on the eternal flow of power among the ruins of ancient Rome ..."

"I knew it," Milton said. "You met at the baths!"

There were some giggles.

Milton thought he was being funny, but I didn't like his tone. And of course I didn't like being interrupted.

"It was at a party, Milton," I said dryly. As it happens, the last time I was in Rome I had cruised the forum, late at night. There were a few things to say about alfresco Roman sex that would have given my story an amusing, respectable air, I thought, not to mention context.

"What kind of party?" Milton roared.

"A summer party, I think." I felt like I was under attack.

"You *think*? Steve, we need details. Where was the party? What was the very first thing you felt from KJ? What attracted you to him?"

KJ's eyes widened. Was he really expecting to hear a vivid description of his cocksucking technique?

"It was in the Pines, actually. On the deck of a friend's house, on the ocean. A benefit for something."

"Nothing wrong with the Pines," Milton said, oddly satisfied.

"We used to go out there for years when we had the boat."

Later, Julia found KJ and me in the library, looking at a piece of sculpture.

"You boys were absolutely lying through your teeth, weren't you?"

KJ made a mock grimace. He had just forgiven me for doing so.

"I could tell," she laughed. "So what's the real story?"

"Julia," I said, "KJ was sucking off some guy in a park one night, when I came along and pushed the other guy out of the way. It was love at first blow job. The end."

"That's priceless!" she said.

"Sometimes it's hard for me to tell the story in public."

"Milton can be such a bully," Julia said, lighting a cigarette. "You know, the truth is even naughtier about him and me. They always refer to me as a beauty queen, because for a year, when I was eighteen, back in Tulsa, I was 'Ms. Black Gold.' But when I was in college in L.A., I was with an escort agency, one of the top agencies in the world. Isn't that so much naughtier than just being loose? I was essentially paid to be at that party in Morocco. Though once I met Milton,"—she sang the words—"'love walked right in ...'"

"He knows very well that I'm no more ashamed of my escorting than I am of my degree," Julia continued. "I learned plenty about men, like how their sexual habits fit with the rest of their personalities—which is one reason why I've been able to make this marriage work."

She took a long draw on her cigarette, then exhaled.

"Is it any wonder that most marriages explode? Women know as little about men as men do about women."

"Do you tell people?" I asked.

"If it comes up, sure," she said. "I even called one of the gossip columnists once, to correct him after he repeated the beauty queen thing. He never printed the truth. Probably because no one cares. And if anybody does, screw 'em, honey. We've all got loads of nicer friends."

In the living room afterward, I wound up talking with an entertainment lawyer who represents several well-known movie directors and producers. She told me about the house she and her husband had recently bought in Connecticut, just ten minutes from the town where they'd both grown up. They'd met on a high school hayride. I didn't know that people really went on hayrides.

"And you said you and your boyfriend met on Fire Island?" she asked.

"Um, you know what? We met right over there," I said, pointing out the window, in the direction of Brooklyn Heights. "About a mile down the river. It was actually in a park—a little playground of a park built by Robert Moses ...."

Simon's Chair

I don't know what the fuck is up with Simon. For some reason, he's not returning my calls or e-mails—which is hugely inconvenient, because I don't know how I'm supposed to get the cum out of my body.

I've come to depend of the little cocksucking "salon" that Simon hosts over at his apartment on weekends when his boyfriend is out of town. Sure, I like the guys I meet over there— the very hot, straight- and bi-identified janitors and schoolteachers and bartenders and doctors and high school soccer coaches whom Simon meets mainly online now, as well as the plain old gay guys who have been referred to Simon by other serious throat addicts. Moreover, especially now that my relationship with KJ is getting serious, I like the convenience of a fairly strings-free opportunity to get my nuts drained, which provides a welcome supplement to my program of combined romantic lovemaking, group-scene sex sport with Chelsea muscle boys, and masturbation. Simon's like a doctor. He just gets the cum out like a pro, without shame or social fuss. With him on his knees in front of me, I feel safe, relaxed—and I like being in the company of other guys who enjoy the same kind of recreation.

Simon lives a few blocks away, and I've been seeing him once or twice a weekend for many years. There are often a few other guys over there, either sitting in that legendary chair (lined with a fresh towel for each occupant), or resting on the sofa between rounds, or just arriving or leaving. When Mark came back to town a few weeks ago, I knew that Simon was occupied with him alone. That's the way Simon and Mark are together. Though Mark is married and has a grown daughter, I know that Simon is totally boyfriends with him in some corner of his mind, though Simon's been with his real boyfriend, Joe, since the '70s (when Simon was this superhot number and Joe was a Marlboro model or something). Simon gets off on: (a) those real-life Army stories Mark tells, (b) the fact that Mark is more completely addicted to having his cock sucked than anyone else on the planet, and of course (c) Mark's nine fat inches and his explosive skull-fucking technique, which always propels him out of the chair at the last minute, all poppered up, grunting gutterally, knocking furniture out of the way, to pin Simon to the wall, clamp down on his head with both arms, and pump a load down his theatrically gulping and choking, though nonetheless supremely capable, mouth hole.

But Mark's gone back to England and Simon's still not returning my calls. I need to figure out why and get back in that chair. Like many of the fifteen or twenty guys who will be invited to sit there during the course of a weekend—to have a cocktail, to smoke a joint, to watch videos "over the top of Simon's head," as it says in his online profile—I usually achieve nirvana in my sessions with Simon. Though I'm not at all explosive. Unlike Mark, I stay seated during my blow job. Simon's talent and dependability have granted me the space, as it were, to contemplate and explore in depth dimensions of sensation and physical response that had previously been unclear to me, even though before KJ (who is great sex) I had had a lover for fifteen years (who was also great sex).

Simon is something else. He's not particularly hot by the superficial standards of contemporary gay party culture. I always tell guys to whom I try to pimp Simon that he's a "Grizzly Adams" type—6 foot 3, maybe 220 pounds, husky (not fat), forty-something, dark hair with a bit of gray. I mean, he is a handsome guy, but to me, the most attractive aspect of Simon is that, like some kind of spiritually advanced sex Buddha, he is so fully uncondescending to this cock hunger of his that he has set up his whole life accordingly. (And his scene is not about drugs, either. He did a lot of Quaaludes and cocaine in the '70s, but doesn't do that stuff anymore.) I was not attracted to Simon the first few times I encountered him, late on summer nights years ago, in a nearby neighborhood park where lots of guys, straight and gay, would go to get their cocks sucked and hook up with other guys cruising in cars. He would nod hello, then watch as I hooked up with somebody; he would maybe hook up with somebody else, nearby, and attempt to indicate in that wordless, universal gay language of outdoor cruising that if I liked good head I would certainly be interested in meeting him. Then one night, Simon mimed an invitation I couldn't refuse. I had gotten out of a cab at the park, smashed after some party, and needed to dump a load big-time. No one else was around, and there was Simon on the other side of a fence of metal bars. He sank to his knees and braced himself by grabbing the bars. It was right out of a porno movie set in prison. I figured, *What the hell? Might as well try it out.*

I went nuts with ecstasy during that first session, and I make it a point of some kind of erotic philosophy to say that the pleasure has been amplified tenfold each time we've done it since. I have learned that such multiplication is possible for the human body and mind. And Simon and I have done it together almost five hundred times, I was informed by Tony, another of Simon's customers. Tony and I have gotten friendly after running into each other occasionally at Simon's. (He'd be resting on the sofa, freshly de-loaded, playing idly with his soft cock, whenever I arrived; I'd get in the chair, start up with Simon, then see Tony restiffen, get up from the sofa, and bring his cock over to my chest, where he'd make his piss slit "suck" my right nipple. I swear he can get his cock, which is huge, to make a true sucking action. This has happened a number of times.) Tony told me that Simon once confided that he keeps count of everyone who visits him and how many times they shoot. The historian in me was relieved to hear that some part of Simon's extraordinary practice is being recorded, but the mouth hound in me was a little disappointed to learn that I still hadn't deposited a thousand loads of sperm in his body.

It was Tony who suggested that Simon might be punishing us

both for not taking our pimping responsibilities seriously enough. Simon hasn't been responding to Tony's calls or IMs either. Simon likes being pimped. Actually, he kinda demands it. From Tony, Simon has wanted a picture of that huge cock, to help lure other guys over—but Tony is slightly phobic about having his cock photographed and has repeatedly refused. From me, Simon has wanted a hook-up with a long-haired bodybuilder who's been connecting with me and KJ. Now, I send a lot of men Simon's way, but the flip side of his admirable single-mindedness about all this cock traffic is that he doesn't seem to understand that the bodybuilder is just not interested in him—I did ask once—and that there's nothing I can do about it.

Anyway, I suppose this'll blow over in a week or two. Little tussles that have arisen between me and Simon in the past—like the time I let somebody else suck my cock at his house: a big no-no!—have always been resolved soon enough. This connection between us is too strong to lose.

Among the Believers

When Mack got home from Bed, Bath & Beyond, around noon, there were five messages on his machine. All were from members of the circle, confirming they would be coming to that evening's ceremony. By six, he knew, there would be at least four more confirmations from the core group. And since two members had said they were bringing guests, it looked like there would be about twelve men in all.

Just the right number, Mack thought. Less than ten feels thin, and at around fifteen a cockworship ceremony can begin to feel like an orgy, which it most definitely is not supposed to do.

OK, he thought, *What needs to be done and how much time do I have to do it?* Mack still thought like an actor-slash-director, even now, in his mid-fifties, years after audience and theater industry indifference had sent him into semiretirement. The show must go on, and tonight that meant selecting music, deploying candles, repositioning the coffee table, and laying down the new king-size flannel sheet he had bought to serve as drop cloth.

People would arrive around nine-thirty. Promptly at ten Mack would turn off the phone's ringer and call the ceremony to order. The whole thing would take around an hour and a half, following a sequence that Mack had created himself. It began with an invocation and "unveiling," proceeded through discussion and blessings, and culminated in a round of "offerings." There was always a different nominal celebrant—a guy whose cock was the focus—but it was always Mack who led the ceremony, as a kind of deacon. Through commentary and chanting he tried to share with the others, without getting hokey about it, a vision of God that emerged for him during the process. Some got it, some didn't—probably in the same proportions as at any Christian service. Afterwards, if people wanted, they could play together free-form, or, as had been happening recently, move to a neighborhood bar for a few genial cocktails. Mack was thinking of doing next month's ceremony a little earlier in the evening and serving dinner afterward.

In his tiny, ground-floor West Village studio apartment Mack tried to create as warm an atmosphere as possible, one where his guests could feel protected from the outside world. Just as he did when he commanded theaters full of people and ordered the lights to go down and the curtain to go up, he did his best to enable members of the circle to break their connections with daily life as the proceedings began, to relax their bodies so attention could be focused on other realities. Yet Mack could still smile during moments of the ceremony when the sound of pedestrian footsteps or a car horn intruded from the outside world. He savored the idea that while ordinary people were rushing around doing ordinary things, just ten feet and a brick wall away, his group of twelve men were sitting naked in a circle on the floor after a busy day of managing staff, negotiating deals, editing manuscripts, sculpting metal, or operating machinery, their thighs and knees and feet pressed together, their cocks in their hands.

This time, Mack would be bringing important news to the circle. He'd just bought a new place upstate. In four months, for the summer solstice, the circle would be invited there for a ceremony in the country, perhaps even outdoors.

Getting a new place upstate had been a dream of his ever since his lover, Stuart, had died. Two years before, as Stuart's long and costly fight with terminal cancer was drawing to a close, Mack had been forced to sell their large Upper West Side apartment and the country place in Stone Ridge that they had owned for thirty years. Stuart was a writer. Mack had met him in the late '60s, when both were students at Cornell. They had moved to New York together and began collaborating on their own shows in cafés and small theaters. In the early '70s they'd had a big hit, which brought them a lot of attention and allowed them to buy Stone Ridge. A kind of gay *Hair,* loaded with nudity and messages of communal love and pantheism, the show started off-off-Broadway, moved to Broadway, won a Tony, toured successfully, and was bought by Hollywood and made into a movie. The movie bombed—its message warped by a closety director—and Mack and Stuart never managed to create another hit. Stuart was against returning to "alternative" themes, possibly because his prominently social Presbyterian family had been so horrified by the show, and audiences didn't respond to anything else he and Mack did. Gradually a million dollars leaked away, in living expenses and on much-publicized projects that went nowhere.

For a while after Stuart's death, Mack's finances were dire. But the moment that payment of Stuart's life insurance policy was arranged, Mack had begun looking for another place upstate. And it had taken him only a few months to find just what he was looking for: a small, year-round camp on fifty acres in Krumville, with plenty of trees and a stream.

Mack didn't want, and anyway couldn't afford, the prosperous queen's country home they'd had before: an historic stone house, painstakingly restored, with a terrace, garden, and heated barn. The new place was comprised of an undistinguished but serviceable main house plus six scattered cabins that could comfortably sleep thirty people. It would be more a base of operations than a luxury retreat, and also a source of income. Mack had been talking to the directors of several gay organizations about renting the place out for various social, spiritual, and theatrical activities.

Krumville signified a return to some of the revolutionary ideals Mack had espoused at Cornell—ideals that were as spiritual and artistic as they turned out to be sexual. What Mack envisioned for Krumville was the sort of tribal experience he realized back then felt more normal to him than family life. He had once hoped that this kind of experience would fill a large part of his life—though he used words like "movement" and "men's commune" to describe it in those years, not "cockworship cult," the terminology he preferred to use today on the Internet. Stone Ridge and that whole social whirl of celebrity houseguests never felt like his life; that was more

Stuart's thing. Most of the trappings of celebrity felt unpleasantly superficial to Mack, and Stuart's death had finally freed him from connections to most of the people they knew during their boldface years. In fact, over the last two decades, during which he "fell from the heights of pop culture fame," as an interviewer from *The Advocate* had recently put it indelicately, Mack felt he had come back to normal, and that was fine with him.

Stuart's loss, moreover, had the inexplicable effect of thrusting Mack back psychologically into his early twenties, when he and Stuart met. He'd heard about this effect from other widowers. Suddenly, Mack was seized by young-man feelings again, and the result was an unforeseen wave of midlife spiritual growth. As he drove around upstate looking for a new place, inspecting property after property, Mack was engulfed by a flood of flower-power memories and they stuck in his head like mantras. The most powerful was of a day during the summer of '67 or '68, when Mack and other nature worshippers went swimming in the nude in an Eden-like reservoir near Cornell.

Actually, the reservoir experience was about more than just swimming. It meant walking around naked in the woods, greeting friends and strangers, and possibly having sex with them. You drove out to the reservoir grounds, parked your car near the gate, and climbed over the fence. You left your clothes in a tree or stuffed them into a knapsack. On a warm, sunny day you'd see scores of people out there, walking or sitting around, alone or in groups, talking or silently meditating, sometimes kissing or even masturbating or fucking—the sex was straight and otherwise. An improvised code of outdoor etiquette enabled all of this to happen smoothly. You were expected, when walking around, to produce loud enough footfall to alert others to your presence. You tread swiftly enough past people to give them privacy but slowly enough to allow them to invite you to join them, if they wanted. You observed but you didn't stare. You could be half erect but you had to smile.

For Mack, the reservoir was also a place to explore a new kind of spirituality that had been liberated in him by his friend Ellie, who was the first person ever to speak to him of witchcraft and other pagan traditions (and the first person ever to feed him brown rice with tofu, shredded carrots, raisins, and nuts as a meal). Often Mack would go to the reservoir to meditate and masturbate. He resisted calling this prayer, as some did, or linking it to gay liberation, then newly in the wind. He thought that any answers to questions about what, precisely, he was doing would arise from the practice itself.

One day, Mack was walking on the upper path to the dam when he came across a muscular man with milky-smooth skin and a blond crew cut, lying back on a boulder overlooking the stream, naked except for beat-up Keds tied low with broken laces. He recognized the man as a well-known varsity wrestler he'd often seen dating popular women—a man one of his friends once described as "a god." The wrestler was absently playing with his cock and continued to do so, as if lost in reverie, as Mack padded by. Mack caught the guy's eye and smiled, and moved on. A glance back revealed the guy sitting up a bit and actually jerking harder, looking in Mack's direction but not precisely at Mack. The guy would have stopped altogether if he'd been uninterested, so Mack said hello.

There was no answer, but no change in posture.

"Great place, isn't it?" Mack continued. "You can breathe. People are free. You can really feel a part of nature."

"Uh-huh."

The wrestler's body was right out of the sexy swimwear ads Mack used to surreptitiously rip out of the back pages of *Esquire* as a boy, in the barbershop, while waiting for a haircut.

"Can I ... sit down?" Mack said. He made his voice sound as casual as possible.

"Sure."

The wrestler glanced at Mack's cock as if to make sure it was hard and that Mack had begun to handle it. Then looked away again, toward the stream. Mack knew this wouldn't be the kind of automatic fuck-and-suck encounter he was just then learning the rules of, as a member of Ithaca's newly consolidating gay scene. He put his knapsack aside and lay back on the boulder, close to but not touching the wrestler. They were parallel, though at sightly different levels, and the composition of figures and stone might have reminded an observer of one of those dramatically posed, outdoor photographs of modern dancers from the 1930s and '40s, at Jacob's Pillow in the Berkshire mountains, in which the lithe male bodies seem to express—understandably, given male roles in the society of that time—just a bit more exultance than the lithe female bodies. The same observer might have described Mack and the wrestler exulting in response to great natural beauty.

"Mmm, that breeze ..." Mack said.

"Yeah," said the wrestler.

The wrestler was pumping his cock faster; Mack his, slower.

"The earth," Mack drawled.

"The earth," said the wrestler.

"It's heaven!"

"Heaven."

Soon the wrestler shot his load onto his contracted abdominals, his eyes nearly closed, body stiff, legs apart, feet pointed almost balletically, the veins at the top of his ankles pulsing. Mack waited until he saw the wrestler's cum, a small blob of which landed near, then leaked into, the sweat pooled in the guy's navel. Then he slid himself off the rock into a semi-standing position, so his own cumload could fly out onto the ground where, in the nature worship scheme of things, it might do some good.

The power of that memory had been blunted for years by the pressure of a "promising" career. But the memory was back now, and blazing, and it had led him to take nature very seriously again, which led to cockworship. Mack had read all the men's spirit literature, researched the history of faiths and heresies, investigated group sex scenes, attended masturbation seminars. All of it felt wrong—either too social or too clinical, too traditionally religious or not religious enough. Then it dawned on him. If he wanted to develop this idea of his, he was going to have to script, cast, direct, present, and star in a vehicle himself.

The phone rang around three. It was Thorpe, Mack's attorney. "Bad news, I'm afraid," Thorpe said. "It's Celia. She's decided to contest the insurance payment after all."

"Damn!" Mack said.

"She says she wants to quote-unquote do something for Stuart."

"What does that mean?" Mack said.

Celia was Stuart's sister, and the marketing director of a small but successful cosmetics company based in midtown. Comfortably ensconced with her husband and three children in a nearby suburb, Celia had never been particularly close with Stuart and Mack, even during their lush years. But during Stuart's illness she had appeared several times at the hospital to pray and occasionally probe into legal and financial matters. Stuart had weakly explained to her, from his bed—when he should have been able to expect comfort from Celia instead, Mack thought—that his and Mack's relationship was like a marriage, and that all his assets and benefits would go to Mack. Thorpe had created documents to this effect, he said. Celia had seemed to acknowledge all that and, when Stuart died, made only minimal appearances at the funeral and memorial service.

"I thought she agreed she wouldn't contest," Mack said. "Anyway she can't, right? I mean, the language is ironclad. I'm the sole beneficiary ...."

"Look, I get the sense that we're dealing with someone who's a bit hurt," said Thorpe. "The will held up and the policy is quite clear. She probably wouldn't win a suit, but we don't want the nuisance, do we?"

"No! I'm closing on the place in Krumville this weekend!"

"Then let me talk to her attorney. I have an appointment with him tomorrow at eleven. I'll call you the moment I'm done."

Mack went out to buy candles. Poisonous thoughts of Celia gave way to the pleasure of seeing scores of gay men on Eighth Avenue pushing the season by sporting tank tops even though it was still barely 60 degrees. Pair after pair of glistening cannonball gym delts muscled past each other on the sidewalk, scarcely less brilliant than the sun. The parade looked both ridiculous and noble.

At 18th Street Mack ran into Joe, a darkly handsome Italian guy in his forties who was serving as the evening's celebrant. The publisher of a major monthly fashion magazine, Joe had turned up one night several years before on AOL, in the "ritualJOm4m" chatroom that Mack created from time to time. The two had become friends.

"We'll be twelve tonight, I think," said Mack.

"Good. I can't wait," Joe said. "I'm just going over to make myself presentable." Across the street was a so-called "full service" salon, which in Chelsea meant that besides a shampoo and haircut you could get your cock shaved and butthole waxed.

Joe had served as celebrant in past ceremonies. He had a great body—hairy, thick, and hard; worked out but not obsessively so—and a wonderful cock, long, chunky, and lavishly uncut. But what made Joe such a great celebrant was his approach to sex—as a necessity in everyday life, like food, water, and air. Sex for Joe was good, as in "good and evil." He was very centered on his cock and happily gave himself over to its needs as often as his duties at the magazine allowed. Even if he weren't in pursuit of some particular sexual adventure at any given moment, he found he could go about life in a erotically hungry way, and that this hunger tended to amplify his curiosity and imagination and emotional openness about everything, including career and friendships. This approach fit well with the role of celebrant as defined in the cockworship "Hagaddah" that Mack had written (and, with characteristic industry, illustrated, printed, and bound). The fruit of a month-long research into several possible religious and therapeutic models on which to base his new ritual, Mack's Hagaddah, with footnotes and appendices, called for the celebrant to embody "the holiness within the hot."

Didn't it make sense to try and make something holy out of the desires that powered the parade on this nine-block stretch of city street—out of the gay talent for adoration and instinct for finding worthy subjects of it? Shouldn't we look for God through any kind of adoration and if we do—if we believe we *can*—won't we find a side of Him? These were some of the questions Mack had asked himself during his research. As Joe and Mack stood there talking on the sidewalk, men passed them with looks and smiles indicating that either or both would absolutely do for something transcendent that moment, or that night, or the next time. Mack recognized some of these men as former one-on-one cockworship partners he'd hooked up with either via the Internet or the phone lines—smart, creative, well-adjusted men whom he suspected weren't going farther with this particular brand of sexual recreation because, like Mack, they hadn't found anywhere to do it besides random living rooms and bedrooms. Circuit parties and backrooms were temples more to commerce than to eros or spirit. Men kept expressing to Mack their interest in some different kind of group event or institution devoted to cock; they kept calling and e-mailing. Mack was amused to think it was probably his instinct as an entertainer, stirring deeply perhaps for the first time in decades, that had inspired him to respond to this demand by developing the ceremony. And he wondered now if it were this instinct that was quietly urging him to explore how much farther the ceremony could go.

That night in New York was clear and fragrant. A light breeze hinted at the summer to come. Citizens were rushing home to have dinner, watch TV, read to their kids, prepare for the next morning's meeting. In a fluorescently lit lobby of an apartment building in the West Village, several men arrived simultaneously and were allowed in by a tired doorman who was indifferent to the casual vibe they were trying to project.

Mack was setting out another ashtray when Joe arrived. Four men came in with him: three who had taken part in a previous ritual that Mack hosted, plus a new guy, Andrew, a sexy, skinny twentysomething with a buzzcut, wire-rim glasses, and a Scottish accent, whom Mack had never seen before.

"You're the last ones, boys. Everybody's here now," he said. "You know what to do."

The others were already naked, sitting in a circle on the floor. A joint was being passed. While the newcomers stripped and seated themselves, warm greetings were exchanged and newcomers introduced. The area immediately surrounding the circle was aglow with candlelight. Golden flesh tones predominated. Furniture and collectibles receded into shadow. A John Hassell CD from the early '80s, *Possible Musics*—Mack's favorite—played softly in the background. At the crown of the circle was a chair, and next to it a stool.

The joint made a final round, then was put aside for later. Joe took his place in the chair, still wearing his boxer shorts. Mack alighted next to him, on the stool.

There was a wave of clasping hands and shoulders, of brushing thighs and squeezing forearms, as Mack began to speak.

"Our bodies are for the universe, our bodies are for ourselves, our bodies are for each other ..." It was a short invocation he'd delivered on several previous occasions.

After the invocation Mack asked everyone to take hold of their cocks and look at them—everyone but Joe, whose moment would come later. The eleven cocks were as different from each other as the men displaying them. One was thick and stumpy, uncut, and brownish except for slight bruises that were probably the result of excessive recent vacuum pumping. It looked tough and feisty, ready for anything. Another cock was skinny and pinkish-white, with an incandescently red, bulbous head. It looked almost too hard and had an alarmed look about it—like one of those plastic thermometers that pops when the turkey's done. Stroke styles were equally individual. Some cocks were being pumped, others squeezed. One cock, rather long, curved to the left with a twist, and looked, especially as kneaded by its owner, as if it were writhing to get somewhere. Another rested, semisoft, on the thigh of its owner, who stroked and teased it like a beloved pet. And the balls—there were shaved balls that dropped low, obviously heavy and warm, with great baroque swags of lushly smooth, buttery-looking scrotal draping; others that were barely descended, crinkled, and bristling with whisker-like hair.

Andrew's cock attracted a lot of interest, since it happened to be the largest: it had a long, thick shaft, veiny but not alien, and a magnificent, proportional head. Mack knew that those in the habit of sucking and getting fucked—all of his guests, since they had all grown up gay in the modern world—had instantly calculated the volume of Andrew's cock as off-the-scale.

Outside the circle—say, in the corner of a sleazy bar, late at night—any of these cocks, if pulled out of a fly as an invitation, might strike you as interesting or not interesting. "Here," Mack told the assembled group, "each body is your own body." Mack always urged members of a circle, in the plainest, non-titter-producing language he could muster, to temporarily put aside their individual standards of physical attractiveness; beyond these standards lay the possibility of a powerful kind of communion. Several of them knew this already, having attended previous ceremonies and experienced that sudden ton-of-bricks hunger for a stranger they might not have looked at twice, outside. They were the ones who were the greediest *and* most generous.

Each man stood in turn and spoke briefly about his own cock. The idea was to try to amp this hunger as much as possible.

"I've always been proud of being hung," one said, "of showing off this fucker to other men and seeing their reaction to its size ..."

"My cock is my lover," another said. "Since I can't French kiss it I let other guys do it, then kiss them ..."

"I need to get drunk on cock as much as I can," said a third guy. "My cock, other guys' cocks, *any* cock, *any* time ..."

After they'd gone around the circle, Mack cued Joe, who stood and pulled his cock and balls out of his boxers. The shaft was soft, but thickening. He moved about the circle, handling himself with the seductive confidence of someone who'd performed this kind of stand-up act many times before.

"I guess I've always known I have a show cock," Joe said quietly, "and the responsibility to share it and let as many people as possible be inspired by it ..."

All eyes were on it. All breathing seemed regulated by it. During this, the blessing round, Joe gave each man a chance to come face to face with his freshly shaved meat, to kiss it, fondle it, sniff it, lick it, or suck it lightly. At the end of each interaction, Joe pressed the underside of his cock head onto the man's forehead and drew it off between the eyes.

Some were stroking themselves up to a certain point of arousal. Others were holding back, having built up to the point and attempting to stay there. Guided by Mack's gentle verbal cues, their rhythms were converging into a single masturbatory pulse.

"Keep it going, keep it going," Mack said. "Stay with me."

Once Joe had seated himself again, Mack began the round of chanting. A voice well trained in the theater came in handy here. In wording the chants and developing sequences of them around themes—"I live for cock," "We live for cock," "Cock is life," etc.—Mack worked improvisationally, the way a DJ or even a square dance caller does. He tried to reflect and amplify the energy of the room, to find the direction in which people were willing to go, then go there. But Mack knew that chants can sound silly until their hypnotic resonance tranquilizes the critical mind. So he made an effort, when leading chants, to let his body and face, as well as his voice—his whole instrument, as they say in the theater—express full commitment to the moment.

He usually started with a simple, back-and-forth, call-and-response pattern. Then, when the momentum got going, he let the responses repeat more lengthily, jumping in at the sixth, eighth, or tenth repetition with a new variation.

"Me and my cock. Me and my cock. Me and my cock ..."
Very quietly, at first—almost whispering. Candles glowing.
"My cock and me. My cock and me. My cock and me ..."
Voices joining. Hassell's blunted horns wailing.
"You and my cock. You and my cock. You and my cock ..."
Glances locking. Volume building. Precum gleaming.

"Look at my cock. Look at my cock. Look at my cock ..."

A spicy scent rising from the candles. Drips of sweat.

"*My* cock. *My* cock. *My* cock ..."

Bodies beginning to rock in unison.

"Cock for *me*. Cock for *me*. Cock for *me* ..."

For some, an underground choir, suddenly audible, voiced primal hymns.

"*Listen to cock ...*"

All were listening. *Listen*.

"*Believe cock ...*"

Men believing. *Believe*.

"*Obey cock ...*"

Ready to obey. *Obey*.

"*Cock is God is cock is God is cock is God ...*"

It was a thundering whisper.

"*God is cock is God is cock is God is cock ...*"

A glance at the clock showed more than an hour had passed since they had first sat down. It was time for the offering.

With a tap on the knee Mack invited Joe to choose the guy whose offering he wanted. Joe looked at Andrew, who nodded.

"You're returning power you've borrowed from the source," Mack said quietly. "Just give Joe whatever you have for him—your mouth, your hand, a song ...."

Wordlessly Andrew strode over to Joe and planted himself over him, standing, his legs apart, straddling Joe's. His enormous cock soared in Joe's face, and both men continued to stroke slowly in rhythm. Every so often Andrew went into a little squat so his perineum could just be bumped by Joe's bobbing knuckles and moistened by the head of Joe's cock. Andrew reached down and dabbed a bit of this moisture from his perineum, then brought his finger to his lips.

All were rapt. Chanting had given way to waves of nonverbal sounds.

After five minutes Andrew slowed up. Bracing himself with one arm he hunched slightly forward and positioned the head of his cock over Joe's cock. Everyone understood.

Suddenly a voluminous load of cum was hosing out all over Joe's cock and hand.

"Oh!" and "Wow!" the others murmured in unison, as if some spectacular trapeze trick had just been completed.

The others' loads popped at the same time all around the circle, except for those of three men: Joe, who proceeded to lean forward and suck Andrew's dripping, softening cock; a little muscular guy named Louie, who had wiggled his way under Andrew's legs and positioned himself on the floor in front of Joe; and Mack, sitting on his stool, leaning forward both to better see this spectacle close-up and put some pleasant pressure on that sensitive area between his balls and his asshole as he stroked.

Mack released his load at the same moment that he saw, from Louie's bobbing Adam's apple and Joe's shallow breathing, that Joe, who usually came very silently, was unloading deep inside Louie's throat. Louie made an attempt to lean over and take Mack's load too, but the angle was wrong. Besides, Mack's load was already on the floor, in great gobs, soaking into the flannel sheet. Louie lay back on the floor and jerked off onto himself.

There was deep breathing and sighing all around, some laughing, some throat-clearing, and a cough or two. Mack reached behind him and produced a pile of towels. Louie kept jerking his soft cock and after a few minutes shot a second time.

Joe whispered to Andrew, "I want your load next time."

"You can have it later, if you want," Andrew whispered back. "Where are you off to?"

"We're all off to XL, I think," Joe said, out loud. "Aren't we, Mack—XL?"

"That sounds nice, don't you think?" Mack replied. "Andrew? Charles? Raymond? XL?"

After cleanup, they set off in a group. Mack and Joe chatted along the way.

"So you're closing this weekend? That's awesome, buddy," said Joe.

"I want us to be having these get-togethers out under the stars this summer," Mack said. "Really take it to the next level and see where it can go. Maybe hook up the cabins and the main house on a network, so we can webcast."

"Oh my God! A cybercult!" Joe laughed.

"Except for Celia, Stuart's sister. She's making noises about contesting the insurance benefit. That's what's supposed to be paying for the place."

"The skincare lady. I met her at Stuart's memorial service. When she found out who I was, she practically begged me to do a page on one of her lines in the magazine. She seemed like a total publicity whore. But, you know, their stuff isn't bad."

"She what?"

"I said I'd think about it."

"That bitch!"

"Look, would it help if I did do a page—you know, in exchange for her butting out of your business? Make a deal. I'd be happy to support you. It's far from the slimiest piece of journalism ever practiced by a fashion magazine."

"You would do that? I mean, you'd be able to do something like that?"

"Mack, we're friends. Besides, I love what you're doing with these little groups. I like to think we're building something. I know you think of it as religious. I see it as more of an art form."

"Why not both, like ancient Greek theater?" Mack said.

"So let me do this. My contribution to the arts. It couldn't be easier."

"If you could do that, it'd be great."

Joe elbowed Mack and nodded toward Andrew, up ahead of them, talking with several of the others.

"Nice, right?" Joe said. "Totally not my type. You know I like those muscle daddies. But there's something about him."

"Seems like a nice guy."

"I think we're gonna hook up later. He's based in L.A., here twice a month. Content director of the largest gay web site. They grabbed him away from cable TV. He created that big reality show—you know, 'Felon Island.' You should tell him your cyber idea."

"Which product?" Celia snapped. Mack called promptly at ten the next morning.

"I don't know which product, Celia. I don't know your line well enough. Whatever's the hottest, I guess. But he really wants to do it."

"Age-Defying Creme with nanospheres," she said. "For the September issue?"

"Sure, why not?" Mack said.

"And he'll shoot the product specially?"

"I think so. Celia, talk to him. I gave you the number. He's expecting your call."

"And in return you want me to drop my interest in the policy?"

"Frankly, that's what it boils down to. I don't even understand why you were trying to contest the payment in the first place."

She thought for a second.

"OK. I'll do it. I'll call him right now."

Max's caution gave way to curiosity.

"Why *were* you contesting anyway, Celia? Stuart and I were together longer than you and Harvey."

"Why? I don't know," she sighed. "I guess I wanted him to be remembered for something important, not a thirty-year-old musical about men taking their clothes off. I was actually thinking of donating the money to an arts organization, in his name."

"I may do something like that myself," Mack said.

When Thorpe called that afternoon, he was jubilant.

"They're backing off," he announced.

"I know," Mack said. "I made a deal."

"Oh? And when were you going to tell me about that?"

"Drive upstate with me on Saturday for the closing. I'll tell you all about it. Meanwhile, Thorpe, do me a favor. Check into how quickly I can form a not-for-profit corporation around a small, interactive performing arts, or possibly religious, group I'm thinking about starting."

By May, Mack was spending half his time in Krumville, supervising renovations and hosting small groups of friends. By the beginning of June, the work was done and Mack was occasionally renting out five of the cabins to gay groups—dance companies, spiritual retreats, massage workshops. In the sixth cabin lived the full-time caretaker/gardener/cook he hired, a young printmaker who'd quit his day job as a proofreader to pursue his art. That same month, Mack purchased a new computer and, with the help of a circle member who was a porn star with his own web site, began webcasting ceremonies to large and growing audiences. *HX* listed the webcasts in its "HomoMusts" column.

At the end of June Mack convened his first outdoor circle. It was late on a warm Saturday afternoon, in the middle of a gloriously clear weekend. The group was all regulars this time, and they had the place to themselves. After a day of swimming, hiking, eating, and reading, they gathered in the middle of the lush, expansive main lawn with sheets and pillows, and conjured among themselves an enormously strong, body-filling energy, particularly during the chanting, when at one point they were singing at the top of their lungs. *"Cock is God is cock is God is cock is God ..."*

The celebrant was Andrew, who had become boyfriends with Joe. In recent months Andrew had been featured in *Advertising Age* and *Variety* as the content director of one of the few viable, mass-audience Web enterprises still operating. The guy who got to give the offering was the caretaker, who started out a little shy but surprised everyone—Joe cheered!—when he throated Andrew to the balls, breathing effortlessly through his nose while basically jerking Andrew off with repeated swallow contractions. Nearby on a tripod was the webcam, connected to the main house by a cable snaking through the grass.

On Sunday night, Mack drove back into the city with Joe and Andrew.

"Fun weekend," said Joe.

"Incredible," Mack said.

"Listen, Mack, tomorrow morning I'm talking over some ideas for reality entertainment," Andrew said. "I'd like to mention your group. I think it's a show."

Mack hadn't mentioned the cybercult idea to Andrew, but Joe had.

"A show," Mack said.

"A Web show. Classic heretical cult meets feel-good pornography. It would be a dream to market, especially in today's climate."

Mack was silent.

"We can webcast the ceremony to a much larger audience than you're reaching now and we can get people to join each other in subgroups. If it goes well, as my gut says it will, we'd partner within a year with a cable channel that's been wanting to develop content with us. We think mainstream cable is ready for reality sex. You could host; you'd get a producer credit and own a piece of the project. And we'd shoot it in Krumville, so you'd get a rental fee."

"Wow," said Mack. He tried to think about it.

"Maybe build a little temple by the stream, with an attached control room?" Andrew said.

"Can my little ceremony really find that wide an audience?" Mack asked.

It was tickling, the idea of having a hit again after so many years. And sad, the dawning awareness that he might have had more hits all along, if only Stuart's weirdness about gay stuff hadn't kept them from going deeper ....

Andrew chuckled.

"You're asking if can I apply media savvy to an edgy gay sex ritual, conceived as theater, and sell it as a wholesome religious cult in top twenty U.S. markets? I think I can. It's not exactly what Jesus and Mohammed were peddling, but I think it'll find an audience."

Last Night at the Spike

$\mathcal{I}$ hadn't heard that the Spike was supposed to close, so when Wayne, a guy I met on a phone sex line on Saturday afternoon, said that we could probably "still meet there tonight after all," I asked what he meant. Wayne told me that the Spike had been scheduled to go out of business last week but that the owners had delayed closing so it could be open for Labor Day weekend. My first thought was, *God, the Eagle and now the Spike!* Why should we feel lucky that there's one last night when we can piss on each other and suck each other's cocks? Shouldn't we feel deprived if we can't do this every night, especially those of us who remember doing so at will in any of several neighborhood sleaze bars? Shouldn't we be organizing, or protesting, or publicly debating the further marginalization of gay male sexual space?

Part of me—the party-goer, the art writer—loves what's been happening in far west Chelsea. I know a lot of people who own galleries and live there, a lot of artists who show there. I don't particularly hate the real estate interests that have developed the neighborhood, or even the process, inevitable in Manhattan, by which crummy neighborhoods are turned into nicer ones. But I believe in what planners call "mixed use," and that, as far as I'm concerned, should include public sex. Having sex casually in a bar, or outside, in the street, is not at all like going to a sex club or a privately organized sex scene. I don't want to have to enter a private space for sex. I mean, sometimes I do that, but then you're playing with a lot of private men, some of whom can radiate an unattractively high level of gutlessness, even if their pecs or cocks or arms happen to be configured in an appealing way. What I want is to walk around in a fully charged state of sexual possibility and freely connect with others so charged. I want to express a vision of the whole world as an erotic playground and validate this vision in others, instigating scenes and inspiring neophytes when necessary, though without offending people who don't see the point. If I could give a class in public sex at the New School, I would do it in a minute. I'd explain how to train the body for public sex, how to sharpen the hearing, eyesight, and most especially that other special, unnamed sense that people who have public sex quickly discover within that alerts them simultaneously to both danger and the proximity of other people.

It's so weird now, being in that part of Chelsea. By day, even the most sacred sexual memories—those you would have thought were etched forever into the stone facades of garages-turned-galleries— seem scoured by the corrosively entitled glare of art consumers. By night, those memories are dissolved in the social scene. You can be entering a star-studded Fashion Week party at Lot 61 without remembering, at least at first, that a only few years ago when the place was being built you were blown on the sidewalk outside, in back of a dumpster, where the velvet rope is now. You can be chatting there with fashionistas and suddenly be distracted by the thought of just how much sex you had on the streets of west Chelsea during the '70s and '80s. Back then it was a quiet, industrial neighborhood on the edge of the city. At night, on West Street and on side streets where noisy door scenes now flourish, men prowled silently back and forth between the Spike and the Eagle, looking to hook up *now,* with leather jackets open, shirtless, even when the harshest winter winds blew off the river. They were able to select from an encyclopedic array of possible nearby outdoor trysting spots affording various degrees of protection from view and the elements. Today you can be drinking at Open, the buzzy little art lounge newly opened at the corner of West and 22nd, and realize only after the second martini that you're sitting in the formerly boarded-up shop in front of which, on many summer Sunday mornings at 5 A.M., when you were getting blown at the loading dock across the street, a crazy guy used to show up naked, recline on the pavement, then flog himself, muttering incomprehensibly. You can be ordering supper at an outdoor table at the landmark Empire Diner and catch yourself remembering the time two years ago when you and two other guys were getting blown in darkness on the front stoop of a now brightly lit house diagonally across the street, all of you merrily fucking throat right out in the open, while the Empire's sidewalk crowd munched burgers not far away.

It's scary how fast you can forget what used to be in a particular location in this city, after buildings get renovated or new ones go up. That's one reason why I agreed to meet Wayne at the Spike on Saturday night. I wanted a last chance to burn the place into my memory. Another reason was that I felt like getting pissed on by a big-dicked muscle daddy, which Wayne said he was, and another was that KJ was out of town.

It's ironic that I feel so affectionately toward the Spike. The place meant nothing to me when I came to New York, in the mid '70s, an unsophisticated kid from upstate. My boyfriend, Barry, and I didn't drink much, or stay up late, or identify with the leather lifestyle. "Fern bars" were more what we looked for on those rare nights when our gay socializing took the form of bar hopping. Most of our social time was taken up by volunteer work with some gay organization or other. In fact, the first time I visited the Spike I was delivering programs for *The West Street Gang*, the Doric Wilson play produced there in 1977 by the gay theater company Barry and I volunteered for. Doric's play was set in a bar very like the Spike and depicted men very like those who showed up in leather later that night for the opening. I stood through the performance in a Levi jacket and wondered if gay life were truly segmented into mutually exclusive clans of "daddies," "boys," "tops," "bottoms," "renegade bikers," and "editorial assistants from upstate who volunteer for gay causes."

Over the years I'd go back to the Spike when friends more interested in leather than I was suggested we meet there and I came to see how friendly the place was. Moreover, I learned that like most of the men who went to the Spike, I could belong to many clans at once—an important theme of Doric's play (which, by the way, set an off-Broadway record at the time, by running at the bar for five months). I returned to the Spike throughout the '80s, as public sex established itself there—in the men's rooms, in the back areas, sometimes out in the open—and receded with the growth of AIDS and the appearance of sex monitors. I was there when sexplay reestablished itself secretly, among true sex hounds who were happy to define "safe" for themselves and take responsibility for shielding each other from monitoring.

On Saturday night, I wound up getting pissed on not by Wayne, who never showed up, but by another even hotter guy who'd clearly been a regular at the Spike for years. His name was Larry. He was six feet tall, fortyish, very skinny, tight, and tattooed, with long brown hair, pierced nipples, a mammoth cock, and, as I discovered later, a "guiche"—a piercing of the perineal area. He had a regular spot where he planted himself at the main bar, around back, near the phone and the men's rooms, and as we stood there, drinking beer (him) and vodka (me), he told me several stories about bar sex over the years.

"I've seen guys getting fisted on the pool table while other guys slow-danced in the corner like prom queens," Larry said. "There was a guy who used to crawl around on all fours kissing boots, even when it was so crowded you couldn't move. And then there was the guy who only liked to blow guys who were passed out; I think he used to own the flower shop at the Stanhope."

Larry and I got our cocks sucked together by a guy who came over and sank to his knees between us and the bar. Wedged down there, the guy stayed through several cum and piss drainings, and we shared him with a few of Larry's buddies who came over to say hello. No big deal; just bar banter, a few laughs, and a mouth. Larry was a church organist. He said that staying up late on a Saturday night required pre-arranging a substitute for Sunday morning—something he did only on very special occasions, like this. After an hour, Larry and I took off in his Volvo and headed for the Promenade, near where I live in Brooklyn Heights. I was going to show him the famed quarter-mile-long pedestrian walkway overlooking the skyline of Manhattan, where I'd had sex a thousand times. But there were no parking spots nearby, so we drove down the hill, parked near the Fulton ferry landing and wound up in a secluded little park half a block away.

It was a hot, humid night, and the park was arranged on several lushly planted terraces, protecting us from the view of any passersby, though there were none, because of the hour. We took our shirts off, let our shorts fall, and sucked each other's cocks in a perfectly relaxed way, right out in the open, for an hour. It was fun—even when, uninvited (though I may have been sending him a different signal), Larry let a load of diluted beer piss start draining down my throat.

The following day I called Larry to thank him for coming all the way to Brooklyn Heights with me (he lived in New Jersey). He told me that he had just learned from a friend, a Spike bartender, that we'd *almost* been there for the bar's final party. Saturday night was to have been it, but the owner was, in fact, planning an unadvertised *final* final party for that night, Sunday. Larry suggested we go. I was up for it, since my dogging around tends to go in cycles and this cycle was intensifying because, as I say, KJ was away and because Larry was hot. And the guiche that I had come across the night before in the park, that I had apparently intuitively known *exactly* what to do with: that was something I'd fantasized about since I was a little boy. Not that I dreamed about that exact method of piercing, or that precise piece of hardware. After consulting numerous piercing web sites on Sunday morning I decided I probably wouldn't risk the six-month healing period that a new guiche sometimes requires. But that area has always been central to my erotic potential, as far back as the fifth or sixth grade, when I used to jerk off with my friend Howie after school and always tried to get him to kneel between my legs and press under my balls with his thumbs while I stroked.

The crowd on Sunday night was sparse but randy. I guessed they were longtime regulars. Like me, they seemed to have been summoned by word-of-mouth. And I could tell that everybody else was feeling what I was feeling: So what if I take my cock out? So what if I get sucked off? So what if I pee in my pants? So what if someone sees? What's the worst that can happen? This place is as good as closed.

Again, Larry held court at the end of the bar. A steady flow of friends came by to greet him as if he were a politician, introducing themselves genially. And I have to say I felt privileged to be standing there with Larry, feeling for the first time like an insider at the Spike. I was sad that it had taken me so long to reach this pinnacle and sorry I could be there only for this final night. Circling the bar and lurking in the poolroom, where *The West Street Gang* had been performed, were two or three lone sharks with a predatory, private energy. But for the rest of us, it was everything out in the open at the bar, the way it used to be before AIDS, before Mayor Giuliani. I got sucked off a few times and pissed on a lot, on the long side of the bar, a few steps away from the door. I pissed on a few guys, too, including one named Paul, who introduced himself as a professor from Boston University, who said, when I asked, ridiculously, that he'd known my friend George, who taught French there. After a while, kinda drunk, I wound up trying to suck the *hugest* cock in the place, which was hanging off of this older, skinny guy with a shaved head, who seemed bored but enticeable. He didn't mind when I went down on him near the pay phone and knelt there for quite a while with his cock jammed down my throat, though it was clear that I was not up to the challenge and we both enjoyed, instead of a blow job, providing our brothers with an inspiring tableau vivant.

I left an hour before closing time. Larry and his circle had already mostly gone. We never said goodbye. The only people left were the sharks, who were beginning to look better and better, now that I was getting more and more in touch with my hunger ....

Keep Up the Good Work

I've just seen a screen-size picture of my cock on the Web's largest vacuum pumping message board site, www.newart.com, and I've gotta admit that nothing thus far in the Internet revolution has thrilled me as deeply.

I posted the picture there on Sunday night, after spending a few minutes alone at my office that day teaching myself how to use the digital camera, with my freshly pumped cock as subject. Five minutes ago, I went to the site and looked at the picture again for the umpteenth time. There it was: my ultra-beautiful cock, eight thick cut inches, hanging semisoft out of the fly of my striped Brooks Brothers boxer shorts, my jeans open, my balls freshly shaved, a computer keyboard in the foreground, a monitor in the background. I posted the photo with the headline, "Hanging Around After Work."

It feels great to show my cock to the world this way—and the response has been amazing. I received dozens of e-mails from guys all over the world, and there were ten or so follow-up postings at the site itself: advice and encouragement from veteran pumpers, praise and questions from novices, and a sprinkling of inarticulate but sincere come-ons. It made me understand why pumping is like, say, owning a Jack Russell terrier: it's about showing, looking, discussing. Cock fancy.

Like the good little sex hound I am, I've been answering every e-mail. And I've been responding to the follow-up postings with follow-follow-up messages of my own, thanking people and giving further testimony, since I feel that, as with any cult, it's important to profess the faith—though I admit it's surprising that, for someone who has been sex hounding for decades, I'm only a recent convert. I explored the site just a few weeks ago: on Christmas Day, actually, during a visit to my sister's roomy, trappingly comfortable house in suburban Jacksonville, Florida. Nephews, grandparents and everybody else were downstairs playing with new toys; alone, upstairs, at the computer in the hall-slash-den (where my nephews do their homework) I was online, idly attempting to dismantle some of the family cheer that had accumulated. A few clicks and there it was: message boards, advice columns, advertisements for Newart products, and pictures of cock, cock, cock. What I loved was that, instead of porn shots, these were homemade pictures of big, fat cocks on regular guys, both straight and gay, plus earnest captions like, "I started pumping with a 2 $^1/_4$ x 9 tube and now fill a 2 $^1/_2$ x 9. Got a Monster Jr. tube to pump my balls. Looking for a buddy to pump with and watch movies."

Within days of returning to New York I was dipping into the Newart site every day, having advanced my cock hunger by hearing other men discuss theirs. In fact, I'll bet there are whole demographic segments out there that are now identifying and working out, via the Web, new sexual appetites that in real life would be difficult to explore. It's earthshaking that anyone can use this new mass medium to tell the whole wide world what he or she does and what he or she wants—let alone that anyone can see what vast numbers of us are doing in common. How different that is even from thirty years ago, when the late Boyd McDonald and a very few others were collecting "real," meaning reader-written, sex stories and publishing them "underground" in chapbooks. The Internet has put desire on its own electronic superhighway.

(As a young interviewer on assignment for *The Advocate,* I got to meet Boyd. He received me in the room where he lived in a shabby residential hotel on New York's Upper West Side. There was just a bed, a hot plate, a table and chair, and skinny, shambling Boyd, who had left everything behind in the '70s, he told me—Harvard, family, the army, a career on Wall Street—for sex. When I asked him the question that everyone wanted answered—Were all those *Straight to Hell* letters real?—he walked unceremoniously to the closet, opened the door, and showed me bags and bags of correspondence. Inside were all kinds of stationery, postmarks from all over the world, all types of handwriting telling stories of everyday sexual adventures that were just beginning to reach a mainstream audience.)

I first came across the Newart site a year or two ago, but I wasn't inspired to bookmark it then, which is probably because pumping as I first experienced it seemed ... harsh. I have a MityVac non-electric model, with trigger grip, plus a 2-inch starter tube. My boyfriend KJ gave it to me last Valentine's Day, on what I guess you'd call a whim we both had. I pumped as per instructions maybe eight or ten times, always in two or three very strictly observed ten or fifteen minute sessions per evening, alone, at a moderate level of suction. But it never seemed fun that way—sticking my cock into a yanking void and pulling out something sore. I was never able to grow *fervent* about it.

I think I was afraid that if I pumped too much or too hard, I might cross some line and become obsessed with turning my beautiful cock into something alien—like the basketball-sized, silicone-filled thing I once discovered between the legs of an East Village guy I hooked up with one night after meeting on a phone sex line. This guy had created a monstrous entity the likes of which I didn't want to own but nonetheless felt drawn to observe—and sit in front of, and talk about, and talk *to*, and *honor* as if it were some kind of liege lord. This guy said he had started pumping years ago and couldn't stop; his cock had become his life's work. He now proudly posts pictures of himself under the name of "The Meat Master" on various pumping web sites.

(Though already committed to sexual exploration as a young man I was uncertain about how far real erotonauts need go. Even as I was pontificating about the "importance" of the work my shit-eating, flesh-cutting, and boy-loving friends were doing, I was also unnerved by it. I must have encountered some of the century's pioneer cock fanciers when I first came to New York and had the time to explore sex endlessly; now that I find myself a cock fancier, too, I could kick myself for not pursuing some of these guys further! Many of them must be gone by now. Like the massively hung, craggy-faced, exhibitionistic janitor I met in the subway men's room at 23rd Street whose giant, rubbery foreskin I filled with my cum in about a second when we docked. Or the mature but frisky French guy, André, I met in the Metropolitan Theater on 14th Street, who not only pumped his cock but his nipples—his "chest cocks!"—whom I subsequently saw pictured in *Drummer*. Or the distinguished-looking Beekman Towers daddy with the Satanic artifacts collection, whose whole midsection was tattooed with the Devil's face, his penis the tongue.)

What finally ignited my pumping soul was discovering, on a Newart message board, an exchange devoted to warm water pumping. Now that sounded nice. I couldn't quite envision the hydraulics of the process but one night I figured, *What the hell?* and I just jumped in the tub to see what would happen. Well, what happens is altogether *slower,* and *warmer*. Your cock doesn't blow up; it *swells* nicely. Afterwards it feels bigger, yes, but also more ... *companionable*. Then I heard about combining pumping and JO, and group pumping scenes with cocksuckers who specialize in freshly pumped cock. And then I met a guy with an electric pump—which is like sinking into a Cadillac after bumping around in a Jeep.

Now that I am up to speed on pumping, I know that doing it doesn't necessarily mean ending up with a monster. One horrified friend, a sissy who's not all that comfy with sex in the first place, told me that he'd heard pumping breaks down the tissue and eventually "turns your cock into sponge." And another friend says that he knew somebody who committed suicide after pumping his cock into something so huge that it couldn't get hard. But most of these horror stories are bullshit, according to hundreds of apparently normal Newart fans who've been pumping happily for years with no effects they consider ill. Frankly, I trust their empirical evidence no less than I would the official urological line. Besides, more than facts about physiology, pumpers share a kind of manliness support—something I find I want and definitely won't get at the art opening I'm going to tonight, or the product launch I went to last night, or the screening I'm going to tomorrow night.

One guy from South Carolina sends me advice about cock photography—tips on lighting and composition. Another guy, in Florida, explains how to pump while driving around in a convertible, a towel draped over the lap. Two other guys—a self-described "pagan priest" from Long Island and a Citibank executive from the Bronx—tell me all the best ways to show off a pumped cock when clothed. Who else would tell me these things? One of my new best friends is a retired plumber who lives outside of Cincinnati, a straight guy, who e-mails me every day with pump lore and tidbits of medical information he's picked up over the years. Apparently, he gets up before dawn and pumps for an hour while his wife is still asleep. He says he's up to 9 x 7 inches and loves to show it off to women *and* men, often in social nudist settings like the private resort on some secluded riverbank that he's told me about, which he visits with his wife and other couples. (Occasionally, he admits, some of the men sneak off for a bit of same-sex cock fancying.) This guy finishes his e-mail when it's time to get off the pump and go make breakfast. He usually signs off with something motivational, like a coach would: "Keep up the good work, Steve!"

I suspect that these are the same people who are buying groceries on Priceline and trading collectibles on eBay. In other words, this is a mainstream thing, beyond straight and gay. And that's finally what interests me about pumping: you can do it with straight guys. That is, you don't necessarily have to do it with gay guys. Meaning that guys are doing it irrespective of sexual identity. Pumping is a gender identity thing, and I guess that feels refreshing to me, since I've long since checked out of a lot of feelings in common with men in general. Pumping seems to connect me with what connects men at some primal level—and I love that it doesn't involve shooting, cutting, or batting.

Field of Vision

All I know is what I can see, so let me start by describing the apartment.

"C'mon in and watch your head," Jack said. "Can I ask you to take off your shoes?"

Ducking under the low stoop of the nondescript, turn-of-the-century building in New York's West Village, I entered a front room that apparently serves as both gym and art gallery. I dropped my jacket on a bench-press machine, and perched on a Donghia side chair to remove my sneakers. On the opposite wall hung a series of cheesy, Russian icon-like paintings of naked men, each in its own pin spotlight. The whole place was so dark that it took a moment to figure out that both floor and walls were carpeted in industrial gray carpeting. Gray, black, and silver were the predominant tones: the rack of iron dumbbells, the stripped steel physician's cabinet, the mountain bike stowed on a wall mount. None of this was exactly decor news.

Jack gave me the tour. A long hallway led past the bathroom to the living room at the back of the house, which gave onto a large yard with statuary that I could see, even in the fading late-afternoon February light, included quite a few startlingly priapic figures.

"The garden looks better in the summer," Jack said—a hostly apology doubling as a reminder to stop peeking through the blinds and pay attention. He was telling me where in India he had found the stone lingam displayed in a glitzy, mirrored, circular niche, also spotlighted. My God, I realized, it's just as he promised on the phone: there are cocks everywhere. But if part of me was wondering whether this man could be a little crazy—the sum total of my experience with him amounted to one chat session on AOL, three e-mails, plus the phone call—I realized that he was obviously so house-proud that there was no question of mucking things up with body fluids leaking out of a drugged or murdered visitor. Everything here was scrupulously maintained, not at all like some of the makeshift, spare-room dungeons I've seen that could pass for crime scenes.

On one side of the living room were a few pieces of contemporary black leather furniture arranged around a giant video screen, in what some shelter magazines call a "conversation group." On the other side, where anyone else would have put a dining table, Jack had a large, black vinyl-padded massage table neatly punctuated with two holes—one where your face would go, if you were lying facedown on it, and the other for your cock. I noticed that the table had been prepared with a fresh, folded, black terry-cloth towel near the upper hole.

"I keep the smaller equipment here," Jack said, dramatically throwing open a set of louvered doors, to reveal a walk-in toy closet custom-fitted with shelves, racks, and pull-out bins of dildos and butt-plugs; lubricants and oils; condoms and latex gloves; straps, harnesses, cuffs, clamps, chains, rings, ropes, and other necessities. Beyond, through the galley kitchen and spare, tiny bedroom (the door between which featured another glory hole), was the office. His appointment book sat open on the desk, with a dozen or so names penned in for the week. (And there I was, down for Sunday at five.) The computer screen was flashing pictures of cocks, both naked and in various stages of bondage.

Though I found the design of the place downright tacky and old-fashioned, I did think it interesting how the residential aspect blended seamlessly with the commercial—or should I say blended *shamelessly*, since in addition to the lucrative consulting position he holds with a British corporation, Jack uses his place as the site of a discreet body grooming business. He shaves and trims some of the city's most pubically public men.

"I started the practice because I love playing with cock in a very focused way," he explained. "And I only like being with guys who are also obsessed with their cocks—hustlers, porn stars, party boys, professional masters, et cetera. I have those guys coming over here all the time now. I hardly have to go out anymore, which is OK because I hate bars and the whole late-night thing. I have to be up early to talk with London, but by afternoon their business day is over, so I'm done and have the rest of my day."

He chuckled.

"My friends call me cock-crazy. And I agree with them."

I'd asked Jack if I could see his place because I was scouting. Having written for *Elle Decor* and *Casa Vogue*, I'd been asked by the editor of a gay lifestyle magazine to do a series on people who work at home. Jack's was the first place I had looked at. But as we sat there in his office, talking about his "practice," the idea of my writing about the place as design seemed pretty much out of the question. *This is a boys' clubhouse*, I remember thinking; *I won't have anything to say about it.* An author I knew uptown had a "Louis Louis" showplace that would make a much easier assignment.

But I said that I'd have a drink before going.

"This way," Jack said.

He made a point of showing me the bathroom again. This time I went in. There was the usual sink, commode, and tub. Then I noticed that off to the left, through a glass door etched with mermen, was a slate-tiled steam room large enough to seat eight.

In the living room, Jack poured me a vodka and settled into a chair opposite me. A fiftyish guy with hair too long and wavy for its thinness, he was not particularly hot by my standards, but he seemed nice enough. He was dressed for sex the way men his age do if they haven't kept up with trends in sexwear: in gray sweatpants and a plaid sleeveless shirt. I met Jack through another guy I know from AOL—a Philadelphian with a mammoth, tattooed penis that Jack assured me is famous. I knew a little bit about Jack's obsession, because, for one thing, he had mentioned that, like several men I know, he was writing a user-friendly pamphlet with step-by-step instructions and commentary, for use among small groups of like-minded men. But I hadn't realized how persuasive exposure to his obsession might be. As I sat there on that leather couch, growing more relaxed, I think it was the fact that all those hustlers and porn stars had been there before me that produced a palpable pulse between my legs—the idea that their steely asses had dented the leather seat that my ass now occupied, that their freshly-shaved balls had rested, or hung, or bounced, in the space where mine were now. It was funny to think that I could be seduced as much by the house as the man, yet the more I looked around at the glory holes and custom-made equipment, I couldn't help fixating on the point of it all: penis traffic.

I pulled off my jeans and boxers and started fondling myself. He came over and settled on his knees in front of me. With a smile meant to encourage me to lean back, he began handling me appreciatively, apparently by way of overview, to get the weight and density of the thing. Then he began licking and sucking, sometimes stopping simply to look at it and beam, sometimes giving voice to some inner, spiritual laughter.

A few minutes later he rose and suggested we move to the table. I mounted it facedown—rather, my face to one side, cradled by the towel; my cock hanging through, feeling not so much hard as full. Jack got underneath and seated himself in some way I couldn't observe. After some adjustments he was sucking again contentedly. Half an hour earlier I might have been tempted to ask if he knew whether it was Louis XIV or Louis XV who had commissioned a special *chaise d'amour* to be built for a certain royal act. Now, though, I was silent, except for a low, intermittent moan.

It occurred to me after a while that I wanted to be looking at something. Pornography, maybe. There was that big, empty video screen, and, nearby, a videocam on a tripod.

"Uh, would it be possible for me to watch somehow while you do that?"

"Why not?" Jack said, after a second or two. He emerged from under the table. "It'll just take a second to set up."

Moments later, Jack was back down below and I was watching myself star in an impromptu porno movie. This was kind of a dream come true for me, because one of my favorite porn movies is a '70s opus in which a guy named Tom sucks an endless succession of great-looking cocks presented through a plywood glory hole. There's something about the film's tight, unvarying focus that makes it easy for me to project myself into it as the guy being sucked, which always amps the feeling of connection with my own cock. Now it *was* my cock in front of me, and I was decidedly connected. Though I have always liked my cock, seeing it up there on the screen for the first time made me unexpectedly gaga for it—in love with its beauty, proud of its performance, desperate to please it.

"All those photos on the computer—you took them all?" I asked, when we took a break.

"Sure did," he said. "You wanna see yours?"

At the computer, Jack prepared my stills and displayed them on the screen. Nearby was a stack of zip discs, all labeled with men's names and hometowns: John from Dallas; Henry from Boston; Tom, Ray, and Paco from New York; Sammy who had just moved to Florida from Connecticut; several Steves whom I would now join. Many of the photos looked like portfolio shots, advertising his trimming business, about which he told me more.

"I don't need the money," Jack said. "But when guys are paying for it they'll sit still longer and be more passive. Even though I call what I do 'service,' I work from a top energy. I really like when guys let me take control of the worshiping process, especially when I get into bondage with straps and rope."

He paused.

"I could do you, if you want," he said, scrutinizing my crotch.

"You mean ... a trim?" It took me a moment to understand that my weekly, self-administered ball shave might be horribly inept by his professional standards.

"C'mon. Let's see what we can do."

He led me back to the living room couch, dimming the lights as we entered the room. As I sat back, I discovered there was a pin spot above, aimed to highlight a client's pubic area like the site of a miniature formal drama.

"I'd bring that trim line down a bit closer to the shaft," he said pressing the shaft down, then shifting it from side to side diagnostically, fluffing the hair a bit. "And I'd definitely take down some of this volume." He disappeared for a moment and came back with a pile of towels and a slender, cordless beard clipper. Chattering like a small-town beautician about other clients, he knelt down and began swiping away at the hair above my cock, between my legs, and under my balls, pausing occasionally to brush it away lightly with his fingers or blow it away with little puffs of air.

"Of course, whenever Morrie's in town"—the guy from Philadelphia—"I invite a few people over to watch me groom him. It turns into quite a little scene. Sometimes we all go out for Thai food afterward. Morrie's a great guy. You really have to meet him."

He knelt there chatting, clipping, pausing occasionally to consider his work. "Ready for some vapors, then?"

He'd already switched on the steam room, and it was there that my little day of beauty came to a climax. Now I've visited lots of public baths—sweated with patriarchs in the tiny, tiled cubicles of the Russian baths on Manhattan's East 10th Street; soaked with off-duty army officers beneath the soaring fourth-century arches of a *hammam* in Cairo's Old City; showered with Navy boys in the strip-mall splendor of the Jacksonville Club—and in these places I have done my best to allow the effect of their design to work itself on my entire body: to release it from everyday tensions and concerns and expectations, or at least shelter it from them; to suggest, if you will, that in ritual attention to the body we can discern the reflection of a state of existence we might call godliness. But no place was so effective in this as

Jack's steam room. The impulse to build it had clearly come from something as deep as the faith of medieval cathedral builders, and it gave me, as I sat there—naked amidst hot, wet clouds and the scent of expensive rosemary-olive oil soap—more loving permission to feel divine than I'd ever felt before.

Jack positioned me on the slate banquette, my back to a tinted-glass window into the living room (!) that I had mistaken earlier, from the couch, for a full-length mirror. My limbs had gone almost limp with relaxation and Jack manipulated them with great care, like a nurse, spraying, soaping, and rinsing me. Kneeling in front of me, he massaged my legs, spreading them gently, kneading the tension from my feet, then working up to my calves and my quads, then easing back down to the toes, to which he devoted elaborate ministrations. Woozy with comfort, I found myself following his lead and massaging myself—the inside of my thighs, my pecs and shoulders. He ran his hand over my abdominals and brought my hand over them as well. He kissed my biceps, one at a time, then held my arms up so I could I kiss them, too. He gathered my hand around my cock, and together we squeezed and released, squeezed and released.

His gaze remained on my cock as I masturbated. His voice reverberated in the chamber, over the hiss of steam vents.

"Yeah, Steve. Be an orgy, man."

His wet feet and butt slapped on the floor, as he kept repositioning himself for a better view.

"Look at that. *Look* at that!"

As I stroked, he cock-ringed me with his hands, the pressure of his thumbs just under my balls turning into a slow massage of the perineum. I could feel the valleys between my fingers go electric as he whispered details of the last party he hosted, at which guys playing in the living room watched guys playing in the steam room.

"Look at that," I breathed.

"Yeah. Orgy for me, Steve."

My grip weakened, my erection ripened into something rubbery,

I was doing little more than holding myself in a cupped hand.

Before long, I had finished building and spent some moments experiencing that state of fully charged calm beyond the horizon of everyday language. Then, almost casually, I asked if he wanted me to shoot in his face. His face gave me the answer.

"Then this is for you," I gurgled.

I half stood. I did little more than slide my cock forward in my palm. It was more like peeing than shooting.

I released everything, even the duty of seeing. During the massage Jack had tenderly removed my glasses and set them aside— an intimacy I always perform for myself, before bed. I am so nearsighted that my cock marks the farthest distance from my eyes at which I can make something out clearly. I have worn glasses since the third grade, and even while they sharpen my view of the world, they have come to enforce my distance from a certain reality. Jack knew, I guess, that I had gotten to a place where there was nothing I needed to see that couldn't better be seen without correction.

OK, maybe there's a story here after all, I thought as I got dressed. What's funny is that Jack and I had been positioned in roughly the same way as the two people in an old photograph I noticed he had pinned to his bulletin board, in which a small boy is helping a handsome young man build a tool shed in the backyard of a suburban ranch house. The man is dressed in baggy khakis and a sweaty, unbuttoned shirt whose rolled-up sleeves show off manly forearms. The boy's head is exactly level with and a foot away from the man's crotch. It was obvious that these were Jack and his father. It made me smirk to remember that I have practically the exact same picture of my father and me, only we are raking leaves. Jack told me his picture was taken in 1952. That's maybe three years before mine was taken.

The following Sunday, Jack phoned to see whether I might be free. I was glad he called, since I wanted the opportunity to look more closely at some of his artwork, walk around in the garden, maybe see what it was like to get my cock tied up ....

"Morrie's in town," he said. "I want you to meet him. He *really* gets into cock. Next to him, I'm an amateur."

I was back at Jack's door within an hour. Even before knocking I was breathing more deeply. Beaming, too. I pulled off my glasses and slipped them into my shirt pocket, at which point all I could see was that silly door knocker in the form of a naked man sporting— I hadn't noticed this the first time around—a boner.

Spurt

This is not like me, going upstairs in the middle of the day to jerk off. For the second time today, no less. I used to love to masturbate—not just for the pleasure, but the idea of giving it to myself. It *was* like me, years ago, to spend hours at it. But that was before my career took off, before the writing and teaching schedule began to strain under my responsibilities as what *Vanity Fair* calls "best-selling author-slash-talk show dependable." And it was way before Josh, who's made it his business to give me all the pleasure I need.

How many times have I climbed these stairs? Until now, I might have said a million. Today, as it happens, I know the real figure. During the thirty-one years I've owned this house, I've climbed the main stairs four times a day, on average, meaning that it's been 117,180 times in all, so far. I didn't do the math. Josh did, last night. We were having sex, during which, as often happens, he was focusing on my legs. After licking and massaging my thighs for half an hour, he climbed halfway on top of me and began rubbing his tight, hairless gymnast's body all over me, his cock jamming against my left quad, shooting as soon as I started flexing. Afterwards, as part of the ongoing narration he likes to provide during sex, he told me all the reasons why my legs were so great for, quote-unquote, a man my age—which happens to be sixty-three, as Josh never tires of pointing out to people whom he thinks find me unusually vital, or surprisingly unwrinkled, or *something*. He took into account the gym and the work I do in my garden. But it's the number "117,180" that comes to mind at this moment, as I climb these stairs, since I know it's at least 100,000 times that I've said I would fix that split baluster on the landing and at least 100,000 times that I've just put it out of my mind, as I'm probably going to do once again, right now.

Spurt

Only, damn—that split looks worse than I remember it. Now, when did that happen? I don't remember bumping it, though back before I gave up drinking this whole staircase took a lot of punishment, as I stumbled up to bed at night—alone for years, then occasionally with a stranger, or with someone who became slightly less strange during a short, ill-fated parody of courtship, then later with Josh, during the first year I knew him.

It was during the second year that Josh helped me go dry. One day he's this cute grad student at the other end of the table in my "Novel to Film" seminar. Two weeks later he's stopping by my office on a pretext and inviting me to lunch off campus. Ten months after that he's driving me across state lines to Hazelden and housesitting until I get back. And three weeks after I get out of Hazelden I'm telling Josh it's OK if he moves his stuff in. We've been together now as partners for two years. Partners, lovers; I still don't know what words to use. Josh likes saying it's a marriage, and I do love him enough to sign a contract, if it ever comes to that, and I do believe that despite the difference in our ages he can love me as fully as he says he does—though this relationship is turning out to be no less labor-intensive than my first one, with Andrew, years ago, when I had far less experience living with people.

God, when *was* that?—and how different it all was, once! Andrew and I met in the late '60s, back when gay men were so sure that the only path to couplehood was political. So there we were, Andrew and me, each struggling to be a good Ozzie Nelson-meets-Emma Goldman-type husband, while plenty of our friends, the real revolutionaries, were rejecting "dyads" entirely and clumping together in tribes. Something of that struggle stayed with Andrew and me even into the '80s, when death did us part, and by the time I met Josh I thought I had evolved beyond the romance of doctrine. *This time*, I thought when God finally saw fit to send me another contender, *I will be wiser about love.* Yet here we are, just as doctrinaire, in our own way: the sixty-three-year-old man and the twenty-four-year-old man agreeing explicitly and repeatedly to put

aside their baggage about age—finding common ground on which
to discuss Stonewall and hip-hop with a minimum of smugness—
and coming together as spiritual equals.

It almost works. Though this morning the nature of the gap
between us became a little clearer to me, when for some reason,
after Josh left for the airport, I jerked off alone and really got into
it. I mean, I *really* got into it, for the first time in years. Josh has a
gymnastics meet tomorrow in Boston and I feel somehow, I don't
know, like I've cheated on him. Christ, we'll probably have sex
tonight, since I'm taking a later flight to Boston. Yet here I am,
walking up these stairs again, to jerk off again, feeling guilty
again—and feeling a little stupid for having forgotten how much I
need this form of recreation, a little ashamed for having neglected
it for so long, and even, in some juvenile corner of my mind, a little
fearful that now God is going to rethink his lovely gift to me.

Of course, God might also just be trying to remind me of something else lovely. Lying there on my back, my legs spread wide, cock
in hand, playing with my balls, building and edging for forty minutes, catching sight of myself in the mirror, and finally blowing a
load all over my stomach, I felt like a teenager again, all atwitter.
Actually, no, this is how I used to feel in my thirties, with Andrew,
when all the options for living first seemed truly possible, sexually
and otherwise. (Or should I say, sexually *thus* otherwise, since it
was only after I fell in love that I found the faith to start writing
about "eros as a beacon of truth"—as a friendly critic once put it—
and my career took off.) I looked down this morning and saw the
body that Andrew cherished—and I'm happy to report that there's
so much of it left: the waist that's exactly the same size it was
thirty years ago, thanks to dietary discipline; the pecs that are as
defined as ever, if not quite as hard; the toes that have not gotten
all gnarled and ghastly; the hair that has stayed mostly dark, like
my mother's did, and is still on my head.

Josh doesn't savor the twitter in me. I'd say he likes my youthfulness but is indifferent to my Inner Youth. He likes it when I show command. He loves the fact that I'm this established older guy who, by the standards of his generation, is nonetheless cool and tuned-in and in-shape. In fact, Josh kinda expects me to demonstrate all these qualities constantly, and until recently I didn't think too much about doing so, because his expectation itself probably helps keep me cool and tuned-in and in-shape. On the other hand, the foiblish youth in me is looking more embraceable than ever—a gift of old age? I am not only the bench-pressing, club-attending, Paul Smith-wearing, transgressive novel-producing old guy that Josh wants. I'm also the nerd who sits at the piano every day and practices Bach, like I did when I was a kid, because I was shy. I'm also the fag who spends an obscene amount of money on an urn for the garden, because that's what the pansy teenager dreamed of doing.

Lately, when I see Josh fetishizing my age, I find myself wincing slightly, despite my thrill in being made to feel like a porn star four times a week, and the responsibly intellectual envy of my older friends. I realize that Josh and I always talk about this issue and we never talk about it. God knows, we know plenty of people in his crowd who are in culturally mixed relationships in which fetishization sometimes becomes an issue. Maybe tonight, over dinner, I'll pretend to be all creaky and aged. My elbow *has* been acting up again; I'll fake a motor control problem. I'm sure he'll laugh; he always laughs at my jokes. At the same time, I can ask him about the baluster. I'll *start* with the baluster! My plane gets in around seven. He'll pick me up in the full-size car he took such pains to rent. (Safety nut.) We'll probably go to a restaurant on the way back to the hotel. In the car, he'll tell me about the other gymnasts—who's in shape, who's offering the stiffest competition, who's the cutest. He'll tell me all about his flight this morning, about settling into the hotel and checking out the arena where the meet takes place. He'll ask me about my one o'clock lecture, which he knows I didn't want to cancel even though I do like travelling with him and, in fact, have been looking forward to being in Boston with him for weeks, since I haven't done the strolling tour there since I was, um, his age.

We'll be chatting over appetizers, and he'll have ordered a salad (health nut), and there'll be a lull and I'll say, "Oh, Josh, do you know what I noticed? That split in the baluster on the upper landing looks worse than it used to. What happened there, do you know? Did people get upstairs during the book party? Was it your friends, or my friends ...?"

He'll smile and think I'm some kind of dear for being so concerned about my house. And I'll look into those incandescent green eyes and think how curly that luscious black hair would be if he didn't have to buzz it so short; and I'll notice that somebody across the restaurant is looking our way and trying to figure out exactly what we are; and I'll feel Josh's hand on my knee, under the table, and I'll realize how unexpectedly happy I am, after losing so much. Knowing me, I'll probably also have a thought of my darling Andrew, propped up in his hospital bed, skinny and wan, the time he told me—whenever *that* was; last week? some other century?— that he wanted me to find another boyfriend, that it would be alright with him, that there would be a time when I'd be glad he had said this.

Josh will know nothing about the baluster. If he'd been aware of any fresh damage he'd have mentioned it immediately, I know. And he certainly won't rise to any "your friends/my friends" bait I might throw out. He's too wise for that. God knows that fetishism alone wouldn't have given him the patience to deal with the rather large idea I have about myself and my lengthening personal history. It was soon after we met that Josh got beyond his automatic, good boy's respect for my relationship with my home and his smart boy's appreciation of the fact that I had planned this place with Andrew as a post-Stonewall love nest. To Josh's credit, he understood right away when I first explained what the proportions and materials and pathways of this house mean to me, down deep.

Spurt

I remember the conversation. It was a crushingly hot summer night and we were sitting on the front porch in our tank tops, after dancing at the local gay club. Some kids drove by in a convertible blaring Outkast. Josh was surprised I knew it was Outkast. I was explaining that in college I had studied to be an architect, that the writing happened later. I had grown up in a small town during a world war that everybody talked about but nobody really saw, since this was before TV. Enemy soldiers and bombing scared the shit out of me, despite adult reassurances; and then I had gotten through high school during real-life "Happy Days" by doodling through every class: floor plans of sculptural, free-form houses that I later saw were screamingly womb-like. College for me was about looking to protect myself in something built.

Josh got all that. Then, after a moment, our shirts were off and we were fooling around right there on the porch.

As it happens, I didn't build this house; I bought it. The moment I saw it, I knew that some progressive architect back in 1922 had thought just what I was thinking about how solid and safe things should be, but how light and open, too. Andrew and I had barely set foot on the porch with the realtor before we were catching each other's eye and blurting out something like, "This is it! This is the place!" Going inside was like coming home— Manderly but on a scale appropriate to just-off-campus: warmly paneled entry hall with built-in window benches and its own stone fireplace; inviting archways leading to library, living room, and kitchen; a wide, thickly crafted staircase rising in three landings to the bedrooms. Something in both our minds was able to ignite at that moment, because of those sticks and stones—a long-standing assumption, or maybe it was only a hope, that the world was indeed a place where people like Andrew and me could live happily together. Then we lived happily together, for a few years.

And then I'm getting my quad fucked by a green-eyed gymnast in the very same room where Andrew stopped breathing in my arms, two weeks after coming home from the hospital to die. This is something I've never discussed with Josh, either, though it has come to mind sometimes when he and I are up in bed and he's gobbling my fat, old man's cock (which is his favorite thing *and* mine), or we're playing in an occasional threesome with one of the guys we meet on the Internet—one of whom, now that I think of it, did bump against the railing during some horseplay last month, as we all headed merrily upstairs.

Funny: I remember telling hospice workers and ambulance attendants and all kinds of other strangers who went up and down these stairs every day when Andrew was dying to please be careful of the balusters. I was such a pill about scratches, stains, messes, when all that was happening. I was always doing laundry, straightening furniture, I suppose as a way of coping. Wrote up a storm, too; one of my worst books, very unsexy.

Well, maybe we can talk about that tonight, too. Maybe this whole Boston trip will prove a nice little overdue growth spurt for our relationship, whether or not I have really "outgrown growing," as I thought I had, like the Jules Pfeiffer character. Here's the thing though: I find this dialogue habit so much work, and so much time away from my *work*. Love should be easier by now, I keep thinking. Sure, I can't complain about Josh putting me in a category if I put him in one labeled, "Won't understand the twittery nerd within, which I am just now coming to accept," or, "Won't appreciate the fact that previous boyfriend died where we fuck." Sure, we're both big talkers, but I'd also love to have the comfort of being effortlessly *known*, at this point. That's the old man in me. I'd rather talk about my roses, and we all know I can do *that* in some depth. The habit his generation has of endlessly "interrogating" themselves on positions and assumptions—planted there, of course, by well-meaning educators of my generation—takes too much time away from what I consider to be real introspection and even, when we are in the middle of one of those week-long conversations about some issue between us, from my gardening.

Really: it affects my gardening. I mean not only hands-in-the-earth but that garden state of mind I struggle to achieve in the Buddhist sense, in which all possible me's, all the stages of my life, the goals achieved, the dreams lost, feel wordlessly knowable and present at once in some sunny, green place. There's the two-month-old me in a pram, outdoors during my very first summer in my parents' backyard; the fifty-year-old me helping Andrew up the porch steps for the last time; the 104-year-old me, doubtless a Pulitzer Prize-winner, being wheeled onto the back terrace by an attendant not even born yet; the me standing here right now on this staircase; all observed in one view if not by some ideally empathic lover then by a movie camera, as during the final scenes of *Dark Victory*.

Well, tonight I'll simply have to keep it from becoming interrogation, that's all. We'll *discuss*. And what am I talking about? Josh is completely not a typical member of his generation. And besides, they're not so bad as a whole. So after dinner it'll be something like, "No dessert for me, just coffee," and "Hey, Josh, isn't it odd that as the years go by you can become both more yourself and less the self you once, 'at last' discovered?"

My agent called this morning. "Have you got it yet?" she asked. For eighteen months I've been promising her the idea for my next book. "Yeah, it's about jerking off," I said flippantly. I was half-propped up in bed, toweling cum from my navel. "It's about a guy who jerks off and in that one moment of cumming he encounters the wholeness of his life. He sees this huge urge to cum and the memory of all his sexual adventures and the cumming itself as moments in time that are somehow unified by an achievement called joy." There was a silence on the line. "That's a book?" she said. "A book about jerking off?" "No," I said. "It's about how we live. But jerking off inspires the guy. See, there's only one character. He's survived World War II, and Vietnam, and AIDS, and now he feels lost in time. Sexual drama gives him the only through-line there is."

After a second she said, "I hate it. It feels juvenile. Go back to the drawing board. Good about World War II, though."

It was a joke—but here I am thinking, why not? Actually my next book was supposed to be about the murder of a sex club entrepreneur in Amsterdam, but who knows? In the past, I've often bashed off with one book idea after spending several months developing a different one. Josh keeps telling me I should write about him.

OK, no more moaning about endless silences. I'm saving any further interior monologue for the flight. I'm moving my butt up these stairs. I'm jerking off again. I'm showering and packing. I'm getting in the car and going to the airport and flying off to see Josh, and sharing all my masturbatory, old man maunderings. And tomorrow, well, I'm calling a contractor and getting that baluster taken care of. I mean, blah-blah-blah.

Dirty Postcard

The entrance to the club is in a small, dark alleyway, off a grimy main artery in the Marais. I knew the address but it was helpful to spot two hot-looking guys in the otherwise deserted street. They were obviously going to the same place. It was almost four in the morning.

Since my French is so feeble I had been concerned about getting in smoothly, but talk was unnecessary. I nodded hello to the door guy and was wordlessly admitted—grateful that I'd allowed Jed to dress me in the jeans, T-shirt, and sneakers he correctly assumed would conform to the dress code. Inside, I paid my fifty francs, checked my shirt, and ordered a double vodka.

Literally underground, the club occupies several interlinked cellars of buildings that appear to date back to the Revolution. To reach the main cruising areas you go down an ancient staircase and through a dark, stone tunnel. The banister is jerry-rigged and the floors unpaved and uneven. The place is definitely not up to what Americans take for granted as code. And if you're the slightest bit claustrophobic you notice, after making your way into the depths of the club, that there is no way back up to the street except for that one stairway.

The place was packed, and for a few minutes it looked promising.

"This is where you should go to have sex with the hottest, most sophisticated men in Paris," Jed and I had been told. But after an initial look around, my impression was that while the men there may have been sophisticated intellectually or in other ways, their behavior was stiff and unfriendly, which in any American sex club would be taken as fairly unsophisticated. Though the club was as hot as a furnace most men had elected to keep their shirts on— some, despite the code, even wearing neatly pressed, long-sleeve dress shirts with collars, the kind you'd wear under a suit. Two or three men said hello to me but were ultimately more interested in discussing my business in Paris than in getting down to business. Some men were huddled in nooks, already coupled but doing nothing more than chatting, looking very private, while practically everyone else was standing around in a disappointingly unpredatory way. There was none of that obsessive curiosity, or shameless exhibitionism and voyeurism, that propels the traffic in really fun sex clubs and relentlessly clumps and re-clumps bodies. This place seemed a patch of static, decorous, personal spaces—an absurd intermission.

The scene was almost as prim as the late-night cruising that took place in the Tuileries thirty years ago, when some men perambulated for hours before acknowledging anyone else amidst the shadowy greenery, when they smoked cigarettes and looked at statues solitarily while attempting to register someone else's, and perhaps their own, desires. Why had this backwardness gone unchallenged for so long—the Church? The tradition of Cartesian rationality? An attachment to bourgeois convention? Why has there been so little progress in gay public sex in the world's most civilized city?

The question rang in my mind when I first encountered Alain. He was standing alone against the wall in one of the club's passageways. Five-foot-ten and maybe 230 pounds, he was extremely well-muscled, with a small waist, like a real bodybuilder, and a shaved, bullet-shaped head. He wore green army pants and a black leather motorcycle jacket, open with no shirt. A meaty paw clutched a beer. He seemed remote, but in a tentative way, as if he might welcome the right opportunity to smile and greet a stranger. He was attracting no one's attention that I could see, but to me he was the hottest thing in the club. And since I was obviously the second hottest, our destiny seemed clear.

I glanced hungrily at his smooth, superhero cleavage as I passed. Casually I brushed his thigh. I was about to feel the bulge of his cock when he reached down and firmly pushed my wrist away.

Stephen Greco

"How ya doin'?" I said, in my best American.

He smirked dismissively and said nothing.

Fuck you, I thought, and moved on. I went to the bar and ordered another double vodka.

I was in Paris on a press junket, along with several other American journalists including my old friend Jed, to see and gather background information on a Delacroix exhibition on view at the Grand Palais museum, that would be traveling to the United States. Jed and I both had magazine assignments centering on the show.

Paris had changed for me, over the years. In the early '70s, when I first arrived there with my boyfriend, Barry, the city opened my eyes to everything: noble boulevards and spot-lit monuments that had witnessed the creation of deathless works of art, science, and literature; tiny hotel rooms and modest restaurants that had blessed other passions as great as Barry's and mine. For many years I viewed Paris like the rest of the world did, as the world capital of ardor and enlightenment, and Barry and I vowed to return there together every year, forever—which we did until 1987, when he died. Then, somehow, I wound up desensitizing myself to the city's glamour, rather than trying to savor it alone. Through the '90s I continued to go there, but only on business. I gave up the stylish attire that Barry and I always lovingly planned for Parisian visits and stuck to plain suits. I went to bed early and stayed away from cruising.

I never consciously decided to do so, but I started losing touch with the spirit of the city, the seductive Paris of both clean and dirty postcards. My current boyfriend, KJ, and I have often said we *must* see the City of Light together, but so far our trips abroad have been quite intentionally to places that neither of us has seen before, so we can create our own nostalgia, independent of any potentially confusing, pre-existing memories that either of us still held from previous relationships. Yet on this trip I had been ambushed by memories more visceral than mere nostalgia—like one that made me weep one day when Jed and I, walking down the Rue des Saint Pères, came across a small luxury hotel I recognized: a memory about sneaking a cooked chicken into a shabby student hotel room though food was forbidden, dining royally for ten minutes, being sniffed out by a very vocal cat named Whiskey, chucking the chicken carcass out the window, and being chastised by the hotel's redoubtable manager, Madame Dufour, notwithstanding the invitation to come in and search the room. I had begun to remember that *being there*, surrendering to the enchantment of chicken or any other flesh, is a ritual to be performed always, at all stages of life, alone or with any manner of friend or lover.

I certainly would never have entered a sex club there, at this stage of my life, had I not been traveling with Jed. For one thing, Jed, unlike me, speaks fluent French. He went to school in Paris and still has friends there. Then there's Jed's boyish good looks and his infectiously charming need to be in the middle of the action—which on this trip automatically differentiated us from the scores of sheepish, slightly under- or overdressed, guidebook-toting gay tourists roving around the city. By the end of our first day together Jed and I had struck up conversations with several Frenchmen we'd met in the street, or in shops and restaurants, who'd clued us in to new night spots and DJ performances, invited us to a few parties.

On the night I met Alain, Jed and I had dined early at a trendy new restaurant in the Marais. We'd not been allowed to pay the bill, since Jed had attracted the attention of the restaurant's owner, who came over and had a drink with us. Did we know, the owner asked, that he also has a space downstairs that much later in the evening turns into one of the city's hottest dance clubs? We did not know that, but four hours later we showed up at a discreetly marked door to the left of the restaurant, found our names on the list, and spent an hour or so among a capacity crowd in a small, basement-level, neon-lit box, while cloud after cloud of lightly scented disco mist washed through the space. Jed found the owner and made out with him. We left around two with the addresses of three highly recommended, semiprivate sex clubs.

The idea was to check out all three clubs. The first was tiny and empty—just a neighborhood bar. Jed and I bolted down our drinks and left. The second was much larger, comprising three floors designed as a menacingly high-tech, sci-fi fantasy world, with lots of pods and cubicles that said a lot—to me, anyway—about how the French love to mix their horror of dehumanization with their secret thrill in it. This place, too, was fairly empty, though Jed wound up meeting a sexy man there, Laurent, and we all cabbed back to his place, a luxuriously restored eighteenth-century private house not far from the restaurant where we'd had dinner. At first we said we would all do some drugs and go out together to the third sex club, but when Jed and Laurent began making out more seriously, I excused myself and set out alone.

The third place wasn't far away. As I walked there—maybe it was the hash—I realized that the night air was redolent with a powerful Parisian fragrance I remembered, both leafy and petro-chemical. I entered the club determined to find or create my own kind of sex and not pose for an hour, discussing Delacroix.

Half an hour later, after being rebuffed by Alain, I was standing against a timber support in a little pen in the club's deepest recess. My third vodka rested nearby on a narrow ledge. Fire was the last thing on my mind. I was watching a group of men who had finally started playing among themselves. Two naked boys—one blond, one dark-haired—were working as a team of provocateurs. They would kiss, suck, and fondle each other, then go around the group and do the same with other men. Then they'd come back to each other for more fondling.

Watching this got me hard. I loved the boys' attitude. I unbuttoned my jeans, which fell halfway down my legs, and took out my cock and started stroking it intermittently. Soon I was included in the boys' circuit: one or the other would come over and fondle my cock or suck it briefly, rub my pecs, or rub my butt and thighs.

At some point I noticed that Alain was also in the pen, standing opposite me, a few feet away. He still looked rigid, his shoulders back in an almost military posture. His jacket was a bit more open now, and enough of one of his square, bulging pecs showed to expose a nipple. But he still looked aloof. I suspected that because my pants were down he might now be a bit more attracted to me, but I avoided looking at him until the two naked boys started devoting themselves to my body exclusively—which met with the obvious approval of the other men, who stroked their own cocks as they watched. At that point, naked boy flesh all over me, I began staring at Alain squarely, immobile, with narrowed eyes, as if stoically enduring a torture.

I thought he'd enjoy this display: me showing publicly that his presence made me indifferent to anything else. And sure enough, within a few minutes, one side of Alain's mouth was curling slightly into a half smile.

Meanwhile the boys were proving effective. They were kneeling in front of me, taking turns on my cock. I had hoped that Alain might stride over, take hold of me, and say something gutteral in French just as I was about to shoot, but the timing was off. When Alain finally came over with the obvious intention of joining the action, I was already pumping my load deep into the eager throat of one of the boys—who I think was surprised I had gotten to that point so undetectably.

Alain planted himself opposite me, so close that I could smell the beer on his breath with an undertone of garlic. He brushed away the boy's attempt to grab his cock but he let me touch it, through his pants. He grabbed mine and apparently didn't notice that I had cum. But it was over. I needed to collect myself. The boys went back to each other, while Alain and I began talking.

"My name is Steve."

"Hello." He was suddenly beaming like a little boy. "Alain."

"Hi. I just came, you know."

I could tell that Alain's English was as limited as my French. I suddenly felt a little responsible for him.

"What's French for cum?" I said. "Uh ... *jouir!*"

Alain smiled knowingly.

"No, I mean I just ... *J'ai déjà* ..."

I was trying to scrunch down and pull my jeans up as we spoke, but Alain was standing too close to me and he wasn't budging. Finally I had to ask him for some room. He seemed to find this charming.

We went upstairs for a drink, doing our best to communicate. I couldn't understand what Alain said he did for a living, but I did get that his family was German, from Alsace. He was sweet and a little oafish, sharp but not terribly intellectual. And he was that rare thing in France, a nonsmoker—because of his bodybuilding, I gathered. I knew he didn't understand that I had cum and he probably expected that our discussion would lead to sex. In fact, I got the impression that his goal was taking someone home, but another session was out of the question for me. In three hours I had to appear, showered and fresh, in the baroque breakfast room of our expensive hotel, just off the Champs Elysée, ready to tour the French senate, where Delacroix had painted some murals.

I knew I'd kick myself if I didn't have some kind of sex with Alain. And so would KJ. Alain was a type that both KJ and I flip over and sometimes hook up with for threesomes, one of several, carefully negotiated sexual "extensions" that have been instrumental in keeping us together as a happy couple—though in other times Barry and I pursued a different romantic ideal and never imagined such behavior.

But it was late. I made it clear to Alain that I was leaving and we exchanged phone numbers.

I called the next day. He wasn't there so I left a message, saying hello and also good-bye. The day after that, my last in Paris, there was a phone message waiting for me when I got back to the hotel room, around eleven, after my final morning's appointments.

"You like Alain's cock, yes? You come to the place?"

A charming invitation, but he hadn't understood. In my message, I'd explained I was leaving. I had also mentioned that fact at the club. There was no way I could get to the "place" where he told me he lives—he used what sounded like the English word—and be back in time for my flight, even if he was the hottest man in France I almost had sex with.

I dialed his number.

"*Allo?*"

"Alain, it's Steve."

"*Oui*, Steve! *Comment va?*"

"Fine, thanks. *Merci*. Listen, *peu-je parle en anglais s'il vous plaît?* It was great to hear from you, but as I mentioned I'm leaving today—actually in an hour or so. So it's going to have to wait until I come back to Paris or you come to New York. Do you think you'll be in New York any time soon?"

Alain said a few sentences in French that I couldn't understand but took to mean, "Come to my place because the resident isn't home."

Did he mean his landlord or something? For a moment I considered what it might cost to change my flight. If it were only a second round of sex we were talking about, I might have found it easier to say no. But we were still talking about a consummation.

Just then, Jed knocked at the door and popped his head into the room.

"If you're packed, we have just enough time for a quick lunch at that nice bistro around the corner. Laurent is meeting us." It was now love between them and they were planning an extended American sojourn for Laurent.

I pointed to the phone and mouthed, "It's him."

Jed raised his eyebrows. "Your muscle guy? How exciting."

He entered the room and flopped down on the bed, singing the theme song from "The Love Boat."

"Exciting and new ..."

"Wait, Alain," I said into the phone, "Say hello to my friend.

Souviens-toi mon ami Jed?"

I covered the mouthpiece.

"I don't know what he's saying," I said. "Will you talk to him? I'm trying to say good-bye. Ask him if he ever gets to New York."

Jed got on. He started rattling away in French, punctuating the conversation with plenty of *ouis, nons,* and very Gallic-sounding grunts of understanding.

"*Attends, attends,*" Jed said to Alain, laughing. Then, to me, "So do you know what he said when I asked if he would be in New York anytime soon?"

"What?"

"He said, 'Maybe in three months, when Monsieur le Président plans to visit the United States.'"

The president?

"He's a bodyguard at the Elysée Palace," Jed continued. "That's where the President of France lives. He wants to know if you have time to stop over there right now. He can meet you at the gate. We're only three blocks away. But think fast, because I don't want to be late for Laurent."

It took me a while to process this new information and the extraordinary invitation, but finally, through Jed, I said no. I wasn't surprised when I learned what Alain did for a living. When I first saw him I thought he might be a cop or work with his body in some way. Turns out, I was right on both counts.

Neither Jed nor I was quite clear on whether Alain was proposing a quickie somewhere on palace grounds. We didn't resolve that issue. We gave Alain my phone number and address in New York and made him promise to call before he came. I insisted that Jed mention that he could stay with me.

Lunch was epic in its way. The fish was a poem and I enjoyed seeing Jed so head-over-heels about Laurent. I left the table early, to go back to the room and call KJ.

"We're jumping on the plane in an hour," I said to my boyfriend. "I'll be home for dinner, your time. I just called to say, having a wonderful time, *wish* you were here."

"That's sweet," KJ said. "So you love me?"

"I do, and I think we have to check out Paris together sooner than we planned. Picture you and me in a steamy, after-hours sex club, playing with a muscle god who ranks as one of the greatest monuments of Western civilization ...."

The Trout

This is the tale of a young man who didn't figure out what his heart and body really wanted until it was too late. He swam in several different New York social streams and was thought to be a great catch for any guest list, so gossip columnists often referred to him as "The Trout."

His name was Jason and he was twenty-three years old. He smiled easily, flashing green eyes and arcs of perfect white teeth, and he had the squarish jaw and horizontal slashes of eyebrow that cartoonists give men they mean to be handsome. He powered his athletic, 6-foot-1, 190-pound body through a room as if the place were as large as the Colorado ranch he grew up on, and his manner was charged with an easygoing sexual vibe that registered equally with women and men. "A young Harrison Ford" was how people sometimes described him; he had the same artlessly masculine thicket of brown hair.

The moment Jason arrived in New York, right after college, he was taken up by a young, rich party crowd. They were attracted by Jason's casual seductiveness and were always inviting him to the right parties and hottest clubs, where his charm gave him entree with fashion and magazine people, celebrity artists and actors, and other scenesters. Paparazzi sensed he was someone, or perhaps that he would one day be someone, so they always shot him arriving at or leaving places. Jason returned all this attention by being good company. He conversed lightly with everyone, knowing when to make jokes and when not to. He could drink without losing control and behaving badly. He didn't tell long stories about his childhood and college years. His sexuality was best defined by his favorite word, "whatever"—he got taken home by everyone who wanted him, didn't seem to want anyone back that much, enjoyed what was done to him, and didn't do too much back. Every now and then someone fell for him for a weekend, but no one ever made him feel the same way, and soon it was all laughs again and the party kept going.

He didn't know what the word "love" meant and didn't really think about it.

His family had money, but he chose not to depend on his family, so he sometimes worked as a carpenter. And he was a pretty good carpenter, too, having worked all his life in a friend's dad's custom cabinetry business. He hadn't given much thought to a "real" career until arriving in New York, when he decided to become an actor. Selling his Rolex allowed him to enroll in classes at the Neighborhood Playhouse. One of the toughest challenges he encountered there was learning to avoid overplaying the cowboy thing—which explains why, at six in the evening one day in July, after working eight hours with a construction crew in the kitchen of the Park Avenue apartment of the well-known playwright Porter Allen Douglas, Jason was wearing a pair of beat up cowboy boots and a sweatshirt that read "Boulder" with a dirty pair of painter's pants.

It was the last stage of an extensive renovation. The men were packing up their tool bags and checking their cell phones, while the forty-seven-year-old playwright stood there at the door, letting them out.

"Oh, Jason, do you have time for a drink?" Porter said. "I found that speech we were talking about."

Jason bid the rest of the crew goodnight. In the library, Porter mixed gin-and-tonics.

"It *is* Thornton Wilder, but from a novel, not a play."

"Hey, great, man."

"I'm not sure it would work as a monologue, as it is. If you like, I could make a few interpolations myself and create a version for you."

"Damn, Porter, that's really nice of you."

"Nice has nothing to do with it. I like helping young talent."

They had met once at a party and spoken a bit. Then both were surprised when Jason showed up months later as part of the construction crew that was building Porter a new kitchen using antique and recycled materials. Porter Allen Douglas, unwilling to vacate while the work was being done, had been underfoot almost every day, inspecting everything. While most of the crew found this annoying, Jason thought it funny and joked with the playwright about it. Porter allowed this because Jason's work was so fine and ... the boy had those flashing green eyes. Sometimes, after work, the two of them talked about the theater, the difference between the art form and the industry. Sometimes they talked about the difficulty of making it in New York. It had never been much of a seduction either way, until now. Today Porter had decided to do the boy a favor with the monologue and take him to dinner. Then, afterward, he would ask Jason to do *him* a big favor.

Some people are desperate and don't even know it. Porter was one of them. He had been seriously depressed for months and tried to deny it by doing things like buying $600 loafers and designing custom drawer pulls for his kitchen. Not exactly a has-been, Porter had never bested the series of successes he had off-Broadway in the '80s: bitterly amusing, largely autobiographical plays about growing up impoverished and unhappy in Kentucky. Toward the end of the series critics began complaining about the cynicism and monotony they saw taking over his work, and Porter knew they were right. He stopped writing for a while. The only thing he did in the '90s was work on his photography, which he knew was not much more than competent, despite the fact that a photo book he did on life in rural Kentucky became a best-seller and was made into a documentary by The Learning Channel.

"You have no idea how hard the business is nowadays, especially for an established playwright," Porter said, returning to one of his favorite subjects. "I'm trying to get my latest one produced. It's a completely different kind of play for me. I wrote it this year after not writing a thing since—well, you know. A completely new direction, and I can't get anybody to read it. They're always looking for *young* playwrights. 'Who's the hot *young* playwright?'"

"What's it about?"

"Life. Not my life, though! I'm sick of talking about that. No, it's about life-life, hopefully from an amusing point of view. The characters started out as total strangers to me. I made up events that never happened to me. I was terrified to work on it, but I felt I had to try. I'm petrified it's awful."

"I'm sure it's brilliant, Porter."

"We'll see. I need to get it read."

For a moment, Porter imagined Jason's large hands on the keyboard of a laptop.

"Have you … ever thought about writing a play?"

"I wouldn't know what to write about."

"For God's sake, don't write about what you know!"

They both laughed and put down their glasses.

"Come," Porter said. "Dinner. And if you ever do decide to crank out a draft of something, you know I'll be perfectly happy to help you with it …."

Dinner led to the casual kind of sex that Jason stuck to with men: he let himself get sucked a bit and he jerked himself off. Neither of them talked about it before or afterward. It was the next morning, in Porter's bedroom, after Jason had showered and dressed, when Porter asked his big favor. He had been cooking up the proposition for weeks, so by now it sounded reasonable to him. Jason thought it wild at first, but then, after listening to Porter lay out the terms and possible results, and considering all that he could do with the $10,000 that Porter was offering in exchange for his cooperation, he decided it might be fun. Jason would pretend to be the author of Porter's new play. Posing as the hot young playwright, he would take it around to various agents and directors. When the play was produced, and Porter never doubted that it would be, everyone in Jason's crowd would add to the buzz. Jason and Porter would keep the ruse going until the day after opening night, at which point they would reveal the truth. They'd talk to the *Times* and tell everybody what great fun it had been to administer a good poke to the establishment.

It sounded fine to Jason. Hell, he felt honored to have been chosen. Porter assured him that any theater would happily weather the controversy as long as ticket sales remained strong, which they would because the playwright was famous and New York loves a scandal. The only thing Porter didn't tell the boy was that if the play bombed on opening night, he intended to kill himself without revealing anything. Failure was not something Porter was prepared to face. Whatever the outcome, he would at least have given a young actor the role of a lifetime, to do with as he pleased.

Porter slapped the script down onto the upholstered bench at the end of the bed.

"What do you think?" A new title page with Jason's name on it was already attached.

"I think I'm gonna win a damned Tony with that," Jason said.

Over the next few months, as summer gave way to fall, Jason ran around New York with the play. Under Porter's guidance, he made calls and met with directors and producers. A columnist ran an item about everybody's favorite "Trout" surprising the world with a new play, which she pronounced "fabulous" without having read it. Jason did read the play, of course, and liked it as far as he understood it. But following rules Porter set he never publicly discussed the play's influences and themes, only its plot. They decided that when asked about themes or anything else potentially confounding, Jason should divert the conversation with lines that Porter wrote especially for this situation, like "I want to stay respectful of the play's right to speak for itself," or "Given the great debt I owe those who have obviously influenced me, it's very hard for me to talk about them." As for casting, Porter came up with a list of interesting names and Jason practiced saying them as if he were thinking of them on the spur of the moment.

Jason enjoyed the game more than he thought he would. People in his crowd responded enthusiastically to the idea of his blossoming into an artist. Those who could started talking to him in a different, more serious way, which pleased him enormously and made him try to be more thoughtful in response. As per his bargain with Porter, he let no one in on the secret, but one day, almost as a way of making good on people's interest, he decided to write a play of his own. It would be about a young guy who comes to New York from Kansas and helps an older friend get a novel published. The guy falls in love and ... then what?

He was going to wait until the play was finished before showing it to Porter, as a surprise, but he quickly saw how much he could use the kind of help his friend had offered. Writing was difficult for Jason. He had expected telling stories on paper to be as easy as recounting social exploits, which he did every day with his friends. But it wasn't easy at all. Writing seemed to require a kind of judgment alien to him. Even the simplest choices were perplexing, like what to put in and what to leave out. Should the guy in Jason's play be like Jason or not? How did an author decide how much of himself to put into a play—for instance, could the hero be someone who, as a boy, had enjoyed playing roles in little plays his girlfriend wrote; had been ridiculed by an angry father the night he performed in a play about fairies; had thrown himself into every sport offered by his high school; had learned to ride horses, date girls, and out-cowboy all the other cowboys?

Jason worked on his play when time allowed, but characters and motivations eluded him. He wrote in short sessions that ended in distraction, his thoughts jammed.

In October, Porter's play was taken by the Little Theater in Tribeca. It was a small but prestigious theater whose famous artistic director had close ties with Hollywood. Almost immediately, the play was cast with Ryan Philippe in the lead, rehearsals began, and the run was set to begin in early December. The director was thrilled to have a playwright with so little interest in giving input.

Porter and Jason had made it a point not see too much of each other after the kitchen was finished, so no suspicions would be aroused, but they talked often by phone.

"It's looking good, Porter." It was the afternoon of opening night, during a break in the last-minute tech rehearsal. Jason was calling from the theater lobby. Dress rehearsal, the night before, had gone very well.

"Is it?" Porter sounded distant and distracted. "I'm living in complete fear, you know. Not just that the play is bad, but that it's the kind of bad that will make people rethink everything else I've ever done."

"That's crazy. It's a wonderful play. I think I'm actually beginning to understand it now. Ryan has made some really interesting choices."

"Oh, God. Listen to you."

"Look, I know I can't convince you to come tonight, but you've got tickets for tomorrow night, and there's our lunch with that writer from the *Times*. It'll be fun. She thinks she's interviewing just me. I'll pick you up at your place around eleven, OK?"

"Good luck, Jason."

"The party is at Barolo but I'm only stopping in for a second. It would feel too weird being congratulated all night."

"Good luck, understand?"

The opening was a hit. Sitting in the audience were not only members of the media but every trendsetter and buzzmaker in the city. Jason tried calling Porter a few times from the party, but there was no answer. At ten-thirty the next morning he arrived at Porter's apartment building, carrying an armful of white peonies and the new play of his own that he'd finished the week before. He didn't notice the ambulance double-parked at the curb. The apartment door was open and Porter's housekeeper was just inside, talking to police detectives. Other people were in the kitchen. She'd found the body in there an hour ago, slumped on the banquette, with a glass containing the remains of something nasty-looking on a table nearby. There was a note, addressed to no one, that read, "Keep on swimming."

After speaking with the detectives and giving his condolences to the housekeeper, Jason left, in shock. The only thing he could think to do was call the *Times* reporter and postpone lunch.

II

"It's definitely ... interesting," the old man said, tapping the script with a bony, milky-white finger. He was talking about Jason's play but was distracted by the boy's good looks.

It was a spring day, four months after Porter's death. Jason was sitting with the playwright Seymour Kransky, in Kransky's room in a residential hotel on the Lower East Side. The room contained a cot, a table, two chairs, a desk, several nicked, gray metal file cabinets, hundreds of books in piles on the floor, and not much else. Through an open window came a breeze carrying the scent of Chinese cooking and the sound of kids playing in a schoolyard. Kransky had been popular in the '40s and '50s for soap opera-ish, slice-of-life type plays, one of which was made into a movie starring Lana Turner. He lived high for a while, then cracked up on alcohol in the '60s and spent a decade recovering by living in a Catholic rectory, cooking and cleaning for priests. After the rectory closed, he took a low-paying job as a clerk in the library at NYU. Now, in his seventies, his health up and down, Kransky was "back in the freshman dorms," as he liked to joke.

Kransky knew that most people in the theater world thought him long dead, and that was fine with him. The whole Broadway machine was just too much for a bookish, introspective boy from the Bronx, especially now that star power and gimmickry had robbed big-time theater of the humanity it seemed to have right after World War II. He still went out socially now and then, but mostly to the homes of old friends: distinguished men and women in the arts who were themselves in their seventies and eighties but who still often dressed up in bohemian cocktail attire and got together with the same determined zest they had in the '40s and '50s, when they were on the vanguard of New York's most progressive, creative scene.

Kransky had been introduced to Jason at a party for a new volume of memoirs by one of the women in the group. The playwright thought the boy debonair, yet somehow sad. He had gone with him to see his play, at the boy's invitation, and during intermission they had had a nice talk. *Not gay, or at least, not gay enough*, Kransky thought, *but there's something precious inside him, trying to live*. They stayed in touch, mostly by phone, and Kransky turned into something of a mentor for Jason. They spoke several times a week, though the older man's attempts to go into deeper things, like what made the boy want to be a writer, were always evaded.

Jason had called the day before with "a big problem," a new play he needed help with. He'd messengered it over immediately with a note that said he wanted to meet with Kransky about it as soon as possible.

"So you'll help me edit it?" Jason said.

"Yes, yes. It shows promise," Kransky replied diplomatically. "But I can't help being mystified that it is so very ... different from the play I saw with you."

"But Seymour, can you can help me? Lincoln Center is begging me for something to do in the winter season."

"Let me be honest with you." Kransky shook his head and smiled gently. "Not this play. This needs more work than a week of shaping. I will work on it with you, and perhaps in a few months ..."

"I need something now! What the hell am I gonna do?"

The force of Jason's outburst surprised them both. During the previous four months, Jason's play at the Little Theater had been pulling in sell-out audiences. Press had been great and advance sale was strong. Several stars and celebrities had expressed interest in working with Jason on his next project. In fact, Lincoln Center Theater was putting a great deal of pressure on him to have that honor. Since he hadn't figured out a way to step away from this ruse, he had decided to use it in a way that would help him become the person people thought he was: a writer. Something inside Jason had been wrenched by the experience of playing this wonderful though monstrous role, by lying and becoming famous, by losing someone he'd hoped would become a great friend. He had been trying to get some of his feelings down in this new play of his, because he thought that the most fitting testament to Porter Allen Douglas would be to make a success of himself in the role that Porter had given him. But how? He went through draft after draft, each more reproachingly weak than the last.

Kransky knew something was wrong. He'd seen boys come and go in New York for half a century, boys who were handsome and/or talented and/or ambitious and/or pretending to be something as a way of becoming it. Gently, he put his hand on the boy's shoulder.

"Tell me what's going on."

Jason put his face in his hands and wept. After a few minutes, the whole story was out. Kransky listened with great emotion. He'd heard far worse.

"Darling, do you want my advice?" Kransky said. "You can't become a writer in one season. Perhaps you're on the right path. Perhaps you need more time. Give yourself another year."

"Another year," Jason muttered.

To lighten things up Kransky said, "Look, you've come this far with it. Why not find another play and fake it again?" And he added *sotto voce*, "Take one of mine. God knows I have plenty."

"What do you mean?"

"Oh, let Lincoln Center do one of my plays and say it's yours," Kransky said brightly. "Wouldn't that be delicious?" He walked over to one of the file cabinets and pulled out several scripts. "I've got a *Hamlet* here. I've got a *Cherry Orchard*, I've got a *Skin of Our Damned Teeth* .... I never stopped writing. I've got twenty plays here the world has never seen. Best stuff I ever did. Not that I would try to publish or produce it myself in a million years. No, thank you, ma'am. I wrote these for the future. Though it's clear that you could use a little play right now, couldn't you? Take one. Let it be a gift from someone who has plenty to give away."

He plopped the scripts down on the table, and went and got several more.

Jason looked through the pile. "I can pay," he said.

"Oh, keep your money. We're friends. Besides, there is only one other thing I would want from you and I can *hardly* expect to get any of that ...." Kransky said it coquettishly, but he meant it seriously. And he knew it was one of the most foolish things he had ever said in his life, not because the invitation was so frank but because the pains in his chest had been getting worse and he knew that one day soon he'd have to look into getting, and paying for, some kind of medical attention.

"Are you serious?" Jason said with a laugh, wiping away his tears. "You dog."

Jason selected a play. During the months that Lincoln Center was rehearsing and hyping it, he worked with Kransky on his other play. They met two or three times a week in Kransky's room. They also studied the classics and, sometimes, Kransky's plays. Jason came to see the old man's immense kindness and humanity, to understand how and why some of his extraordinary characters did what they did. Sometimes they traded personal stories—for Jason, stories from his childhood and teenage years he'd never told anyone and hadn't realized he remembered. Kransky talked about New York intellectual life during the '40s and '50s—how blacks, gays, and women led pioneering lives and created revolutionary work that in many ways caused the '60s. Jason was fascinated. He pored over pictures of Kransky during this period and was amazed at the gauntly handsome, poetic-looking dreamer with masses of lustrous, wavy black hair and big, soulful eyes. He thought how great it must have been to live in New York back then, when important cultural tasks needed doing; and he realized that the Kransky who *did* live through that era had been about the same age that Jason was now. In a way, Jason fell half in love with that Kransky, as they worked, because being with the old man made him understand the passion and engagement of the younger one, and that was inspiring.

Kransky was in a kind of love, too. This was the first time he had really *smelled* spring in three decades. So he didn't say no, one evening, when after their usual conversation and a pot of tea Jason quietly took his cock out of the fly of his jeans and started masturbating. Jason was accustomed to rewarding well-wishers in this way—but there was something more going on this time; he enjoyed giving this gift to Kransky; he was excited.... Slowly, as Kransky watched intently from across the room and rubbed his own cock through his pants, Jason leaned back in the chair with a little smile on his face and spread his legs. Handling himself lovingly, he brought his meaty cock from semihard to hard, and then, after cumming into his other hand, to rest. For a few minutes he let his soft cock hang out of his fly, resting to one side, while the two of them sat there in silence. Then Kransky said "Amen" and rose to find a towel.

In the weeks that followed, there were more sexual moments, always wordless, always with Jason initiating and Kransky taking part passively. At first the old man would pull his chair closer, to sit parallel with Jason and rest his hand on Jason's thigh as the boy shot. Then they fell into a ritual that was repeated on several occasions, in which Jason stood before cumming and shot his load onto Seymour's beatifically beaming face. The old man never asked for more, and Jason wasn't sure whether Kransky's rubbing of his own crotch ever resulted in an orgasm.

"You can't write a thing until you know what that 'mass of irritable substance' you are really wants," Kransky said one day, quoting Freud. "One pays an enormous price not just for secrecy but for ambiguity. I marvel that so many creative people, the very ones who make such a big deal out of protecting their creativity from psychoanalysis and the like, think they can play fast and loose with sex and desire."

"Damn, Seymour, you keep saying stuff like that," Jason replied. "I wish I knew what you meant. I just let things *happen*. You'd be surprised, the men and women who have come on to me this year— celebrities, man. And I just, whatever, roll with the punches."

"Then look deeper, darling. Something is there, in your little heart. And the heart is connected to the balls. It's not a matter of accepting offers. It's about knowing yourself well enough to make them. So what if your rich, powerful, cowboy father would flip if you turned out to be gay? You've got to stay loyal to yourself."

The play opened in January and, once again, "Jason" had a hit. Reviewers commented on the vast stylistic difference between this and the previous play, but that was generally chalked up to what people were now calling Jason's Shakespearean virtuosity and scope. The *Times, Talk, Vanity Fair,* and *Interview* all did features. Soon Jason was going not just to fun parties but to the "important" ones, too—like a state dinner at the White House, where he chatted at length with the Governor of Colorado. In February he accepted an invitation from a media mogul and his fashion designer wife to go island hopping in the Aegean on their yacht.

"'The Trout' is swimming among the Greek isles, in the wake of his thrilling success at Lincoln Center," said Suzy in *W*. "He's gotten quite friendly with one of his shipmates, beautiful thirtysomething actress Yanna Kumin, who is accustomed to swimming in better social ponds herself. Who else would tell you these things?"

Jason returned on a Sunday and the first thing he did was call Kransky, to make a date for dinner.

"I'm taking you to Bernardin."

"Oh, nice."

"On Thursday?"

"I'm here. Just feeling a little tired."

"Wait until you see what I've done in the third act. I can write for much longer at a time now. Something about the islands inspired me."

"Ah, Mykonos ..."

"And by the way, Seymour, the next time we do our you-know-what, those pants are coming off."

Three days later, on Wednesday, Jason was sitting in a conference room at the *Times* for an interview with one of the paper's cultural writers. She asked Jason if his new play were intended as some kind of homage to the late playwright Seymour Kransky, whose work during the '40s and '50s was in a similar vein, if not quite as profound.

Jason smiled, having run into this mistake before.

"It's not an homage. Though I happen to know Mr. Kransky and am happy to remind the world that he's still alive and kicking."

"Oh, no," the writer said. "He died yesterday—a heart attack, I think. The obit is running in tomorrow's paper."

III

There's no such thing as Fate. Fate is only chance with a sheaf of good press clips under its arm. People find their destinies when they learn to collaborate with chance, which they can do only after they've come to know themselves, inside and out. This isn't a tale of fate. It's a tale of simple, human matters—like sexual urges and a predilection for cowboy boots.

Kransky left no will and had no family. Jason saw to it that his friend's papers were stored safely until it could be arranged for a university archive to accept them. Lovingly, he packed all the material into boxes himself, sifting through it, trying to get a deeper sense of the life just lost. Among the letters and essays were snapshots of Seymour and his friends in the '40s and '50s, looking handsome, heroic. That wavy black hair of Seymour's, swept back in a way that would still look sexy on a guy who had that much hair. His smile and the smiles of several other shirtless men, on the beach, summering on a then barely developed Fire Island. The immense project of giving yourself permission to be really free during the Eisenhower years ....

Jason purchased an expensive plot in a cemetery upstate, along the Hudson. He was driving back from there one day, after signing off on a design for the memorial, when the car phone rang.

"Darling, it's Yanna. I told you I'd call when I got to New York."

"You're here?"

"I'm here and I'm sitting in Monty's office." She meant Montclair Chase, the producer who owned several Broadway houses and was, as Yanna had confessed one night on the Aegean as she and Jason were kissing innocently, her current boyfriend. "We need a play for me, for next season. I know you have one."

Half-English and half-Pakistani, Yanna was a knockout who had been classically trained at the Royal Academy of Dramatic Arts. She had made a big splash a decade before, as a relative unknown, in a Merchant Ivory period drama and had remained an indie queen until recently, when she successfully opened a big-budget action picture with Mark Wahlberg. She was now someone whom industry people were watching intently for her next move. And her next move, Yanna thought, should be Broadway—something serious.

"I was working on a play, yes," Jason said, "but it's far from ready. I put it aside, actually, until I could think through a couple of things."

"Oh, you're thinking," Yanna giggled. "That's marvelous. Listen, have dinner with Monty and me tonight. We'll talk about it, darling, alright? Balthazar at ten."

The restaurant was packed. They had a corner table and everyone stopped to say hello to one, two, or all three of them: Harvey Weinstein, Gwyneth Paltrow, Dominick Dunne, Stella McCartney. Stella was a close friend of Yanna's. She had designed the little beaded black jacket that the actress happened to be wearing, as well as the long, sheer, black scarf that Yanna wore with everything that year.

Yanna was at her most effervescent. Throughout dinner, as was her habit with favorite accessories, she played flirtatiously with the scarf—wrapping and re-wrapping it about both herself and Jason.

"You *have* to do it," she was pleading, leaning into him. "You're a star, I'm a star. It was meant to be. And Monty can make it happen, can't you, Monty?"

Chase was picking at dessert, his back to them, on the phone with Los Angeles.

"Montclair, darling?"

"Can you hold a sec, Steve?" he said, craning around. "Jason, whatever it takes. We're reserving the dates on 47th Street—that's my biggest house. I know we can make this work. I need to see a script by September first. Can you give me September first?" Chase returned to his conversation.

Jason felt the swept-along sensation he'd experienced a few times before, when important decisions were being made. Thinking he'd be willing to revisit his play over the summer, and halting Yanna's wandering hand under the table just before it reached his crotch, he said yes.

"Brilliant!" Yanna exclaimed.

Through the spring and summer, Jason saw a lot of Yanna. She was almost ten years older than him, still very youthful and of-the-moment yet never lacking that more assured, adult kind of poise that he'd always found appealing in women. In bed, Jason did little more with women than he did with men, but his and Yanna's relationship did turn decidedly sexual one night in the Hamptons. They decided to keep this and a few subsequent intimate encounters secret from Chase, though it was clear that Yanna had an arrangement with the producer that allowed her to play when she wanted to play. Jason's relationship with Yanna quickly became a kind of strategic friendship that gave each of them, without demanding much, what they seemed to want physically—which was sometimes only company or a convenient date for high-profile parties.

Jason continued working on his play over the summer, but he told Yanna he wouldn't show it to her until the new version was finished. She was as comfortable with that condition as she was with the remarkable story of Jason's false plays and false fame, which he confessed to her in whispers one night in bed. She understood. In fact, she thought the whole thing wickedly funny, even philosophically important. "This could be greater than what Warhol did," she bubbled. "It's exactly what our times are about, isn't it?" Afterward, she showed lavish affection toward the boy whose weakness, or help-lessness, or moral indirection, had led him to get caught up in such a brilliant scheme. And she began to relish her own role of complic-ity in it, and what she called his destiny.

Toward the end of August they flew to the south of France and checked into a small but luxurious inn near Cassis, on the coast between Marseilles and Toulon. The trip was a gift from Chase. The plan was for Jason to finish his play and for both of them to get in some rock climbing on the steep limestone cliffs that plunge into the Mediterranean. It was a place that Jason, a rock climber for years, had always wanted to try. Yanna, who said she "climbed a bit," was also eager to have a go, though it later came out she had climbed only once before, on a weekend in the Shawangunk Mountains north of New York City.

For a few days they had fun in Cassis. They climbed the cliffs, swam in secluded inlets, dined in two-and three-star restaurants on the coast, drove inland to view Roman ruins. Then something changed in the way they had sex. Never that passionate or fre-quent, now it didn't even feel like fun. Moreover, friction grew between them that seemed to be about more than just sex. Yanna snapped at Jason several times when, despite his good manners, his actions veered from those of an attentive boyfriend. They had never used those words, "boyfriend" and "girlfriend," but still Yanna grew moody and began going off alone, to shop or play.

Jason found himself wondering what the friction between them might mean. This trip had filled his head with thoughts he at first took for new and then realized had been there for a long time. They were thoughts about men. He began catching himself looking at guys at the beach and around town in the same way he had looked at those wonderful old photographs of Seymour and his friends. But these guys were here now and they all looked heroic, suddenly—the way they squinted in the sun when they surveyed the sea, or slicked back their hair when they emerged from a swim. Jason found himself studying their hands, their arms. Arms are the true sexual organs, he thought. It's not a question of whether your cock should be surrounded by vaginal tissue or throat tissue. It's whether your whole body has the right set of arms around it.

He began wondering what would it be like to do more sexually with a guy than just masturbate or get blown, which was all he'd ever done. He wondered what it would be like to meet someone so magnetic that you'd want to be with him all the time, sharing adventures, embraces. One village fisherman—a compact, muscular man around thirty, with a black crew cut and a craggily handsome face—gave Jason a spectacular arm show one afternoon on the dock, when Jason asked, in his rudimentary French, about how fishing nets were repaired. The fisherman showed him all about it, lustily. Jason found it hard to get the experience—those veiny forearms, those thick wrists—out of his mind.

Was this little fever the result of age, Jason wondered? Was it something more likely to occur at twenty-five than at twenty?

He finally presented Yanna with his play one afternoon. He was proud of his accomplishment but wanted to let her respond in her own way, so he left her to read it and went off to get a haircut. When he returned she was already dressed for dinner and they drove up the coast to St. Tropez. During the drive she babbled on about a new movie project she had been offered, and then, over their first glass of wine, she told him that she found his play "unsuitable."

"I'm sorry darling," she said, "I know how much it means to you. But I absolutely need a starring vehicle for Broadway and this play just isn't it."

Jason was stunned. He could say nothing.

"The structure is flawed," she continued. "The action is clumsy. The thing has its moments but ..." She looked down at her wine. "The main character—well, he's hardly what a man in love is really like."

"The play will embarrass us both," she said in a whisper, after noticing that the couple at the next table had recognized her. She admitted that she had been afraid of this possibility all along and, rather as if she had rehearsed it, she launched into the story of there being a certain other play she'd actually love to do, that he could palm off as his, if he wanted. It was a "masterpiece" by an acting coach she'd worked with for years, a Scottish guy who'd died of AIDS in the late '80s. This play was the only thing he'd ever written. He'd done it for her and made her promise, on his deathbed, that she'd find a way to star in it someday.

Now that he thought of it, Jason had noticed Yanna rather intently studying a script she'd brought along.

"Does Monty know about this?" he asked angrily.

"Of course not. He's not going to do a play by an unknown."

"But he *would* do one by me! So you've had this ... other work as your safety play all along?"

"Well, yes, darling, I have. Especially after you told me that long, sad story of yours."

"Jesus, Yanna, didn't you think I could write my own play? Don't you think I'm an artist?"

"*Are* you an artist, Jason? I mean, you know what you are."

They drove back in silence. Early the next morning Jason went out alone, to a café. When he came back, around lunchtime, Yanna was out. The concierge told him she'd gone climbing with one of the pros the inn kept on staff.

Around six, Chase called.

"Cowboy, do you have my play?"

"Yes," Jason said, in a steely tone, "I do. I've just finished it. We'll be back in New York at the end of the week and I'll bring it to you then. It's a whole new thing for me."

"Isn't it always a whole new thing with you? That's your genius, cowboy, and we love it! Now let me say hello to the little girl."

"She went rock climbing."

"Ask her to call me when she gets in."

Jason was getting dressed for dinner, which he was perfectly prepared to enjoy alone if Yanna didn't show up, when there was a knock on the door. It was the police.

"Our deepest apologies, monsieur. There has been an accident—
très grave."

They had Yanna's black Stella McCartney scarf—half of it,
anyway, shredded at one end.

"Does this belong to your wife?"

"Oh my God—she fell!"

"No, monsieur. They were coming back from the cliffs on the
gentleman's moped. The scarf became entangled in the wheels.
Apparently she was ... waving it and trying to put it around his
neck. I am sorry, monsieur. They are gone."

IV

Jason's third success in as many years conferred upon him a kind of
saintly status, burnished by the tragic circumstances surrounding
the production. Montclair Chase took his personal loss in stride and
quickly cast another, younger actress in the lead. Reviewers gasped
at the range of Jason's playwrighting style, his mastery of different
rhythms, his command of language patterns, the uncanny freedom
with which he structured plots and built characters in so many different ways. How could someone who grew up on a ranch in Colorado
during the '80s, they asked, have written first a sparkling parlor
farce worthy of Feydeau, then a gut-wrenching nouveau-social-real-
ist indictment of America's health care system, and now a pene-
trating look beneath the surface of genteel life in a vicar's house-
hold in the Scottish Highlands between the Wars? Jason had flown
back from France not only with Yanna's body but with her RADA-
inflected critique of his work ringing in his ears. It was the dead acting coach's play that he'd submitted to Chase.

Jason was desperate. Somehow he'd have to repay the three
gigantic spiritual loans he'd been foolish enough to accept.
Somehow his writing was the key.

That spring he chatted his way through a full hour on "Charlie
Rose"—not too taxing, he discovered—and with a great flourish of
unsought publicity he enrolled in a master class at the prestigious

HB Studio. He thought if he could only go back and learn more about acting, he might understand more about himself and the play he was struggling to write. Cameras flashed as he arrived at and left the studio on his bike. Chase and his press people were stunned at first. Then they started publicly spouting their praise for an artist so devoted to the theater that he had to seek every bit of wisdom the city had to offer.

It happened that Sammo Kondratiev was in the same class. A popular young actor who grew up in the Russian mob-run streets of Brighton Beach, Sammo had been the MC of a popular, major-label hip-hop group and had recently acquitted himself admirably in supporting roles in several hit movies. His fame was more national in scale than Jason's. Everyone who read *Entertainment Weekly* or watched E! knew that ScreenWorks was paying for Sammo to attend this acting seminar as a way of making him ready for the new, secret Spelvin Steinberg project the studio was developing especially for him. Physically, Sammo was formidable: 5-foot-9; 200 very tightly packed pounds; broad shoulders and small, body-builder's waist. He had trained in a special Asian-Russian form of extreme fighting and his movements were slow and deliberate, though there was something about them that made it seem as though, in an instant, any part of his pit bull physique could trans-mit thousands of pounds of force.

Sammo had a flattering yet somehow scary way of focusing totally on the person he was talking to, of almost making him or her feel guilty about looking away from those expressive brown eyes for even a moment—say, to notice the ugly scar above his right eye. People didn't so much find Sammo charming as fall hostage to his charm. He was the type of guy that certain people, when they were with him in a restaurant or at a party, secretly hoped might erupt into violence at any moment. This was partly because Sammo had a criminal record that he'd never made an attempt to hide. He had been involved in a violent drug deal and had spent some time in a New York state penitentiary. According to the official biography, prison is where Sammo had first started acting. In fact, Sammo worked the "sensitive ex-con" vibe, because he knew it was a major source of his stardom and the huge amount of money that brought him. His current girlfriend, a sexy, fast-rising R&B singer-songwriter, was familiar with this vibe. Her previous man was a boxer who couldn't keep from beating up business associates and members of the media.

Jason thought Sammo was cool. Amused, on the first night of the master class, he wondered if any other HB student had ever been attended by a crew of fearless-looking "associates" who waited outside the building with a double-parked Navigator. After class, on the sidewalk, Jason spoke with Sammo and was glad to discover that the guy was exactly as he seemed on screen: tough and sweet.

"Loved your work in *Terror Squad*," Jason said.

"Thanks a lot, man. You brought some really interesting stuff to the table tonight."

"Hey, thanks. Everybody's working pretty hard in there, aren't they?"

"Oh, and I thought your Scottish play was cool, too," said Sammo, after whispering an order to an associate who then hopped on his cell phone. "How cool would it be if I went, you know, against type and played that priest guy in the movie version?"

"You saw my play?"

"I see everything, man. I go everywhere, I do everything. That's my MO. You got a movie version in the works?"

"We're talking about it."

"Talk about it with me. I just got my own production company."

"Yeah, and what are you gonna do with your production company?"

"Gonna take it for a spin. Gonna see what it can do."

They shook hands and embraced, street-style. Jason unchained his bike while Sammo hopped into the back of the Navigator.

"You free later tonight, man?" Sammo called from the window.

"I'm having some people over, at my loft. Sort of a listening party for a new track by my lady. Gonna be some fun. Bring people."

"Maybe. If I can," Jason said.

He showed up alone. The place was in Tribeca. He knew the address because Sammo's purchase of the loft had been reported in all the papers. Staff posted at the door politely waved him through the lobby to the elevator. The cavernous main room was swirling with at least three hundred guests. Jason was surprised that Sammo had referred to such a big event so casually. There were two bars, waiters passing hors d'oeuvres, music blaring from speakers worthy of a club. The crowd was heavily industry, hip-hop and other music, but there were also a lot of people Jason knew from the magazine and fashion worlds. As he made his way through the crowd, he said brief hellos to a rock star, a clothing designer, a pair of socialite sisters, and a drag queen with her own cable show.

"It's like this around here all the time," Sammo shouted, when Jason found him. "I love giving people a good time."

Sammo showed Jason upstairs to the penthouse study, which was more of a lounge where fifteen or twenty people were smoking cigarettes and cigars, drinking champagne and vodka. The music was more chill. An expanse of glass revealed the glittering cityscape beneath a clear, starry sky. Sammo showed Jason to an empty sofa and poured Cristal for the two of them.

"So tell me what you're working on, man," he said, sinking into the sofa.

"Oh, another play," Jason said wearily, looking off into the night. "I've been working on a play for a long, long time."

"Yeah? About?"

Jason sighed. "About I don't know. About me. About 'life-life.' "

"Show it to me. Is it a movie?"

"No, it's not a movie. It probably isn't even a play. I may have written my last play. I'm actually thinking of retiring and going off to build cabinets somewhere. I need to build back some calluses." Jason stuck his hand out, palm up.

"A genius like you, man? No way. I'd kill for your talent. You know, when I was inside we did a few plays. I wrote most of 'em. They stank, but they got me thinking. They got me acting. And now these places like the Mark Taper Forum are saying, 'Yo, write something for us and we'll do it up right.' You know? ScreenWorks says it would be good for my image and will help the next movie. They only wanna make some money off my ass. Though you know, it might be fun ..."

"Stick to acting, Sammo. To write, you have to know what you want, way down deep. How many people know that?"

"I know what I fucking want, man."

In the months that followed, Jason and Sammo got to know each other. In addition to the soul baring that takes place in any acting class, they did some martial arts together and spent several evenings palling around town, introducing each other to friends. Often, late at night, around a low table and a bottle of Stoli in a VIP lounge, they wound up sharing thoughts about art and life, frequently in the company of slender young women in clingy dresses. Though it was clear the young actor was enthusiastically heterosexual, Jason noted how easily he expressed physical affection with men—a palm to the back of the neck during private conversation, or whispers in the ear so close that you could feel his lips. *Maybe it's a Russian thing,* Jason thought. Sammo referred openly and with surprising understanding to the sex he'd seen in prison. He had no problem with the gay men they ran into on the party circuit and seemed to take in stride Jason's growing admiration for him.

Sammo's girlfriend sometimes joined them on party nights, sometimes not. Jason loved Sammo's juicy descriptions of "banging" her; he also found touching the almost theatrically tearful remorse the actor sometimes expressed for hurting her by succumbing to other girls. Jason could accept all this, while still growing more enamored of the guy. *Wow, is this what it's like?* he thought at one point, when Sammo said to him lightly "You know I love ya, baby," and Jason thought seriously about being loved. They called each other friend and agreed one night that the bond between them should be beyond trivial definitions, and Jason accepted that as reassurance that Sammo understood the situation and was cool with it. Jason knew full well what an operator Sammo was; his natural talent for giving people what they wanted often brought out the faker in him. But he liked Sammo anyway and felt lucky to be around him. If it couldn't be "real" love between them, then maybe it could be that other timeless thing that men sometimes have together, Jason thought—like friendship, but definitely more.

"So you're not gay, man, right?" Sammo popped the question one night, as they were eating Vietnamese food in the window of a dive around the corner from Sammo's loft. They were alone, without entourage. Blue neon reflected off Sammo's muscular forearms. "Weren't you were going out with that Indian chick who died?"

"I was never gay," Jason said quietly. "Sometimes I let guys do me, but I always had women. Lately I don't know what I am. Do I have to have a label? I'm just trying to live my life."

"Way to be. Labels fuck things up."

"Yup, they do. But I'll tell you, Sammy, if I were ... well, I've never met anyone quite like you."

"What do you mean?"

"You bastard, you know what I mean," Jason said, with a laugh. "You have ... I don't know, some quality that you don't see in a lot of other men. I can't put my finger on it. I guess it makes me think things."

"Yeah?" Sammo smiled. "Like what kind of things?"

Jason reached across the formica table, took Sammo's hand, kissed it, and let it go.

"Things," Jason said curtly.

Sammo snorted in amusement.

"You got guts, Jacey-boy. *Def*-initely."

Things were not much different between them after that, and Jason was thankful. There would have been no point in hiding. The two of them still palled around, still did martial arts. There was no question of actually having sex, but in a funny, Damon-Affleck way they were seen in the media that season as a kind of all-American power couple.

Toward the end of the seminar, as summer began, Sammo mentioned that ScreenWorks was serious about having a play of his produced at the Mark Taper Forum. They had rejected everything he'd already shown them—"the fruit of my penitent years," he laughed—so he lied and told them that he'd just finished a new one. Actually, he'd only begun. Would Jason help him work on it, please?

They decided to begin the following week, which both of them cleared expressly for that purpose. They would write together every day in Sammo's study. Sammo would work on his play and Jason would tweak his. Every day over cocktails they'd discuss their progress. Jason read Sammo's draft and thought it lame but promising. Their time together would clearly be more about turning that into something plausible than doing much to Jason's play, which was now pretty much done. Sammo felt sure—and by the second day of that week had confirmed with his agent and some ScreenWorks people, to whom he secretly sent copies—that Jason's play was incredible. Cowboy had put his play through a final revision. Principles that Porter and Seymour preached, and that Yanna had revealed, had finally been properly applied. They had functioned, like time-released medicine, to cure the play's ills. Characters were now true, motivations clear and honest. Moreover, how love drove the main story and how it transformed the hero were dazzlingly, profoundly apparent.

Toward the end of the week Jason and Sammo were having dinner after working all day. It was just the two of them in Sammo's study, their manuscripts and notes in front of them. A buffet supper had been laid out. They were drinking and joking around.

"You know, man, you've been making me think some things myself ..." Sammo said, out of the blue.

"Yeah, like what?"

"Like I don't know."

Sammo showed Jason through his nylon training pants that he had an erection.

Jason smirked. "Gimme a break."

"We could see where it goes. We both know what we do with women. We could just vibe it out, see what happens."

"Sure we could." Jason was incredulous. But game.

"Cool. Let me go grab another bottle of Cristal."

"I'm not gonna do anything stupid, Sammy," Jason shouted after him, kicking off his boots and pulling off his socks.

"I'm excited about your play, man," Sammo yelled from the kitchen.

"Thanks, but to tell you the truth, I'm packing it up with me next week and heading out of New York for a while."

Sammo returned with two new glasses, the champagne already poured.

"A toast," he said. "To what guys want."

"To what guys want."

They emptied the glasses.

Shirts came off. Jason knew what Sammo's body looked like, of course, having seen that naked musculature both normal-size, in locker rooms, and gargantuan, on movie screens and billboards. Then Jason was touching it, allowing himself to touch it. Timidly but with newborn trust and courage, he reached down and felt Sammo's erection. It was firm, warm, immense. Jason was reaching for Sammo's tricep when he realized his hands were going weak, his thoughts icing over in a weird way. Everything seemed to spiral down into little breaths that were hard to take.

He tried to get up but he couldn't. Sammo had picked up his cell phone and was dialing a number ....

Some Brooklyn boys Sammo knew took care of the body. The unsolved disappearance of America's hottest young playwright was a big story in the press for a while. Then it died down, as a scandal erupted involving the city's star real estate developer and a high school girl.

The memorial service was held on a Monday evening in the 47th Street theater where Yanna's acting coach's play was still running to packed houses. The stars and celebrities turned out. So did the party kids, the assistant editors, even the stagehands Jason had been nice to. Sammo came, of course, with his girlfriend and several of the boys in his crew. The young actor stopped at the door to deliver some touchingly elegiac words in front of E!'s camera. The mayor spoke. Hollywood and Broadway people read passages from Jason's plays. The Emerson Quartet and pianist Alex Slobodyanik performed a movement of Schubert's "Trout" Quintet. At the afterparty in a nearby club DJ Cam remixed the Schubert, which was live recorded by Sony and featured on his next album.

The rest of the tale belongs to Sammo. He submitted Jason's play as his own to Mark Taper Forum, got a production, and had a big success with it. Audiences wept at the play's depth of feeling, its honesty about one man's struggle for personal truth and humankind's eternal quest for meaning. Critics praised it lavishly as a call to arms against civilization's dehumanizing forces. Feature writers explained how this essentially Russian vision had been nurtured during Sammo's darkest hours in prison. ScreenWorks made the play into a movie that opened huge and made Sammo a ton of money.

With part of the profits he bought a big, gaudy house in Miami that he kept filled—after ditching the R&B girl—with sexy bitches of all description. Sammo had always known what *he* wanted.

The Last Blow Job

By May, a month and a half after my lover Henry was admitted to Sacred Heart, it was clear that he wasn't going to come home as quickly as we had been hoping. They eliminated the pneumonia within the first few weeks and knocked out the peskiest of the other, "little" infections that had bloomed under its influence, but Dr. Ehrlich said that before we could think of transferring Henry to a "home setting," his mysterious low-grade fever and recurring cough would have to be brought under control. This didn't happen right away and, by late spring, it didn't seem likely to happen at all. Managing Henry's condition had begun to seem as difficult as shoring up a big plate of softening Jell-O.

Still, Henry remained optimistic. Attached to an IV pole, he continued to work on the TV talk show he produced by staying in constant touch with his office by phone. He had a small fax machine installed on the table next to his bed, received and dispatched several messengers a day, and even had prospective guests for the show come by the hospital for the standard interview—something he always took mischievous pleasure in suggesting to them. His universe, like that of all hospital patients, may have shrunk to the size of a room, but Henry's room—private, of course; we had the best medical insurance possible—encompassed the world.

There was a steady stream of friends and colleagues who stopped by—visitors whose appointments it was my responsibility, as Chief Care Partner, to coordinate. Henry was, after all, not as strong as he used to be and needed to conserve his energy for crucial things, like breathing and thinking and praying. His attitude about being sick was philosophical. He accepted the death that was clearly impending but tried to embrace life as vigorously as ever, since it was still in progress. Not only did I never hear Henry curse the sex-in-the-fast-lane lifestyle that some mistook as the cause of this whole mess; more than once, both to me and among friends who loved to hear him talk this way, he affirmed his faith in eros. Eros is not what got us into all this, he would say; eros is what can get us beyond it. Not that he expected his disease to be cured by this force, nor did he think his body would be "healed" by it (to use a fashionable term he found annoyingly unscientific). There was simply nothing Henry had discovered in his predicament to put him off the conviction that what Freud described as "binding together" with others, whether for work or pleasure, was the highest expression of the life instinct.

I guess that's why I was so disappointed when, after the pneumonia was over and he began to gain back a few of the fifty pounds he had lost, Henry rebuffed a gentle request I made to bind with me. We were slouched together in his bed one night, watching TV, and I fell into the kind of lovey-dovey nuzzlings that had been typical of late-night rerun-watching behavior in our home over the last ten years. But Henry wasn't interested. He stopped me with a limp squeeze of my hand. I let it go at that, not wanting to tax him with a conference, but the next day, as I was shaving him, I brought up the question of sex.

"Honey, do you ever jerk off after I go home?"

"Uh-uh."

"Have you done it at all since you've been here?"

"No."

"Why not? Not enough privacy?"

"There's enough privacy. I just haven't felt like it."

It struck me as odd that the man who had gone to so much trouble to reconstitute his work life around his newly diminished capacities should not have done the same thing with his sex life, which was just as important to him.

"I tried once," Henry continued, "but I got interrupted by Rachel." Rachel was the head nurse. "I know she's seen everything, but still I felt weird. Another time, I couldn't stay awake long enough to do it. And then once I thought I was getting turned by a muscle magazine that somebody brought, and that was the moment when a patient down the hall decided to go Code Blue. The commotion killed the mood for me."

I put down the electric razor and took his face in my palms.

"I could help you feel like it," I whispered.

He smiled wanly. Shaving now not only made my Henry look neat but, since the structure of his handsome skull was so much more visible than before, it also brought a clarity to his looks that I had never imagined.

"Can I tell you," I purred, "that I'm as totally turned on by you as ever?"

"Baby, you can tell me anything you want," he said, his smile disappearing suddenly into a fit of coughing.

We'd always been creative with sex. When Henry had his wisdom teeth taken out, when I broke my leg, when we were both paralyzed with sunburn, we were still able to do figure out some way to do it when both of us felt like doing it. And we were proud of our secret history of making love in romantic places on storybook occasions, like the garden of the Taj Mahal at midnight during a full moon in July, or a cramped compartment aboard the Orient Express in the middle of the Alps on New Year's Eve. I was sure there must be some way for me now to be with my lover sexually—pacifically, of course; only so far as his energy and strength would allow; in a modulated manner, the same way I got him to eat in the hospital by dining with him slowly, or, when the meals put before him looked too enormous or too monolithic, by cutting things up and putting them individually into his mouth.

I knew the problem: Henry needed time to adjust to the fact that if he wanted sex, as with work, he was going to have to do it here, in this sanitary environment, because he might never see our Joe Durso bed or the antique oak kitchen table again. It might take time; it might also never happen. I would have to try and remain understanding.

"Well, I want us to keep talking about this, OK?"

"Us having sex? Maybe someday, honey," he said. "I just ... don't know how. I promise I'll work on it."

He reached over to give my pec an appreciative tug, then turned away abruptly as the coughing started again.

Henry was the one who got me going to the gym. He was one of the original converts to the pectoral lifestyle, at the dawn of the Nautilus Age, and was one of the first people I knew to fill out the sleeve of a polo shirt with a properly pumped tricep. Now, installed for weeks in his bed at Sacred Heart—perhaps never to stand up unaided again, as a physical therapist rather insensitively blurted to both of us—Henry continued to take great care in his appearance. He made sure I shaved him three times a week and insisted I speak with a nurse if there was the slightest delay in his sponge bath. He groomed his fingernails daily—much more than they needed it—and somehow managed to contort his semi-wasted self into a position to tend to his toenails, too.

And his body, I thought, still looked great. Was I only seeing him through the eyes of a devoted lover, or was Henry beautiful in a new way? Of course there were detriments galore for us in this damned hospitalization, but there were benefits, too: new strengths, new ways of looking at things. We'd made a pact when he was first admitted to be aware of whatever unexpected good could be found in this new phase of our life together. I thought Henry looked like a statue of the emaciated Buddha we'd seen in Japan, a sexy/saintly figure whose every muscle, vein, and bone was legible beneath a shrink-wrap of skin that seemed a gracious concession to corporeality. Most of the weight that Henry had lost was unsuspected fat, I swear; there was a new tautness that gave his impeccably gymmed physique a refined, essential look—as if he'd been madly training for some bodybuilding contest in which bulk meant nothing and definition everything. His complexion was radiant—probably the side-effect of drugs he was taking, Ehrlich told me—and when Henry sat there in bed, now that it was spring, draped casually with a sheet over his waist, no shirt on, his chest looking like something out of a George Platt Lynes photograph, his feet out of a Michaelangelo drawing, I could hardly deflect the thought that these were nipples I still wanted to lick, toes I still wanted to suck. And I was not ashamed of this thought, because desire was the only way I could think of to keep sanctified this piece of flesh that had been turned by diagnosis into an object to be poked and prodded and palpated by an endless parade of technicians.

Henry often said how glad he was to have suffered only pneumonia so far and no skin mutilations. He detested any kind of physical disfigurement and was horrified when I told him about the guy down the hall who had been so transformed by black-and-purple lesions that he was unrecognizable as the cute boy-next-door in a snapshot his mother had put in a frame near the bed. Henry was intact and proud of the fact.

I, on the other hand, felt like I was disintegrating, physically. Cramming a full day's work into four hours at my own office, then rushing to the hospital to serve as traffic cop, baby-sitter, physical therapist, and master of ceremonies; squeezing in quick workouts now and then; getting home late and sleeping fitfully, because I couldn't adjust to going to bed alone for the first time in a decade. I was often so tuckered out that even looking twice at boners bulging invitingly under sweatpants in the street seemed too hard to do, let alone striking up a conversation and going home with someone—which I almost felt I *should* do, since I hadn't had sex with Henry in months and sex is usually one way for me to refresh myself. Anyway, it was Henry I wanted—*those* arms, *that* face. Despite brief escapades that we agreed must remain "only physical," could never take time away from the relationship, and were not to be spoken of, Henry and I had always been true to each other, and now that our relationship was probably in its final months I felt less like hooking up with a stranger than ever.

I hope I don't have to explain why sex in a hospital is such a thinkable proposition. Hell, sex has got to be the most therapeutic thing in the world. Other longtime companions I was meeting in the corridors of Sacred Heart told me about salutary bouts of love-making they'd enjoyed with their sick boyfriends on hospital beds. In fact, to hear some of them tell it, the hospitals were hopping with sex. One had a friend who, over the years, had been a faithful client of one of the city's top porn-star-hustlers. When the hustler became ill and was occasionally installed in hospital rooms, the client made it a point to go on seeing him. It wasn't so much about money being exchanged for services as it was a special kind of friendship remaining intact, I was told. The client would arrive for a visit with a bouquet; the two of them would chat aimlessly for a while, then swing into a highly verbal bodyworship scene that centered on the hustler's cock; those famous ten fat inches would inflate and be deflated in a manner that was usual for them; and the cash would be found later in a get-well card tucked into the flowers. Gay men are nothing if not adaptable.

Another guy told me that the ritual group of men he belonged to had recently visited one of their members who was hospitalized and in a coma. After words being spoken and hands being laid on, the group masturbated onto the man's motionless body, exactly as he had asked them to do when he was able. And *everyone* was saying that there were nights on the phone sex lines when it simply wasn't possible to avoid at least one connection with someone whose conversation testified to bed confinement. One guy I was talking to told me he had to hang up because an orderly had arrived to wheel him away for an X ray.

I was trimming Henry's hair one day, finishing up with a little peck on the cheek, when he pulled me close to him and inserted his hand under the waistband of my jeans.

"Oh, really?" I said. "Frisky today?"

"I don't know," he said with coyness that outside the room would

have seemed inconsequential but here seemed practically monu-
mental. "You're so good to me."

"You're good to *me*," I said, "letting me take care of you ...."

"Hmmm," he said, snuggling into my armpit.

After a moment he reached over to get his wallet from a drawer
in the night table and took out a twenty dollar bill.

"Listen, it's not five-thirty yet, is it? Go out to where they keep
the linens and give this to that cute nurse with the crewcut and
goatee. His name is Eric. Ask him to watch our door for twenty minutes. He's cool."

When I returned, Henry had kicked down the bedding and was
stroking himself through his Brooks Brothers boxer shorts. I
perched next to him and slipped a hand over his chest and down
around his back. He smelled very old but reassuringly Henry-like.

"He's cute, right?"

"Very," I said, kissing Henry's ear. But I was nervous. "Has
Rachel stopped by with the afternoon meds yet?"

"She came at four. Ehrlich's due around six. Now, I can't guarantee that someone's not going to come barging past Eric, wanting
a cup of my blood or a picture of my brain ..."

"Let me check once more."

I hopped down and went to the door. The corridor was quiet. Eric
smiled confidently when I peeked out. He reassured me that this
was a good time and shooed me back into the room. Inside, it was
suddenly the baths. There was this sexy guy spread out on a bed,
giving me a look and a half. I bee-lined over to him and applied my
skull deftly to his cock.

It was like conversing in your native language again after a year
among foreigners. Henry's cock was big, but it was articulate. It
spoke to me. And I was very good at listening to it. The language
was that subtle, nonverbal kind that occurs between body parts
that are lavishly endowed with a zillion times more receptor nerve
cells than other parts. With the delicate skin of head of cock nestled into the lining of mouth and throat, both of us were acutely

attuned, like human polygraphs, to minute fluctuations in each other's temperature, electrolytic balance, and galvanic response, forget grosser signs like pelvic thrust and breathing rate. The taste of him drove me crazy; the very elements he was made of, in their exact proportion to each other, I have craved since the day I met him. And he simply *looked* hot: Mr. Big TV Producer lying there on his back, his weak little limbs as immobile as if they had been fettered by leather straps. Now, Henry and I had never done much bondage, but I think what really worked for us this time was this expression of his passivity, with an undertone of resignation.

He took no longer to come than he ever did. Maybe fifteen minutes. If Erlich had burst in with his chart, or Rachel with a needle, or that perky, surrealistically well-groomed patients' advocate woman with one more questionnaire, what they would have seen was me kneeling over this muscular skinny guy, his head thrown back in ecstasy, the plastic urinal bottle empty on the floor where it had fallen when knocked from its hook on the bed rail. What they would not have seen, but surmised, was the presence of the thick, warm, veiny shaft plugged up inside my head, emptying itself. Henry gave my hair a little tousle when we'd finished. He was beaming like Howdy Doody. I kissed his navel and covered him with the sheet.

"Cold?" I asked.

"Hot," he said, letting me tuck him in. "I've so much missed being that close to you. Listen, honey, can I say something serious? I want you to make sure you have another lover when I'm gone ...."

"What!? Henry, I can't believe you're giving me that speech. It's entirely premature."

"Just remember that I said it. Be sad when I'm gone, but get another lover. Think of my saying that as a little gift to you, like the one you just gave me."

We talked for a minute about my not wanting to talk about the matter, then it was time for Henry's nap. I put the room back in order and took off. Eric said goodbye as I left.

That was the last time Henry and I had sex. The *last* last time, that is. The time before that—which I remember fearing, when it happened, could itself be the last—took place a month before Henry went into the hospital. We were in London for the opening of a new play. He had already begun to lose weight "mysteriously" and sleep through any performance we got tickets to. We'd returned to our hotel room in the afternoon for a nap, and upon waking fell into each other's arms with a hunger I recalled from our college days, which is when we met. Another lover! That was the last thing I wanted to think about.

Henry never came home from Sacred Heart. Less than a month after our little escapade, Rachel found him one morning wailing about being "at the wrong gate" and waving a towel like a flag to someone on the horizon. Dementia had set in and from there everything got worse. We lost him in August. I am glad to think that, during the last days, though he seldom knew who I was, he still favored me with a kind of infantile sexual intimacy, as if through gathering shadows there shined the memory of love. In the midst of throwing food at the walls and ripping off his diapers, he'd grasp me affectionately and grin as if to say, "I know who you are and I think you're wonderful." And I would feel completely wonderful.

I was surprised when Eric showed up at the memorial service I arranged for Henry that fall. It was a giant affair. Friends and relatives flew in from all over the country. Dr. Ehrlich was there. Rachel came. And then there was Eric, who strode in looking incredibly cute in a smart linen blazer over a tight T-shirt that definitely showed "something going on" underneath, as Henry liked to say. After the ceremony he came up to me and told me something amazing.

"He was a great guy," Eric said, gathering me into a warm embrace. No, I hadn't realized how muscular he was. "I'm sorry I didn't get to know him until so late. But I thought you should know ... that is, he wanted me to tell you, after he was gone like this ... that we fooled around in the hospital. A little bit."

At first, I didn't know what he was talking about.

"Fooled around?"

"Sex. He said you'd approve."

Oh, I thought.

"He loved you so much," Eric went on. "He always said that. He and I used to see each other at the gym all the time, before he got sick. I always thought he was totally hot, and he used to look at me in the shower like, 'Someday, mister.' I'd drop the soap, spend four minutes picking it up, that kind of thing. Well, when he checked into the room on my floor at Sacred Heart, it was natural that we should talk to each other, spend time with each other. You know."

"So how did you fool around?" I asked.

"We felt each other up a few times, jerked off," Eric said brightly, "and once I blew him. Mainly in the room, when I knew there would be no one around. Once he asked me to put him in a wheelchair and take him to the solarium. We did it right there, next to a visitor guy who was asleep on the sofa. Your lover was a very sexy man. Now, he said that this would be good for you to hear ...."

"Yeah, yeah, it's good," I said after a moment. "So the day you watched out for us ...."

"He told me later that until then he hadn't been able to feel aroused in the hospital. It was only after that that he and I did anything. He said that you had, quote, restored his body to him and that after he was gone I should buy you a drink and tell you all the details."

So it was not with me that Henry had his last sexual experience. Well. It would take some getting used to, but I realized even then, in my stressed-out state, that Eric's story hardly detracted from my memory of Henry. It embellished it, really: Heroes of Eros, welcome Henry into your midst.

I wanted to hear more, but I was being summoned by the rabbi. I asked Eric to call me. We would have a drink, talk more. And I was thinking: I'm as happy to go out with Eric as Henry thought I would be. Any excuse to keep talking about my lover was OK with me.

My Poor Furniture

The daybed in my living room, where that muscle guy from Staten Island tried to fuck me a few years ago (was that rape?)— that's exactly where my lover Barry died, fifteen years before. Cleaning up after home care, once Barry's body and all the medical equipment had been taken away, was scarcely more difficult than putting that whole section of the living room back in order once I finally got the Staten Island guy to leave. The daybed's position had shifted and the floor was scratched. The upholstery was smeared with lube and cum. Pillows were strewn all over the room, some with boot marks on them. The bookshelf was dripping with spilled poppers. As I vacuumed and mopped, I noticed the daybed's legs were getting a little banged up, so I tried to go around them extra-tenderly.

Barry and I had just moved into the apartment when we bought the daybed. We wanted something "good," so we went to a studio that makes custom furniture. We ordered something modern, in blond oak with black canvas upholstery. We were told that the super-high-density foam of the cushion would last for years, and it has done so. Barry and I were together for fifteen years. We had some other furniture made, collected some artwork, bought a few antiques. A year after Barry died I was telling a guy much younger than myself that I loved him, reclining right there on the daybed, after a candle-lit dinner. The guy wasn't gay, but he was curious; as we fumbled with each other's shirt buttons we knocked over a small, rather valuable, Cycladic marble sculpture. No harm done. Then there were equally clumsy candle-lit dinners with a dancer, a book reviewer, a Santeria priest, and a model. And then there was KJ, whom I knew I would love forever as we kissed suddenly one night on the edge of the daybed after he blew me, though we'd agreed that sex was to remain "meaningless" because neither of

My Poor Furniture

us was the other's type.

Somewhere during those years I ordered new black canvas upholstery, but now even that's begun to look a little ratty, since I flop
there all the time to watch TV, and KJ and I sometimes host threesomes and group scenes in the living room. My poor chairs, too, have
seen wear-and-tear. They're commodious, well-made armchairs in
woven rattan, with plump, black canvas cushions, created for
Architectural Digest-type beach homes by the late, "California-
style" designer Michael Taylor— who I'm sure had Nancy Reagan's
or a similar ass in mind when he designed the chairs and not mine,
naked and sweaty, parked slouchily while I jerk off or get blown. I
was given the chairs by a decorator friend who had them left over
from a pricey job. They were new, and I wish I had taken better care
of them. I wish I had reminded guys to keep the heels of their boots
away from the rattan skirts that sheath the legs of the chairs,
asked guys not to prop their feet on the arms and backs of them
when trying to position their cocks for better sucking, or their asses
for fucking. I have often thought I might die in one of these chairs—
my cock in somebody's throat, my head full of poppers, my heart gal-
loping, as I try to stay aware of beats-per-second, vesicular ampli-
tude, and the location of the nearest emergency room.

The chairs have their share of stains, too. The other day a great
blow job turned playfully into a great hand-job, and foop!— cum
and lube all over the arm and seat. I try to take care of sex-related
spills, drips, and smears as soon as they happen, but sometimes,
especially during group scenes, my hostly duty precludes this and
stains are produced. I remain highly conscious of these stains
when KJ and I entertain in nonsexual situations. At a cocktail
party a guest will apologize if a drop of wine or morsel of crabcake
happens to fall onto her seat cushion. "No problem," I will say, gently taking care of the accident with a damp cloth. I know it will not
necessarily put the guest at ease to draw her attention to a large
stain on the same cushion and say, "Just guess what that is."

Poppers have eaten away at the once-beautiful finish of my Alvar

Aalto bentwood table— and I'm sure they also have something to do with the cysts that are growing in my sinus cavities, though my ear, nose, and throat man says this is unlikely. Several of my throw pillows— black chintz with pink, green, yellow, and blue flowers— have been knelt on or stepped on a few too many times. Piss, bourbon, and cum have decommissioned several sisal rugs.

Even so, the apartment is basically presentable. The antiques, for the most part, are fine, since they're in the bedroom, out of the line of fire. (KJ and I almost never do group scenes in the bedroom— the bed makes such a dull place for that kind of sex.) And for some reason nothing's happened to any of the artwork— a small miracle considering I hang junk on the walls and prop the more important paintings and photographs in more vulnerable locations, against walls, at floor level, and on shelves with the books. I clean the place once a week. If you came to dinner and didn't know the rest of the story you might take away a fairly respectable impression— though every now and then, during a proper dinner party, I will tell a story of sex damage and everyone will laugh, just as sometimes during a sex scene someone will ask a question about my Cycladic sculpture and I will answer by saying that it's the only thing in the room that existed three thousand years ago and it will be the only thing to endure long after our bodies and the furniture are dust.

Good with Words

Last night I dreamed I went back to the Mineshaft. I knew I had come home even before entering the unmarked door and climbing the flight of stairs to pay my five dollars. Outside, on the sidewalk—where I'd sometimes linger and survey the street action that was often hot enough to induce me to skip the bar entirely—I savored the exhaust that was being sucked out of the bar's downstairs suite by powerful, industrial fans. Beer, piss, poppers, leather, sweat—the smells blended into a perfume more reassuringly familiar than the Bal à Versailles I remember from my mother's dressing table.

The first beer at the upstairs bar was just a formality. I gulped it down and immediately asked the tattooed bartender for another, the second one to sip—a prop, really, to keep my hands occupied until something better came along. Inside, a typical evening was under way: someone in the sling, ingeniously concealing someone else's arm up to the elbow; onlookers rapt, then moving on casually, to survey some of the other attractions that were taking form in the shadows; assorted human undergrowth here and there, some of it inert and some gently undulating like deep-sea flora. On the platform toward the back, a tall, blond man was getting blown. I stood nearby for a while and watched—evaluating his musculature with a touch, scrutinizing his gestures for a flaw in that impeccable attitude, observing the degree to which his arched posture expressed a belief in this kind of recreation—then I turned and went downstairs.

I always spit in the back stairway, as sort of a ritual of purification, I suppose. Below, things were steamier and I adjusted my fly accordingly. The piss room was packed, unnavigable, with dense clumps of flesh around each tub and growing outward from the corners. So noting who was doing what, I passed along the edge of it all, slowly, as if it were a dream—which it was, of course—though even when it wasn't, back when the Mineshaft was open, it all seemed to be. A wet dream; some kind of prenatal fantasy, dark and sheltered; bathed in the music the management knew was perfect for down there, slowish, hazy waves of taped sound that always struck me as exactly what music would sound like if heard from inside the womb; a dream engulfed, as the evening built to its climax, by the fluids—no, the tides—of life itself.

I walked past the posing niche and entered the club's farthest recess, the downstairs bar. There, on his knees, was Paul. Known more widely than seemed possible as the Human Urinal, Paul had installed himself in one of his favorite spots for the early part of an evening, a relatively open and well-lighted place that invited inspection but did not permit extended scenes. Paul moved around, you see. As an evening progressed he would migrate to increasingly more auspicious locations until, around dawn, you would probably find him in what was by then a hub of the Mineshaft's hardest-core action, the upstairs men's room, where he planted himself efficiently, mouth gaping, eyes glazed, between the two nonhuman fixtures.

How I admired that man and his dedication! What fun we would have in the old days, both here and with the straight boys at the Hellfire Club! Paul is immobile as I pass, but I see by his slowly shifting eyes that he knows I've arrived. And he's glad: even in the dark I sense that his pupils have dilated a fraction when he notices I'm carrying a can of beer. I raise it slightly in his direction in a kind of toast. He understands. I stop for a moment opposite him, the constant flow of men between us. Then, because I feel I should follow through with a sympathetic gesture, I bring the can to my lips while pissing, almost incidentally, in my jeans.

I don't look down, of course, but I know that a dark patch has appeared on my right thigh. And I know that Paul sees it too— but since manners are everything in affairs of the heart, we smile no acknowledgment. Burping unceremoniously, I move off toward the bar ....

I was intending to return to Paul after getting another beer, but then I woke up. A garbage truck was roaring outside my bedroom window and the dream was over.

Later that day I called my friend Albert, with whom I'd visited the Mineshaft on occasion. When I mentioned my dream he was unimpressed.

"Of course you're dreaming about the place, puss. It's because you can't go there anymore. What other options *do* we have nowadays for handling our genius, we who have dared to build a world that allowed us to encounter it repeatedly?"

It was like Albert to use the word *genius* that way, with overtones of "essential spirit," even "demon." Albert's good with words, which he says is lucky. He's one of those people who seem able to enjoy exchanging them during sex almost as much as he did those fluids that are now forbidden. Albert sighed, and added that we should be thankful to have glimpsed the "golden age."

We discussed some of the old faces. It turns out that he'd been talking to the real Paul, whom I hadn't run into for quite some time. I was surprised to learn that my fastidious friend actually once traded phone numbers with the Human Urinal and recently has been indulging in a bit of phone JO with him. It was "nothing kinky," Albert insisted. "We just chat for hours like schoolgirls, about choking bodybuilder cops with the severed penises of their teenage sons. What could be safer than that?"

I was happy to hear that Paul is still kicking. In fact, I was relieved, since it won't do to make assumptions anymore about people we used to see around. Yeah, Paul always maintained that he was exclusively oral, never anal, but the fact is that none of us is sure whether that or any particular limit is enough to guarantee someone's safety under present conditions. Wasn't one of Paul's favorite numbers, after all, to beg feverishly for "clap dick," and to revel in the disgust this elicited from many men who took him literally? I don't know—maybe the request was meant literally; since gonorrhea was so readily curable, it never seemed to matter much. It was strange, I know, but I realized when talking to Albert how fond of Paul's creative perversity I'd become, how much I missed his "genius" in a way that would be difficult to explain to someone who'd never experienced firsthand the catalytic charm of old-fashioned sex clubs.

I knew Paul slightly. Though not a chatty sort he would sometimes expose a portion of his outside persona to me, especially if a biographical detail or two could help add luster to a scene we were building. He was thirty-five, the only child of Polish immigrant parents who were now retired. He lived alone in a tenement on the Lower East Side and was involved with a man he called his lover, a man who also had a live-in girlfriend. All three—Paul, lover, girlfriend—were somehow involved in big real-estate deals and would often go jetting off for weekends in Europe or North Africa, though it was clear that Paul himself was not in the lucrative end of the business, since he spoke of having to take occasional jobs waiting on tables. Thin and darkly handsome, Paul was nonetheless at pains to downplay his appearance. I remember his pride when he arrived at the bar one night with a new haircut, a brutishly uneven head-shave that he said with a grin made him look "even more" like a survivor of Auschwitz.

I was a little apprehensive about seeing this man again. Sure, I had gradually come to understand his unspoken language and to sense how far his attraction to dangerous things really went. But the world has changed. Who knew what mischief he might be up to these days, what I might have to frown upon, what I might even find myself somehow drawn into doing? Yet things have been *so* dry lately, I whined to Albert. Could it do any harm to just *talk*? Albert laughed as he gave me Paul's number.

Paul was napping when I rang. A ballet gala the night before had kept him out until breakfast and he confessed he was still in his tuxedo pants. After we brought each other up-to-date (and admitted indirectly that our health was fine), he said he'd be happy to get together again, "to see what develops." Nothing was said about conditions—more, I think, because neither of us wanted to queer an incipient liaison with ill-timed reality talk. We set a time for later that day. Paul suggested a secluded men's room on a downtown university campus. That's a good sign, I thought—if he's fooling around with those finicky college boys, he can't be too heedless.

When I arrived at the men's room I found a scene already in progress that would have seemed innocuous enough four or five years ago, but now, in the era of AIDS, took on a faintly unsettling quality. Paul and someone else had positioned themselves not in a stall but right out in the open, and they were talking about death.

The other guy, a bearded man in his forties whom I'd not seen before, was dressed in a beat-up leather jacket, no shirt, and a pair of those drab, baggy chinos that janitors wear. Out of his fly was hanging a cock that must be described as substantial as much for its apparent weight and density as for its obvious size. Semisoft and just at the point of unwrinkling, the thing had a thick, meandering vein down the top that looked more like an exhaust pipe than a detail of human anatomy. He was lighting a cigarette when I entered and seemed unconcerned that his twosome had just become a threesome. And he was wearing a wedding ring. Paul was kneeling in front of the guy, his head hung low, dressed only in a yellow-stained T-shirt and a pair of pulled-down sweatpants. After a moment I saw that his legs had been bound behind him with a length of rope, which struck me as risky, since someone else could always just walk in unannounced. His hands were tied too, though in front of him, so he was able to reach and clumsily manipulate his cock. The room reeked of pine cleanser.

I'd entered during a short lull—or maybe they'd been waiting for me. Instantly I found myself shedding the everyday state of mind that allows us to do things like hold jobs and get through city traffic and assuming a more intuitive, timeless disposition that's much better suited to the consumption of pleasure. Respectfully I approached. Understanding that this wasn't the time for a kiss and an introduction, I grunted for them to continue.

"I want it, OK?" Paul said. It was that low, trancelike monotone I remember.

"Yeah? You like this fucker?" The other guy handled himself appreciatively.

"Uh-huh. I need it. Put it in my mouth?"

A pause. The other guy farted.

"Why do you need it?" he asked.

Paul did something obscene with his tongue.

Seeing that this was indeed going to work, I took out my own cock and began to pull on it. Already it felt pleasantly *intrusive*, like a complication worth solving. I couldn't have said exactly why, but there was something palpably right about our little scene, something perhaps reflected in subtle linguistic details like the register of Paul's voice and the rhythm of the other guy's responses, as well as in grosser ones like choice of vocabulary and subject matter. I know from experience that arranging these things is far from easy, which is why even after this preliminary exchange I understood perfectly why Paul had wanted me to meet this guy. The scene heated up rapidly.

"I live for that dick," said Paul, his gaze fixed on it.

"Then tell me about it, man. Let me hear it."

Paul's drone became more animated.

"Please, let me have your dick. Slip it into my head."

Then he looked up at the guy's face.

"I'll take your load, OK? Let me suck it out of you. I don't care if I get sick."

I guess that was what they both wanted to hear. The other guy narrowed his eyes.

"I don't give a fuck about you, cocksucker—I just wanna get off. You gonna eat my cum?"

Paul nodded. "Anything."

Both were pumping faster.

"OK, let me feel that pussy mouth on my meat. I'll feed you my fucking load and get out of this shithole."

"If I get sick ...," Paul began.

"So you get sick," was the reply. "I guess you die, man."

And at that moment—or one like it, since I was too deeply engaged by all this bad-boy stuff to remember more than the drift of the dialogue—the three of us shot. I think we'd all been close for a while, and we shot powerfully—me, off to the side, near the radiator; Paul, onto the floor in front of him, grazing my foot; the other guy, past Paul's shoulder and onto the wall and paper towel dispenser. It took only a couple of minutes for us to button up, undo Paul and perform a thorough wordless cleanup. Then our guest silently signaled his farewell, pulling Paul toward him and grazing him on the cheek with an affectionate peck.

After he left I raised an eyebrow.

"I know," Paul said. "Sweet man."

"Who is he?" I asked.

"Just a man," was the answer.

As I stood drying my hands, I couldn't help thinking how dismal a conclusion a stranger would have drawn simply by reading a transcript of our encounter. And even if he'd been there himself, would a *Times* reporter or a health department official have understood how loving it all was? Or how safe? Paul and his friend must have agreed fairly explicitly, though in their own language, to stay within certain limits. They wanted to raise a little hell, anyway.

I winked at myself in the mirror. *Well, boys*, I thought, *we did it.*

Hearing that word "die" during sex did leave me feeling a little clammy, though. I've lost so many friends. So has Albert, I know, yet afterward he made light of my reservations.

"Isn't the best way to honor their memory to care for ourselves and the friends we've got left?" he asked. "It sounds to me like the three of you were eminently careful. If only you'd invited me."

But using death in that way. It felt so ... odd.

Good with Words

"Look," Albert explained, "is it really so different from the old days, when we used to talk about things like getting worked over by a gang of Nazi motorcycle Satanists? Death by gang rape is hardly more attractive than death from AIDS. Sex is theater, darling, even now. And words are only words, even if they do bring the big, bad world into the bedroom, where we can play at controlling it."

When I equivocated, he grew stern.

"Stephen, if you can't tell the difference between talking about something and the thing itself, then you belong in a cave drawing bison on the wall."

I thought of that remark sometime later, when I attended a play at which I was seated two rows away from someone who was so stirred up by an onstage murder that he began talking violently back to the actors ....

Men and Their Issues

Thousands of gay men hooked up with each other last Saturday night in New York. In beds, on rugs, in men's rooms, under street lamps they got together, shot their loads, and gave their hearts a chance to connect. But thousands of other gay men found nothing. They were just as attractive as the ones who hooked up and they tried just as hard. But something—lots of things—got in the way.

Among the guys who might have connected with each other but didn't were a fashion director, a philanthropist, a plumber, an architect, a building superintendent, a hustler, and several individuals who are doing one thing only until they can do something else. Some of these guys are friends; most are strangers to one another. Some wound up at the same party, club, or backroom. Others wandered solitarily through the night making brief, one-time appearances in someone else's life. Only two of them, a graphic designer named Jonathan and another guy he wasn't planning on meeting at all, managed to greet Sunday morning at least a little hooked up—if not with love, at least with the chance of it.

Saturday, 9 to 10 P.M.
Jonathan is in his Chelsea apartment on the sofa, in sweatpants and a sweatshirt, in front of the TV. He is due at midnight at his friend Seb's place, for a small party before everyone goes off to the Roxy. Before settling into a disco nap, Jonathan makes one last flip through the channels.

"Ash, that transmission. Mother's deciphered it. It doesn't look like an SOS."

Damn, Jonathan thinks. *Alien*. He's a big Sigourney Weaver fan. This is a must-watch.

"It looks like a warning!" Ripley says. "I'm going out after them!"

But minutes later, well before his favorite scene—the one where the baby alien pops out of John Hurt's stomach—Jonathan is asleep.

An average-looking twenty-nine-year-old with a friendly face, Jonathan enjoyed a relatively happy childhood in a small, midwestern city. He's made plenty of friends since coming to New York five years ago, and has a secure position as a creative director in a hot graphics design firm. Though he doesn't turn many heads on Eighth Avenue he is OK about his looks, body, and cock, which are all normal in the statistical sense of the word. And he is OK about sex—he gets as much as he wants. He learned shortly after coming to New York that no matter what gay men look like they can always get as much sex as they want, because in a place where there are so many gay men there are always plenty who prefer any given type.

But sexual exploration and a wide circle of friends hasn't yet netted Jonathan a true soul mate, which is the one thing he wants now more than anything else. He knows this won't be easy to find and often complains to friends that "gay social life wasn't built by men looking for boyfriends"—though in something like good faith he keeps plodding off to parties like the one Seb and his roommate Phelan are hosting.

Sixty blocks north, at Lincoln Center, a good-looking, twenty-six-year-old entertainment lawyer named Coby is standing on the great portico balcony of Fisher Hall overlooking the plaza fountain. It is intermission at a benefit for the New York Philharmonic. Coby is in black tie. So is the elegant, gray-haired gentleman he is chatting with, Meeker—one of the Philharmonic's most important donors.

"The adagio was luminous, wasn't it?" Meeker says, taking a sip of his scotch.

"Absolutely luminous," Coby says. "Apparently Maestro Ono held special rehearsals just for the cellos."

They are not close friends but know each other from their positions on some of the same boards of directors of arts organizations.

Coby, the son of a distinguished black congressman, was raised in Washington and schooled at Harvard. His rise at a prestigious New York law firm has been swift and his entree into the city's more enlightened cultural circles, smooth.

Coby lights a cigarette. A longtime smoker, he resents smoking ordinances, even while enjoying the opportunity to show what a good citizen he is by complying with them. And he generally feels guilty about smoking, though he's trying to forgive himself this time because the company of his distinguished friend—the sixty-four-year-old gay scion of a formidable old New York family—makes him a bit nervous.

"Stopping in at the club tonight?" Coby asks. He knows Meeker sometimes stops in at the Roxy for a few drinks on a Saturday night when Meeker's longtime companion is out of town, as he is tonight.

"Indeed I may," Meeker says. "Mrs. Scovill and I are going to stick around for dinner here, but eventually I may wend my way down there. I could use a little *molto* DJ after all this. You staying?"

Coby shakes his head.

"The lonely bachelor. I think I'll head home and have a nap. But I'll look for you later."

...*Or should I have said* "celli"? Coby thinks as takes a drag on his cigarette and looks out over the fountain.

10 to 11 P.M.
Vince, thirty-three, is embarrassed by his Brooklyn-Italian accent and his job as a building superintendent. He's ashamed of being overweight, balding, and sunken-eyed. He's selfconscious about a certain "femmy" look he sees in the mirror, despite the fact that everyone in his building thinks of him as a macho straight guy. And he's got a habit he'd find mortifying except that he's largely separated himself from family and friends who might disapprove of it—the habit of ingesting massive amounts of other men's cum.

Apart from one other person, no one knows about Vince's habit except those who feed it: the hundreds of men a week he meets between shifts online and at his regular haunt, a drive-in video booth store on Kings Highway, deep in Brooklyn. Vince is a cum addict, not a cocksucker proper. He tries to be clear about this so he can weed out those men who want an all-out, deep-throat blow job, in favor of those who enjoy the idea of feeding a cum pig. Vince would buy cum by the quart at the grocery store, if he could. Why he is a cum addict, he doesn't know or much care. His daily need for cum has been increasing, but where the addiction will lead is immaterial to Vince—though he is thankful that, far from being an addict with any other substance, he has no desire to drink or do drugs.

Vince's activities as a building superintendent and his other responsibilities don't suffer from the many hours he devotes to finding cum because he budgets time carefully and makes precise appointments with feeders. He'd be hard pressed to explain whether his addiction takes away from some potential personal progress he might otherwise enjoy or whether it has actually given him the thing that, as a lower-middle-class kid growing up in Bay Ridge, he feared he'd never have: a purpose in life.

Vince is in the backroom of the video booth store on Kings Highway tonight, on his knees in a booth with the door open. Opposite him is one of the straight guys who come to the store for a quick, anonymous pop—a trim, Italian-looking man with a dark buzzcut and gold ID bracelet.

"Hey buddy," Vince says, "Let me grab a quick load from you?"

The guy steps forward and pulls out his cock. He's wearing neatly pressed khaki slacks and a polo shirt that gives off the scent of fabric softener. After swallowing the guy's cum Vince moves to another, better situated booth. There he takes two more loads, from two different men.

11 P.M. to midnight
Jonathan jolts out of his nap with a snort.

"The ship will detonate in T minus ten minutes."

He realizes he's missed a good part of *Alien* and gets up off the sofa.

"OK, plan," he says, flipping off the TV. He must shower, shave, and dress. He must choose between gel in the hair or not, boots or sneakers, a black T-shirt or a white one. His friend Seb, who always looks perfectly put together in a casual way, once recommended that Jonathan wear only plain black or white T-shirts for gay socializing.

"Since you're, you know, plain-looking you should stick with the classics," Seb had told him. "Maybe vary the fit or the fabric for the occasion."

Jonathan pulls several black and several white T-shirts out of a drawer and throws them on the bed.

"Not that it makes a damn bit of difference whether I wear a black or white T-shirt tonight," he says to himself.

Seb is waking up, too. He lives with Phelan in the lavish, three-bedroom apartment off Union Square that Phelan bought in the '80s and did over completely with built-ins and custom materials. Phelan is the fashion director of a major women's magazine and the best friend of a legendary male fashion designer, so the place is pretty heavily designed. Except for some small artworks he acquired at benefit auctions, Phelan has kept the apartment looking exactly as it did the day he finished it.

Seb is not Phelan's boyfriend, or roommate, or even a guest. Technically, Seb is a charity case. He was taken in by Phelan a year ago after being fired from his last job, as a part-time photographer for a weekly newspaper. Seb agreed to pay Phelan token rent, but most months he doesn't manage to do that. He is still unemployed—and what makes the situation more complicated is that Seb spends lots of money on CDs, clothes, and drugs, and can afford to do so because he hustles. That's how he and Phelan met. A couple of years ago Seb was hired by Phelan a few times for the evening, through a short-lived agency run by one of Seb's acquaintances. Then Seb was introduced to Phelan's friends and became a very popular "date" among that crowd—the fashion designers, actors, artists, and media figures sometimes referred to as the "Velvet Mafia."

At twenty-six, a handsome, intelligent, and idealistic boy from Montana, Seb hopes his access to the inner world of gay power will ignite his career as a photographer—though he often finds himself baffled by the conditions that seem to govern this access. Most of his fancy clients won't return Seb's call unless it's about a party. Seb keeps saying he wants to quit hustling and devote more time to taking pictures, but it's easier for him to make money from one activity than from the other. He also has a problem with Phelan. When he moved in Seb stipulated that their relationship was to be nonsexual, but he knows Phelan still harbors other ideas ....

Phelan raps on the door of Seb's room.

"Time to shine, babe. People are gonna be here soon."

Phelan enters, talking on his cell phone.

"Straight to the airport at 8 A.M.?" Phelan says into the cell, while pawing with one hand through a pile of clothing on the floor. "Jeez, isn't that a little brutal? But I guess you can sleep on the flight ... Yes, I'm sure can't come with you. I told you we're closing the issue ...."

Phelan finds a stretchy blue shirt with his designer friend's label hanging from the sleeve. "Let's see what this looks like on you," he says to Seb. He drapes the shirt over the end of Seb's bed.

"... Seb. I'm waking him up. He's going to wear the blue shirt we borrowed from you," Phelan says as he leaves the room.

Phelan is in the midst of a series of phone calls. On a typical Saturday night he will make twenty or thirty. This time he is rounding up people for a 3 A.M. rendezvous he's planning for the Roxy's VIP room. He's already gotten himself on the club's list tonight, "plus party."

Phelan is always making arrangements—Seb calls him a control freak. Sexually, Phelan's a top, but the kind of top who delights in bottoming out when in control of the person or people involved and when fueled by the proper drugs. Drugs are important to Phelan. His relationship with them started five years ago, when he was thirty-seven. After fighting his body with diets and exercise since childhood, when he was labeled "chubby," Phelan felt there had to be more to do to stay in shape than going to the gym every day. He did some research, prescribed himself a certain amphetamine, and made his doctor authorize the choice. Then Phelan discovered that recreational drugs, especially crystal, were even more effective in helping keep the weight off. Now he's Mr. Crystal—a storehouse of drug lore, manners, and contacts. He thinks he can keep his drug consumption under the same kind of control he exercises in the rest of his life, though he knows that the amount of money he spends weekly on drugs has been increasing.

In the kitchen Phelan slices lemons, sets out vodka and bourbon, arranges ice and glassware. He lines a baking sheet with aluminum foil for the Special K that one of his friends is bringing over in liquid form.

Meanwhile, in a crowded bar in the West Village, TR, a short, heavy guy with a shaved head, introduces himself to a tall, muscular man in a tight T-shirt who's been standing nearby.

"How ya doing there, sport?" TR says. "Packed enough for ya in here?" It's obvious TR's been drinking, but he's cute and his energy is positive.

"Yes, thank you, hello," the muscular man says, in a heavy accent. Genially the man introduces himself as Paolo, just relocated here from Venezuela. His English is not perfect. "I buy you a drink?"

"Buy *me* a drink?" TR says. "I was gonna ask if I could buy *you* one. I've been standing here for the last ten minutes, admiring your traps, like the rest of these guys. Though I was expecting you, because you're such a nice muscle god, to be very gentle about telling me that you were, quote-unquote, waiting for someone."

Paolo smiles. He hasn't understood every word of TR's speech and takes a moment to frame his response.

"I am here alone, so I am good you say hello. And I leave my glasses at home, so I don't see who is here. Which is stupid—to have no glasses in this place ...."

They both laugh.

"I thought you might be a working guy," TR says. "I've been known to spring for a couple bucks."

Paolo doesn't understand. "I am an architect," he says.

Drinks are ordered and a groping conversation begins—though fifteen minutes later, when TR offers Paolo a blow job, he *is* understood and invited back to Paolo's apartment.

In the men's room, a bespectacled haircutter named Marcus is thrilled to discover the largest cock he has ever seen in person. It belongs to John, a skinny, long-haired plumber from Queens who since puberty has enjoyed possessing one great secret that compensates for the fact that he is sexually lackadaisical and generally quite dim.

Marcus is proud of his ability to accommodate large meat, but after several minutes on his knees in a booth, throating John's eleven inches with the door open, his purple plastic glasses hooked through the toilet paper dispenser, he gives up.

"Man, that's some awesome piece of meat you have, but maybe we should take a break," Marcus says.

John just stands there, inert, his eyes half-closed. He waves away Marcus's poppers.

"OK. Damn," Marcus says. "Usually guys with cocks as big as yours are glad to see what I can do with my throat."

John grunts unthreateningly but does not move.

There is nothing else Marcus can do. It's too early to get a group scene going in the men's room with John as bait. He puts his glasses on and stands up.

"Well listen, you have a good evening, now," Marcus says as he checks himself in the mirror and walks out.

Home from the Philharmonic, Coby takes off his tuxedo and hangs it up neatly. He checks his e-mail. There is one message, from one of his colleagues at the law firm.

"Buddy, we couldn't get noon. The club offered four and I accepted. Hope that's OK. Bill and Larry can do it. See you three-thirty? Remember, it's the second exit labeled 'New Rochelle' off the Hutch."

Damn, Coby thinks. *Four is so fucking late to tee off.*

He had hoped to get his golf obligation out of the way early and return to the city in time to both work on a contract and go to the gym. Coby has sworn not to grumble to himself about golf dates with his colleagues, which he knows are strategically valuable to his career, though the dates are excruciating for him. He loves golf, and the guys from the firm know he's gay, but walking on a fairway in suburbia with three straight, white men makes Coby feel his lack of a boyfriend more keenly than any race-related condition. In fact his colleagues, to his frequent amusement, spend much more energy demonstrating their comfort with race matters than with sexual identity.

"Three-thirty it is!" Coby types. Then he removes the exclamation point and sends the e-mail.

He jumps into bed for a nap. It's a dangerous move, he knows, since bed naps are harder to wake from than sofa and chair naps. His place near Gramercy Park is small but comfortable, filled with books, art, and family antiques.

He sets his alarm for two-thirty.

Sunday, midnight to 1 A.M.
TR, the short, heavy guy, can't believe his luck. Paolo, the architect, takes off his clothes and reveals an ideal body—hard, defined, and beautifully proportioned. Now wearing wire-rim glasses Paolo

looks even hotter than before.

They are in Paolo's studio apartment on West 16th Street. TR kneels in front of Paolo, who is seated on the sofa, and allows himself to be pulled onto Paolo's meaty, uncut cock. The fit between them feels natural, eased by warmth and wetness.

It goes smoothly for several minutes. TR's throat is relaxed, his position comfortable. Paolo's head is back, eyes shut, breathing deeply. Then TR begins to fret.

Is this guy just bored? he thinks. *Maybe he's just faking that look of bliss. Why would a guy like this have brought me home, anyway? I'm fat. Guys like this can have anybody they want.*

But TR says nothing. Paolo moans and fingers the crook between the back of TR's neck and his hairless skull.

At the West Village bar, John's eleven inches are now being worked on by Donald, an older man in a crisp white shirt and neat khakis who had been watching John earlier with Marcus.

After a few minutes, Donald gives up, too.

"Are you OK?" Donald says, standing up and brushing off his knees, though he had been squatting rather than kneeling.

"Yeah," John says. "Why?"

"Well, you're just standing there. I mean, you seem a little out of it. I thought you might be having a drug moment or something."

Donald doesn't like the look of John's clothing—baggy, drab chino pants and shirt, somewhat stained. The long hair is greasy. There is a body-odorish smell that's right on the line between appealing and disgusting.

"No, man," John drawls. "I'm just doing my thing. I mean, *you're* doing my thing." He smirks, half-soft cock hanging out of his fly, hands in his pockets.

"*Was* doing," Donald snaps. He washes his hands and leaves the men's room.

At the same time uptown, in a fourteen-room duplex on Park

Avenue and 70th Street, Meeker, the patron of the Philharmonic, is welcomed home by his butler of three decades, a slender, delicate-featured man almost Meeker's age, with carefully parted, gleaming black hair.

"How was the symphony, sir?"

"Lovely, thank you, Ramon. Dinner was a sketch. You know how Mrs. Scovill eats—like a soldier."

The butler smiles wanly. He takes Meeker's coat and gloves.

"I'll have a shower, Ramon, and then the Bat Suit."

Upstairs in the bedroom, the butler helps Meeker out of his dinner suit and pumps. He is handed Meeker's Breguet watch, Asprey cufflinks, and T. Anthony billfold. Then, while Meeker is in the bathroom, the butler lays out a pair of jeans, a black T-shirt, a leather jacket, a pair of boots, and an old, beat-up wallet containing one piece of ID and $200 in tens and twenties.

Before leaving the room, at a small bar concealed in an armoire, he pours a scotch for Meeker and leaves it near the wallet.

On the other side of Central Park, the doorbell rings at the upper West Side apartment of a short, compact thirty-four-year-old man named Mitchell. Dressed only in a pair of gym shorts, Mitchell answers the door with his long, semi-hard cock poking out.

"Hiya!" Mitchell says, welcoming Thad, a college student whom he met fifteen minutes earlier, online. "C'mon into the bedroom."

Mitchell tries to quiet his two overprotective Jack Russell terriers who are not yet sure they approve of Thad.

Mitchell has been on the computer for hours, looking for JO hook-ups at his place. That's all Mitchell likes to do—JO. He doesn't want anybody's cock in him or his cock in anybody else. This has always felt dirty to Mitchell, from boyhood on. An only child, Mitchell has never had a problem putting his preferences— his *everything*—in front of everybody else's.

What Mitchell likes to do best is show off while stroking. He enjoys seeing people's reactions to his large, beautifully shaped

cock. He likes hearing them talk about it, saying that it's out of
proportion to his height, which is five-foot-six. Two others guys
have come over already this evening. Each was introduced to and
ushered past the terriers; each was shown into the bedroom and
started to stroke with Mitchell, watching and talking. Then, when
Mitchell felt the energy of the session go slack, each was asked to
leave after only ten minutes.

Now Thad comes into the bedroom and begins jerking off with
Mitchell. Ten minutes pass, then Thad too gets the bad news.

"Sorry, Ted, it just isn't working. But thanks for coming over."

After Thad leaves, Mitchell checks the instant messages that
have been piling up on his computer screen. Through each visit he
has remained signed into his favorite "m4mNOW" chatroom.

Jonathan arrives at Seb and Phelan's party wearing not a plain
white or black T-shirt but an electric blue one with the words *Wolf
Trap* printed on it. The shirt is a favorite of Jonathan's not only
because it was purchased on a memorable visit to the famous music
festival outside Washington D.C., but because its blocky typeface
and absence of other design elements make it look like Wolf Trap
could be a gay bar somewhere in the northern mountains.

The crowd at Seb and Phelan's is small but studded with A-list
celebrities: a movie star, a fashion model, a gossip columnist, a few
hot models and stylists. There are bulging muscles and blaring
music, clever haircuts and deep tans.

Jonathan finds Seb near the door and greets him with a kiss.
Seb has just emerged from his room in a gray tank top, white cargo
shorts, and shower sandals.

"Bold move," Seb says, indicating Jonathan's shirt.

"Not a disconnect from this fashionable crowd?"

"Sure is—that's why it's perfect."

Jonathan and Seb have been friends since the day, two years
ago, when Seb showed up at Jonathan's office without an appointment, wanting to show his photographs. Jonathan liked Seb imme-

diately—not for his good looks or transparently seductive manner, but for the underlying open-heartedness that allowed Seb to simply show up at a stranger's office.

At the bar Jonathan says hello to Phelan and politely refuses a line of cocaine from several arranged in a pinwheel design on a glass plate. He pours himself a mild bourbon and water and begins chatting with Ethan, a handsome restauranteur in his late thirties whom Jonathan has met before at Seb and Phelan's.

"I see that your new place over on Tenth Avenue is really taking off," Jonathan says. "You must be working hard."

"We've been lucky," Ethan says. "This is the first night I've taken off since we opened—and I promised to be back in the kitchen tomorrow morning for brunch."

"I've heard about that retractable roof you put over the garden. It sounds amazing. You designed it yourself?"

"Helped the architect. Studied engineering for a while."

Ethan hardly looks at Jonathan as they talk. He continues to scan the room. Very good-looking, with squarish, sharply defined features and a white-blond crewcut, Ethan is one of those gay men who seems wired to interact seriously only with other "VGLs"— self-described very good-looking men—despite the screeds he has been known to deliver about the superficiality of gay life.

"Didn't I hear that Donald Trump is going ahead with that hotel deal right across the street from you?" Jonathan says. "That's gotta be great news."

"I'm sorry, what did you say?"

Ethan has spotted a man he's had his eye on for months: Gil, a handsome if slightly worn-out thirty-four-year-old society party planner with a dull tan and well-developed upper body. Gil is talking to Seb, by the window.

Jonathan, seeing that Ethan is distracted, excuses himself and moves on to examine a Ross Bleckner lithograph.

Phelan shouts across the room.

"Seb, you're not wearing your shirt!"

Some of the guests turn to look at Seb. He dismisses Phelan's comment with a wave.

"I gave him a silk knit we borrowed for a shoot," Phelan tells the clump of guests in his corner of the room, naming his famous fashion designer friend. "I thought he'd look good in it. Is that so terrible?"

Seb continues talking with Gil.

"The shirt was for a much fancier lad than I am," Seb says. "This one is more me."

Seb stretches—perhaps without calculating that his tank top would ride up and expose his navel.

"Shameless," Gil laughs.

The two of them have had sex once before and they've been flirting ever since, so there's an unspoken assumption that they'll hook up some time again.

Maybe tonight, Gil thinks. He knows that Seb doesn't have a problem with his small cock, hollow face, meatless butt, or inability to have sex without drugs. He knows that Seb understands that he, Gil, is doing the party planning thing only until he can sell a screenplay. And he knows that Seb will morph from a self-described pushy bottom into a convincing top and be discreet afterward about having fucked him. Discretion is important to Gil because of his eminent clientele—though whether Gil fucks or gets fucked, writes screenplays, or scoops ice cream cones, is hardly of interest to his society ladies, who only want their parties to be fabulous and cheap.

Ice cubes tinkle and cell phones ring. The room crackles with opinions on the latest big business deals, the latest Broadway shows. Waves of laughter sweep through the crowd. Phelan surveys everything from his corner.

It always comes together, he thinks, *even when Seb is being a pill.*

Throwing parties like this helps Phelan maintain an at-a-glance picture of the life he has made for himself: a beautiful apartment, a beautiful set of friends, a beautiful roommate whom many take to be his boyfriend. It's a life that Phelan hungers to believe in, because it's so different from the one he suffered as a child, the oldest son of a suffocatingly prominent Memphis judge. Long since excused from any family expectations and now a success on his own terms, Phelan has everything he wants except the perfect companion. If he were only a little more attractive, and if Seb would relax his "no sex" policy, Phelan would be ideally happy.

On the two occasions when he and Seb did have sex, it felt hot, nonstop, and two-sided. And even though Phelan knew at the time that this was an illusion, he fell for it. In fact, the opulent memory of those two times has haunted Phelan ceaselessly. It's led him to hope that Seb's failure to pay the rent is simply a way of sliding into a live-in boy-toy scenario, which would be perfectly happily-ever-after for Phelan. What really stings—and strikes Phelan as illogical—is that Seb can hustle other men without qualm.

Near the Bleckner Jonathan is talking to Maurie, a fastidiously groomed, doughy-featured yet distinguished-looking man in his fifties, dressed in a blazer, jeans, and Prada sneakers. At first Jonathan doesn't know who Maurie is.

"I've known Phelan for years," Maurie says. His voice is both nerdy and commanding, louder than it needs to be, his enunciation precise. "Since Farrah married Ryan. Phelan was dressing Farrah at the time."

Jonathan suddenly recognizes Maurie as a Hollywood talent manager he saw on the Letterman show a few weeks ago.

"Definitely one of those fabulous, frozen-in-time gay apartments," Maurie says, with an expansive gesture. "It was exactly the same ten years ago and it's going to be exactly the same ten years from now. If Phelan lives that long."

The remark strikes Jonathan as snide but possibly accurate—Phelan has been offering cocaine to everyone all night and doing plenty himself. But Jonathan doesn't know how to respond.

"So, Sigourney Weaver," he says. "Have you ever worked with her?"

The phone rings in Dwyer's brownstone in Brooklyn Heights. It's Vince calling.

"I'm not far away, in my car, on my way into the city. Got any cum for me?" Vince often calls Dwyer when driving into or coming back from Manhattan.

"Sure, buddy, c'mon over," Dwyer says. "I was just getting ready to go out myself, but I'd love to feed you."

Dwyer lights a joint and opens another beer. He is bisexual. At fifty-eight, a semiretired structural engineer, Dwyer loves getting his cock sucked by "real" men—a habit he picked up in the Army. For a long time, while married and calling himself "straight," he met men secretly in a nearby park and sometimes went home with them or, if the coast was clear, invited them over to his place. The more "un-gay" the guy, the better. Vince fits the bill perfectly.

Now that his wife has died and his daughter is grown and married, Dwyer has begun to be more open about his interest in men—but only slightly more open. Part of Dwyer admits that he has been what some people call gay ever since he was a teenager in middle-class Long Island. Still, he calls himself bisexual and knows, even now that he's making small steps like occasionally visiting bars and clubs, that he will never feel at home with "that lifestyle."

1 to 2 A.M.
Dwyer greets Vince and leads him into the den. Framed engineering and architectural drawings line the walls. He offers Vince the relit joint but Vince refuses. Seven minutes later he walks Vince back to the front door and claps him on the back.

"Sorry, buddy. Guess I miscalculated," Dwyer says. "Just got drained an hour ago."

Dwyer's cock didn't get hard so Vince didn't get his fourth cum load of the evening. However Vince did get a pint of tasty piss and for the moment he finds this satisfactory.

"I'll call you again," Vince says. He deflects any further conversation.

On West 16th Street Paolo and TR take a break. They have been at it for almost an hour—Paolo on the sofa, TR on his knees.

"It's my fault," TR says, sitting back.

"What does it mean 'my fault'?" says Paolo.

"You're OK with this?"

"Yes."

"You can cum?"

"Oh yes, all the time. But I am thinking that if we can stop for an hour"—*Here it is*, TR thinks, *the brush-off*—"I can get something to make it better. I mean to do this anyway."

"You mean drugs?" TR says. He has given up drugs.

For a second he considers taking a breather, then reconvening, if that's really what Paolo has in mind, and faking the drug thing.

"Fine," TR says. *And if drugs make you act more like a muscle hustler and less like a boyfriend, then so much the better.*

"So let me go now," Paolo says, standing up and warmly kissing TR's shaved head. "And we will get together again later."

They exchange numbers and agree to call each other in an hour. TR figures that in the meantime he can look in on a bar or two.

Often on weekends, a husky, fifty-two-year-old paralegal worker and part-time law student named Ken maintains regular at-home hours at his place in the East Village, where men from all over the city come by to get blown by him. Adamantly, Ken maintains that this is not a sex party. He bills it as a cocksucking service station for guys who are on their way to or from somewhere else. Hundreds of guys know about it—gay, straight, bi. On a good weekend Ken will have twenty or thirty guys stop by at all hours.

House rules are that the host gets all the loads and that any guests who overlap or accumulate can watch each other get blown but not play with each other.

Ken established his service station years ago—well before AIDS and sex monitors—after it became clear that managers of gay bars would not permit him to install himself in a backroom or a men's room as an establishment's sole, designated cocksucker. In fact, Ken got himself banned from several places for scaring away other hungry hopefuls.

A hard, big-gutted daddy nicknamed Sperm Cow arrives at Ken's place. Sperm Cow gets his name from his habit of hanging around throughout the night, dropping several loads between Ken's other sessions.

"Man, am I bushed," Sperm Cow says, stripping down to black socks. "I worked a double shift today and you know what I'm like after one of those days." Sperm Cow has been known to doze off occasionally, even while getting worked on.

"Relax," Ken says.

After settling Sperm Cow into the lounge chair where the servicing takes place, Ken seats himself on a pillow in front of the chair and gently nuzzles his way between Sperm Cow's chunky legs. A video on the TV screen flickers with nothing but close-up glory hole action.

At Phelan and Seb's place, Jonathan is still talking to Maurie, the loud-voiced talent manager.

"Are you coming with us?" Jonathan asks. Phelan has announced they will all be walking over to the Roxy in a group.

"I don't think so," Maurie says.

"No?"

Maurie pats his belly, which is an inch or two away from trim.

"The shirt must *never* be removed in public, under any circumstances."

"Then keep it on."

"Sure, and just stand around in a blazer, feeling unpopular, like it's a school dance."

"Unpopular? Didn't Letterman just call you one of the most sought-after managers in Hollywood?"

"Yeah. That and a pair of pecs would get someone to say hello to me at the Roxy."

Jonathan is stunned. "C'mon, doesn't power trump attitude?" he says.

"Nothing trumps attitude in a club," Maurie says. "Don't worry about me. I see a shrink three times a week. Besides, I only live a block away and I'm taking *Dombey and Son* to bed. *You* go. *Have* fun."

Across the room, Ethan spots Gil leaving early with Seb.

Seb and Gil have decided to walk to the club by way of Gil's dealer's apartment. As they left the party Phelan made them promise they'd rejoin everyone at three in the club's VIP room, for a champagne rendezvous.

In the West Village they pass an alleyway in which they glimpse a tableau: two men masturbating spotlit under a street lamp, their pants around their ankles, and a third man watching, at a distance.

"Jacob Riis," Seb says.

"Who?"

"The photographer. Early twentieth-century New York. Slice-of-life."

"I'll give you slice-of-life," Gil says, grabbing Seb's hand and clamping it to his butt as they walk on.

Elsewhere in Brooklyn Heights Vince takes Load Four from an elementary school teacher in a fourth-floor walk-up. The guy is another regular cum feeder on Vince's speed dial, who just happens to be home when Vince calls. The encounter is wordless, which pleases Vince. He is let in, drops to his knees, takes the load, then leaves. Afterward, in the hallway, as he walks to the stairway and hears the door close and lock, the Chlorox-y taste of this guy's cum fills his nose and throat.

2 to 3 A.M.

"Remember, everybody, see you at three! The VIP room!"

At the club door, Phelan handles everything. He greets the staff warmly and is given passes for everyone in his party. Then, propelled by an instinct that overtakes them as soon as they feel the music thumping from within, he and his guests press inside, sailing past the line of mere mortals waiting to buy tickets.

Everyone heads to the bar or the dance floor, except Jonathan. On the pretense of having to meet a coworker at the back bar he slides off to the periphery, alone.

Jonathan prefers to wander around a bit when he first enters a club—on the event horizon. It's his way of recalibrating the substance of his body to endure the pressure of so many other human beings and the density of club sound and light.

Jonathan has visited clubs in groups, as he's doing tonight, and on dates, with one other guy. *Alone is best*, he thinks. Clubs are not really about socializing, let alone companionship. They are places to contemplate your lone self versus the universe. Isolated there amidst hundreds, sometimes thousands of hyperactive bodies, your senses charged to their maximum, you can attune to the eternal furor that drives human existence. You feel much more easily than you do in a church that the atoms of your body came charging out of the Big Bang only a few billion years ago and that their present configuration exists for all sorts of random reasons that add up to what some people call God.

From an elevated platform ringing the dance floor he spots Ethan in the middle of the crowd. The very good looker has already found his herd: eight or ten of the best looking men in the club. They are all dancing together as a group, shirtless.

They can't have been dancing long enough to be hot, Jonathan thinks.

At a corner of the main bar Meeker stands nursing a scotch. His doctor says he should go easier on alcohol now that he's over sixty and the blackouts at the end of long evenings of drinking occur more frequently, but Meeker considers scotch an old friend. He looks scarcely less formal in black leather than he did earlier in his custom-made dinner suit. In all situations, even in a dance club that celebrates youth and beauty, Meeker radiates the kind of composure that derives only from money. True, at certain times the contemplation of what his father once called his "lesser" lifestyle can provide a twinge of disequilibrium, despite Meeker's mastery of this lifestyle in the quiet manner of his generation and class. But twinges of disequilibrium can often provide pleasure, which is why Meeker sometimes comes to the club looking for them.

Meeker's best twinges come in the form of black and latino boys. He likes them young, middle- or lower-middle-class, articulate, affectionate, and of course beautiful. For the last thirty years he has been meeting boys in bars and clubs, dating them surreptitiously, buying them books and classical CDs, encouraging them to fuck him, though he never requires this, and in many cases funding projects they are working on—a graduate degree, a movie production, a clothing business. His affairs with these boys usually last a year or two and then dissolve amicably into low-maintenance friendships. Meeker's companion of many years chooses not to be aware of these relationships and besides has his own forms of recreation.

The crush at the bar, men pressing past each other on their way to and from the dance floor—it's almost too hectic for a man his age. But Meeker enjoys knowing that someone he'd never have met at the Philharmonic may suddenly appear out of the chaos.

I do hope Coby shows up, he thinks. *Such a nice boy, so cultivated.*

Meeker is sipping his scotch when a handsome face appears in front of him. It belongs to a twentyish, light-skinned latino with a smile verging on a pout.

"Absolut on the rocks with a twist!" the boy shouts. The bartender doesn't hear him.

The boy seems to be alone. Again he tries to catch the bartender's attention, but without luck. He is wearing an underwear tank top.

"He could use some help, couldn't he?" Meeker says.

"I know," says the boy, barely acknowledging the older man. The voice is educated, the manner polite.

"You're alone?" Meeker asks.

"Here with people, actually."

"Ah. Dancing up a storm."

"In the DJ booth, actually. We're friends of the DJ. Actually *I'm* a DJ ...."

"I see."

As the boy raises his arm to flag the bartender Meeker catches a glimpse of armpit hair.

"Laying down some terrific beats tonight, isn't he?" Meeker says.

The boy studies Meeker briefly. He's unaccustomed to gray-haired guys talking about club music this way. André hates it when gay white guys fake being "down" just to get in his pants.

"I'm John," Meeker says.

"André."

"Can I buy you a drink, André?"

"Thanks, but ... I'm not really into older guys."

Meeker smiles. "I'm not picking anyone up, my friend. I'm here with friends myself. Just hanging about, doing good deeds."

By tipping twenty dollars with his first drink Meeker established a good relationship with the bartender. Within a minute he has ordered an Absolut on the rocks with a twist and is passing it to André.

"Nice to meet you, André," he says, raising his own glass in a toast. "Please give Sensay my compliments."

André registers Meeker's knowledge of the DJ's name.

"He's good, right? OK, thanks, man. Sorry about the mix-up. Enjoy."

André disappears back into the crowd.

"*Que rico,*" Meeker says. With all the noise, no one hears these words.

Meeker orders himself another scotch, knowing he shouldn't, and glances around absently. Another boy is standing opposite him at the bar—a good-looking boy some might take for Asian, others for latino. Asians do nothing for Meeker and he isn't even conscious of dismissing this boy in a split second, then looking beyond him.

The boy's name is Emanuel and he's Philippino-Jewish—the only son of a physicist and a famous classical pianist. Emanuel's alone with a beer. His brow is furrowed and he looks a little hostile, though he's actually only depressed. He's wondering if it was wise to have left his girlfriend, Celia, alone at the hip-hop CD release party where they were an hour ago. The party was fun but Celia was talking a little too warmly to one of the recording artists, so Emanuel bolted without saying a word.

A native of San Francisco and a graduate of U.C. Berkeley, Emanuel arrived in New York only months ago at the age of twenty-one, ostensibly to launch a career in journalism. But some magazine people noticed Emanuel skateboarding in the parking lot of a supermarket in Brooklyn and got him into modeling. Emanuel has large, credulous eyes, great slashes of black eyebrows, and a sensitive mouth that makes him look both vulnerable and ready to sneer. He's been getting a lot of work from a number of influential style magazines in the stratum just below Condé Nast, so now Emanuel's unsure whether journalism is the right direction for him.

He also has questions about whether women are right for him. Celia's a model too, and Emanuel has strong feelings for her. But he often winds up alone in gay clubs on weekend nights. When he's attracted to guys it's usually to much older ones—like the gray-haired guy in the black leather jacket, on the other side of the bar—but he never knows what to say and how to act, so he does nothing.

Maybe I shouldn't have smoked a joint on the way over here, Emanuel thinks. He pulls out his cell phone and dials Celia's number, then realizes that there's too much noise to make a call.

The appearance of a cell phone makes a stranger standing next to Emanuel roll his eyes and make a comment to a friend, though Emanuel doesn't notice this.

At the club's loading dock, which doubles as its back door, Phelan is talking on his phone, looking up the street. Next to him is a club security guard.

"And I haven't seen Seb since we arrived...."

A black limousine appears in the street.

"OK, there you are ... I'm right here on the dock ...." Phelan waves.

The limousine pulls up and out steps Phelan's friend the fashion designer, a once truly handsome, now eerily overpreserved man in his late fifties. He is accompanied by three gorgeous, much younger men. They're all coming from a West Village dinner party and performance hosted by another fashion designer for a young singer-songwriter she is sponsoring.

Phelan and the designer embrace. The designer introduces the younger men—two of them models Phelan recognizes—and they all enter the building.

"So who's here?" the designer says, as the security guard leads the party through a service corridor toward a "secret" entrance to the dance floor, near the stairs to the VIP room.

"You know who's here?" Phelan says. "The Asian boy I was telling you about—the skateboarder model that *Trace* put in the silver parka. The scowler."

"Oh, I love that boy!" the designer says. "Such amazing hairless skin. Only don't say he was scowling. I'm telling you, he was channeling the Stern Buddha! What's his name?"

"I don't remember. Something Biblical. But he's by the big bar, all by himself. I thought ..."

"Alone? Let's swing by on our way upstairs, yes? He'll join us."

The security guard opens the door and the group sweeps into the crowd. They could have used another entrance to the VIP room directly from the street, but the designer likes his two-minute, escorted walk through two thousand dancing men.

In the main men's room Vince has occupied the last stall of a long row for the last half hour. He keeps the door propped open with his knee, giving himself a view of several urinals and the men waiting to use them. He doesn't really like men's rooms in clubs because they can be so messy and he is a bit of a clean freak. But he likes how easy it is to convince men fucked up on drugs and alcohol to let him suck their dicks.

Load Five is delivered by a hairy, lanky kid who is so drunk that he leans against the stall door for several minutes beforehand, silently trying to figure out how to coordinate his need to pee with his intention of getting sucked off. Patiently Vince guides the kid through both processes. Load Six is delivered by a tight little muscle dude on speed who fucks Vince's head like a piston with a small, very hard, upward-curving cock that does not fit well in Vince's mouth.

As Vince works, the room echoes with multiple conversations and corridor-filtered disco music.

Adjoining the men's room is a ladies' room, also full of men. John, the semi-inert plumber from Queens, is getting his cock sucked in one of the stalls there by a pretty blond boy in a girl-cut T-shirt who's straddling the toilet backward. The word *twinkie* is printed in sparkles on the back of the shirt. The boy had darted into the stall and gotten to work instantly when he saw John standing there lazily, with that enormous cock hanging out.

But the session is soon over.

"You're not going to cum, are you?" the boy says.

"You're not going to leave, are you?"

The boy leaves, then John vacates the stall—which is noticed by

Dwyer, who, after downing beer after beer in the club for almost an hour, needs to pee badly and is extremely pee shy. Gratefully, Dwyer ducks into the stall. A body-odorish smell lingers there, which he finds intoxicating.

Could that smell belong to the skinny slob who just left? Dwyer wonders.

Seb and Gil don't go to the club at all. After stopping to visit Gil's dealer they go to Gil's apartment. The minute they arrive Gil puts on some vintage bossa nova and they attack the crystal. Sex for these two is a career sport. They are like famous athletes, trained only for matches like this. They go at each other as if reputations were on the line.

Seb unbuttons Gil's shirt and slowly pulls it off his body. The lusterless tanned flesh is well defined but softer than it looks. Gil pulls Seb's shorts down, revealing the fact that Seb is wearing no underwear and is already half hard. In a moment all their clothing is strewn on the floor. Naked, they cup each other's pecs, grasp each other's butts. Then in slow motion, holding each other, they fall onto Gil's unmade platform bed.

In forty-five minutes they cycle through as many different sexual positions, each demonstrating as much technique and indicating as much hunger as possible.

Gil begins caressing Seb's ass, but his hands are pushed away. *Is his ass clean?* Gil wonders. Next position.

Seb starts to suck Gil's toes, but suddenly Gil pulls up his leg. *Does he have athlete's foot?* Seb wonders. Next position.

They kiss, then both pull away at the same moment.

Bad breath? A gum infection?

They hardly speak. It's not time yet to fuck though both know that fucking is where this match is going.

Coby's alarm rings at two-thirty. His body has sunk more deeply into sleep than he had planned. The bed is warm and comforting.

Getting up feels difficult on a cellular level.

He rolls over and presses the snooze button, while a hundred thoughts race obsessively through his dream-clogged mind.

Do I really wanna go to a club at this point? Did I say for sure I'd meet up with Meeker? Was it a real date? Did I say, "I'll see you there"? Will Meeker even show, himself? What if I go there and can't find him? What if don't go but pretend later that I went and couldn't find him? Can I even wake up enough to get out of bed? Is the Roxy as good as it used to be or do we just go there automatically? Will I being doing anybody a favor if I show up all groggy and out of it? Will the music be good enough to get me up to speed? Would it be OK if I just skipped it? Does anybody go to the Roxy whom I can deal with? Is there ever anybody there who qualifies as a potential boyfriend? Are there ever white guys there who are cool—who can deal with a black guy without making a fetish out of it? Why is this city is so full of fakers? Why should deciding whether or not to go out be so much work? Shouldn't I be using the weekend to relax? Christ, and I have to fucking play golf with those yahoos at four o' clock!— be all black and masculine for four hours. God forbid I should show them a campy moment ....

When the alarm rings again, Coby presses the off button and sinks back into sleep.

In the East Village, Sperm Cow is sound asleep in Ken's chair. He hasn't even shot his first load yet, nor has Ken had any other action. No one else has called or come by and Ken doesn't understand why, though his experience with these service station sessions over the years has allowed him to empirically observe the outlines of a vast phenomenon he calls the "sexual weather." This is a set of conditions that seems to govern whether on any give night scores of men will be drawn to Ken's doorstep by a strong need pulsing through their cocks or whether the doorstep will be barren— conditions including day of the week, time of the month, and the national mood, as well as, of course, temperature, barometric pressure, humidity, and other actual meteorological phenomena.

Ken has come to realize that sexual weather can't be changed. But almost angrily he insists on doing what he can to fight back when the weather is inclement, as it is tonight. So he hops on the computer and joins a New York "m4mNOW" chatroom under a screen name that advertises his cocksucking abilities. After every few lines of dialog among room members he inserts an invitation:

"Cocksucking service station. Loads now being drained in the East Village. IM me for details. Cum by, drop a load or two. Legendary deep throat. References on request."

3 to 4 A.M.

The overpreserved fashion designer decides it isn't worth sticking around in the VIP room, because "no one is there." Phelan understands this to mean that although the place is packed there are no other models or boys cute enough to be models. No one has been able to find the Buddha.

"The boys and I have promised our driver we'd look in on a puppy christening his roommate is hosting," the designer says to Phelan. "It sounds like fun. A baby chihuahua. Apparently they have a priest and everything. But reach me if something develops or I'll call you from the plane."

The designer and his boys sweep out.

At 3:15 the only person Phelan sees in the crowded VIP room whom he knows is Jonathan. In a seating nook overlooking the dance floor Phelan and Jonathan open the bottle of champagne and cut into the cake that have been set out on a low table, along with plates, glasses, forks, and napkins.

"It was for Seb," says Phelan, who arranged the spread. "It's his birthday. Well, it *was* his birthday last week."

Phelan starts offering cake and champagne to strangers.

"Maybe you should have told people it was a surprise for Seb?" Jonathan says.

"No big deal," Phelan says. He is feeding cake to a tall, young

hunk with a blond crewcut and electric smile. "Let's make it—
What's your name? Charlie? Let's make it Charlie's birthday!"

Downstairs, still standing in the same place at the bar, Meeker
is talking to Paolo, who appeared next to him and ordered a bottle
of water. They are discussing the ecology and building materials of
the Caribbean, and Meeker is impressed enough to consider giving
Paolo a business card. Paolo keeps checking his watch and looking
over at a particular spot by a sparsely populated lounge area.
Suddenly, someone is standing over there, wearing a glittering, silver sequined baseball cap.

"Excuse me one minute, please?" Paolo says. "I will come right
back."

Meeker watches Paolo go over, greet the man in a business-like
manner, exchange something, and walk back.

"I suppose that was your dealer," Meeker jokes. He cannot imagine that anyone as reasonable as Paolo seems would be involved
with drugs.

"Yes, exactly," Paolo says cheerfully, holding up his fist, which
conceals something small. "This is for the rest of the evening."

Meeker is aghast. He abhors drugs.

"I'm sorry, will you excuse me please?" he says and walks away.
Paolo is confused but shrugs off the sudden departure.

In the men's room Vince is still on duty in his stall. Load Seven
is salty and comes from a preppily dressed guy from St. Louis who
heard about the Roxy six hours ago in a gay restaurant in Chelsea.
Load Eight is voluminous, from a bookish looking guy in tape-
patched glasses, who keeps turning around to see if people are
watching. Load Nine is thin, from a chunky, older leather man with
a Prince Albert—a type rare for this club, Vince thinks, since
leather daddies don't usually come to the Roxy that often and even
when they do they save their loads for other scenes later in the
evening. Load Ten is rushed, from a muscular and sweaty bartender.

Also in the men's room is very good-looking Ethan. There, he
finds Ron, a very good-looking, salt-and-pepper haired man he has

Men and Their Issues

been trying to track down for thirty minutes. Ron is in a stall sucking on John, the plumber. Ron had been part of the group Ethan
was dancing with; he and Ethan had paired up and were dancing
near the DJ booth when Ron went off to pee.

Now Ethan can't quite figure out how to interrupt Ron, so he
just stares. The salt-and-pepper head thrusts greedily in and out
on John.

I'm not going to compete with that, Ethan thinks. He decides to
move on—but not before John notices him, leans forward, and, gently pulling Ron's head out of the way, pushes the door shut.

The music in the club's chill room is trancelike and merges
gauzily with echoes of the harder stuff pounding on the dance floor.
People are seated around the room in small groups, talking quietly in
a state of buzzed idleness. A spread of fruit and cookies, compliments
of the house, looks treasure-like in the lunar-blue light. On a low, free-
form couch that would be at home in the Jetson residence André the
DJ is reclining with Jaime, a cute young graphic and animation
artist whom André introduced himself to over a bunch of grapes.

Jaime's manner is a little spacey. His eyes—which André immediately thought were the most beautiful eyes he'd ever seen—aren't
quite focused.

"My friends are around somewhere," Jaime says. "We're scouting for a video thing we're doing with MTV." Languidly Jaime
explains that they're looking for young, male, nonwhite models for
a shoot—which is André's cue to begin selling himself to score the
project.

"You definitely have to check out what my group and I are
doing," André says. "Combining turntable sounds with live instru-
mentals. Like jazz. We play at the SoHo Grand on Mondays. You
hafta come hear us."

"Yeah, we should talk more ...," Jaime says.

"No, you should meet my people," André says. "We're all in the
DJ booth, if you want to stop over there with me." He touches
Jaime's shoulder with one finger.

"Yeah, maybe later ...."

"And we're definitely looking for someone to do the packaging for a CD we're putting together."

"Definitely, yeah. We should talk ...."

Jaime's friends appear. They're on their way to a party and have come to collect Jaime. Jaime and André stand up. Introductions are made. André takes a second to evaluate the social cost of leaving without his friends, should he be invited to join Jaime's group. But he isn't invited. One of Jaime's friends takes Jaime's hand and kisses it, whispering something in Jaime's ear.

"How can I contact you?" André asks.

Jaime says his e-mail address. The address involves a pun that's difficult to understand over the noise. André asks Jaime to repeat it. No one in Jaime's party has a pen.

Down in the club's lobby, people are drifting toward the exit. On a pay phone—because he owes his cell phone company a lot of money—Emanuel calls Celia. She doesn't answer her cell and, oddly, there's no message. Emanuel wonders if he's remembered the number correctly and tries again. Still no answer and no message. Emanuel's only got one quarter left and uses it to leave a message on Celia's home machine.

"Hi. Looking for you. Around four, I guess. Check you later. Love you."

Emanuel craves a cigarette and sees a man lighting up at the exit—Jaime. But he sees that the man is with a group of friends and, being shy, lets the opportunity pass. Aimlessly, Emanuel exits too.

Outside the door club kids are handing out flyers for other club nights. Emanuel takes several and examines them cursorily, then drops them on the sidewalk as he shuffles away. Flyers litter the sidewalk between the exit and the street corner.

The screen of Ken's computer is choked with IMs. While Sperm Cow sleeps he struggles to respond to each one.

"hi need draning"

"HEY THRE. WESTVLLAGE DADY HERE NEEDS SERVICE."

"you there? —I have big cock —need to come soon—"

Ken types as fast as he can while checking profiles and trading pictures. Six men have promised to stop over within the next hour or so. Four of them say they are in the same neighborhood. One says he is bringing two friends.

4 to 5 A.M.

The lights are turned up inside the club. Decor elements like the undulating wall of brushed aluminum are drained of their magic. The music is halted and the sound of tired people working hovers over the empty dance floor. Bars are being secured, trash is being gathered.

In the men's room John and salt-and-pepper-haired Ron are asked by security to vacate. John tucks in his shirt and zips up while Ron wordlessly slips him a card and takes off. The card is for a vintage furniture shop in Chelsea. John takes a look at it and tosses the card in the garbage. Then he goes to a sink to wash his hands.

"So what are you up to now, guy?" It's Dwyer, standing behind him.

"I don't know," says John to the mirror. "What did you have in mind?"

"I have a car. I was thinking of going over to the Place."

"What place?"

"A sex club called the Place."

"That sounds like a plan."

In the hallway of a Chelsea apartment building—quietly, so a room-mate won't hear—Vince takes Load Eleven. On his way out of the building he calls another of his speed dial numbers, that of an art dealer in Tribeca. Twenty minutes later in an art-filled loft Vince is doing his best to collect Loads Twelve and Thirteen from the dealer and a friend the dealer has invited over. But both are high and giggly, and neither can stay hard.

"You guys said you had cum for me and I really needed it ...," says Vince as he leaves, making no attempt to disguise his disgust.

"Well, we'll call you later."

"No, another time. I'm on my way back to Brooklyn."

Phelan is home in his fabulous apartment off Union Square, lying on the living room sofa, talking quietly into his cell phone. The lights are low. His new friend Charlie, the birthday boy, is in the master bathroom.

"We just got in. He's in the tub, cleaning himself out. No, I met him at the club. He was right there in the VIP room—six-two, blond crewcut. You must have seen him. I'm feeding him party favors and I think he's going to be a lot of fun. He says he was out for an adventure and sure enough, his little backpack was full of toys. Apparently he knows Tommy and Tommy's magic hands, so I've got Tommy coming over, and he's bringing some people. No, I haven't seen Seb. You want him to do *what?*"

Back at his apartment Paolo sits on his sofa in boxer shorts. He is alone, forlorn. He hasn't done any of the crystal he bought because he doesn't do drugs. They were for his guest. Soon after he came to New York a gay coworker told Paolo that supplying party favors was a host's responsibility and that this was more important to hook-ups than liquor or running water. Now Paolo regrets letting TR go without attempting to discuss this explicitly.

Half-heartedly playing with his floppy cock Paolo dials TR's number and reaches a message system.

"Hey, man, this is 16th Street. I am thinking about you. You know where I am?" He gives the address and phone number. "I forget to ask if you like drugs. Maybe you don't. I'm sorry—my English. You are the nicest man I meet in New York. OK. Call me. I am here."

TR is not far from Paolo's apartment. He's entering an eighty-year-old building in the Flatiron district that for most of its life housed light manufacturing businesses. Today it is the home of design studios, modeling agencies, financial consultancies, and an after-hours gay sex club called the Place. Set in a cavernous fourth-floor loft, the club was launched informally ten years ago as a recurring private party by two biker guys who had been running a photography studio in the space. When the sex parties took off the photo bookings were dropped. Now the biker guys make gay porn films there during the day.

The elevator opens directly into the dimly lit club. TR steps off into the reception area, where several men are either checking or retrieving their clothing, getting dressed or undressed. All seats are taken, so shakily, because he is drunk, TR stands to get out of his chinos, removing and then stepping back into one boot at a time. He tucks his ID into a sock and leaves on his loose-fitting T-shirt.

"That's twenty-five dollars and I'll need your card," drones the shirtless boy behind the reception desk, without looking at TR. The boy has his hands full—handling the checking as well as the admission and the sale of water and poppers.

"Here's thirty. Keep the change." TR is about to explain that he doesn't have his card when the boy looks up.

"Hey!" the boy says with a smile.

"Hey," TR says. The last time TR was at the club, also drunk, he sucked this boy off behind the desk.

The place is packed. Just beyond the reception area, in a lounge, several men are sitting on low couches, quietly talking or kissing. A seated cigar smoker—an older man dressed in nothing but a leather jacket, a jock strap, and boots—is being serviced by a kneeling naked boy in sneakers. Casually the smoker looks around to savor any reaction to this situation. Another seated man is nosing into the ass crack of a tall, hairless guy standing backwards in front of him. The tall man, bent slight forward, his briefs stretched between his thighs, is writing his number on a card for a third guy. Nearby, on line for the bathroom, two shirtless men in jeans with wet legs are simultaneously pissing into the gaping mouth of a fully clothed boy hunched in front of them.

Beyond the lounge naked flesh is pressed into partitioned nooks made of plywood and two-by-fours. Bodies are spread over low, pool table-size platforms padded in fake leather. Walls of black drapery set off two semi-secluded areas, both overcrowded—one holds a pillory, another a bathtub. In a third area men pack into and around a pen pierced with glory holes. From hidden speakers pulses the sound of something slightly less cohesive than music. Above it all flicker video monitors cloning images from a fisting video.

After being rejected by Paolo, TR wants some action. Slowly he begins making his way to the back of the club. This is his element and he slips through it gracefully, instantly registering hot guys and keeping in mind their trajectories with the skill of an air flight controller—though a minor tumble he takes onto the cum- and piss-slathered floor as he tries to squeeze around a clump of fused body parts, reminds TR that his motor control is not 100 percent.

"Here?" Gil says to Seb. They are in one of the club's nooks, momentarily empty except for them. They have been at the Place for half an hour, having decided it would be fun to come here and have an audience for their exploits.

It was Seb's idea to change the venue. At Gil's place things never quite took off.

"Mmm, I dunno," whispers Seb. "I think that annoying guy is right around the corner."

"*Which* annoying guy?" Gil says. He has been following Seb around from spot to spot with increasing impatience, as they look for the right place where they can fuck, be watched, see others, and yet not become engulfed in a mass of the "wrong" grasping gawkers. According to Seb, several of the wrong ones are stalking them.

"If you mean the guy in the glasses who we saw in the tub room then we should let him watch, " Gil says. "He has a great attitude."

"*He* might, but what kind of signal does that send to the rest of the club?"

Gil rolls his eyes.

"Once during a blizzard I sneaked down in the elevator, naked, and did it with some guy in the lobby," Seb says. "Do you think we could get past the guy at the door?"

At that moment the guy with the glasses peers into the nook, then steps in. Wordlessly he begins groping himself but maintains a few feet of distance.

Meeker lets himself into his Park Avenue duplex and pads up to his bedroom. On his dresser there is a note from the butler.

I have a friend here, it reads. *You're welcome to join. Feel free to phone when you get in.*

Meeker hesitates, then dials the butler on the house phone, a relic from the days when Meeker's mother modernized the place, right after World War II.

"Is this the boy from last time—the one from the Bronx?"

"No, a different one. You don't know him."

"But you think I'd like to know him, right?"

"I think maybe so."

"Well, thank you anyway, Ramon, but I'm going to bed. I have to be fresh for the Mayor's breakfast at nine. So make sure I'm up at eight, will you, and have the car outside at eight-forty-five?"

"Of course, sir."

In the background, on the butler's end, there is a loud thud.

"Good heavens, what was that?"

"Nothing, sir." Muffled laughter. "He was just showing me a step from *The Prodigal Son*. He's in the Dance Theater of Harlem."

"A ballet dancer," Meeker says. "Hmmm. You know what? *May* I look in for just a minute? Let me pour a nightcap and I'll be right down."

5 to 6 A.M.

"Aiden, it's Jonathan, in New York."

"Jonathan, darling!"

"I just called to say hello. *Buon giorno*. How's the book going?

How's Rudolf? How's Rome?"

"The book is going well and Rudolf is just fine, thank you. But, darling, I'm just running off to a sort of mass at Princess—well, you remember Ilaria. She's restored the seventeenth-century chapel we looked at in her family's palazzo and now she has some very important cardinals coming over to reconsecrate the place."

"Very nice. I could use a little reconsecration myself."

"Could you, puss?"

"Yeah, but go. We can talk tomorrow."

"Something the matter? Men?"

"It's nothing. Just New York."

"New York men?"

"*A* man, Aiden—as in, Where is he? And if he is here in this damned city how am I supposed to find him?"

"You've been to a party. You've been up all night."

"Been to a party. Talked to a lot of unconnected people. Been to a club. Saw a lot of unconnected people. Went to a fisting scene for about twelve seconds. Came home. Tried to connect with the television."

"'Only connect.'"

"Right. So don't forget to find out from Ilaria what that handsome brother of hers is up to. I might have to fly over there and marry him."

"Oh, he *got* married to Lady Serena something and moved to London. But don't worry. I hear he's still gay."

"Great."

"I wish I could tell you what the answer is."

"Is it me?"

"It's not you. It's them—all of them. Men who marry their ambition and then forget to cheat on it. It's not just a gay thing."

"OK. Go, Aiden. We can talk later. I want to hear all about it. Did they restore the organ too?"

"Yes, the organ too. And Ilaria's booked a choir and a brass ensemble."

"Yikes. Call me after. And pray for me."

"You won't slit your wrists?"

"No. I'm going to try to nap. Then I'm going to go out and buy myself the most delicious breakfast I can find."

"Wear something special, darling. And promise me you'll invite some nice stranger along."

The video booth store on King's Highway is open all night. Vince arrives back there just before six, with a newspaper. He likes the store when it's empty, as it is most mornings, because that's when the management is least intrusive in Vince's lair, the windowless backrooms, and when the guys who do show up—especially the straight guys, who are often nervous about coming there—are most relaxed about getting sucked off.

Vince is standing next to his favorite booth reading the real estate section when another man enters.

"You're up early." It's the straight guy Vince sucked off the night before. Different pressed slacks and shirt, same gold ID bracelet.

"I've been up feeding all night. That's when I get the most, at night on weekends."

"I had to drive my wife to the hospital for her shift. This is on my way to church."

The man gropes himself gently.

"You need more?" he says.

Instantly Vince puts aside the newspaper.

"Sure, " he says, his eyes locking onto the man's hand as the fly is undone.

Vince sinks to his knees. He groans as the meat finds its way down his throat. The night before, this guy came quickly, produced a big load, and let Vince kiss off the very last warm drops of cum. This time the guy cums just as quickly and acts even more like the ideal feeder that Vince is looking for—impersonal but not unfriendly.

"Next time show me my load before you swallow it?" the guy

says, zipping up.

Vince nods eagerly. "You got it."

The guy nods, gives a thumbs-up, and takes off.

Twelve, Vince thinks. *And then there were Friday and Saturday's nine. But it'll never be a record this weekend, no matter what I do.*

Vince's record for a full weekend—Friday night through early Monday morning—is thirty-one loads. He checks his watch and decides he can give it another hour before having to leave, so he picks up the real estate section and goes back to looking through listings for two- and three-bedroom houses in the suburbs.

6 to 7 A.M.

Sperm Cow is still asleep. No one else has come over to Ken's service station.

"Fuck you all," he murmurs at the computer as he scrolls down lists of people who are in the New York "m4mNOW" chatrooms. He spots Mitchell, who he knows is looking only for JO because a few weeks ago, posing under a "neutral" screen name as a JO freak, Ken chatted and traded X-rated pictures with him. Mitchell's beautiful cock has been stuck in his thoughts ever since.

Ken signs on again under the same screen name.

Who knows, he thinks, *maybe I can just go over there and watch him jerk off.*

Ken: Great cock. We've talked before.

Mitchell: East Village, right? Thx.

Ken: Yeah. Been JOing?

Mitchell: All night. You?

Ken: All night.

Mitchell: Feel like stroking with a buddy? Watching?

Ken: Sure. Like to get it worked on?

Mitchell: You mean BJ?

Ken: Love watching, stroking.

Mitchell: Nah.

Ken: Incredible cock. Pic is in front of me.

Mitchell: C'mon over. Check out the real thing.

There's less traffic on Eighth Avenue in Chelsea early on a Sunday morning than at any other time of the week and it seems to flow at a more civilized pace. The street is quiet, almost picturesque, a lovely illustration composed of sidewalks, storefronts, and scale figures. But Eighth Avenue is really two parallel dimensions at this time, deceptively appearing as a harmonious whole. In one dimension shopkeepers swab floors, delivery men unload newspapers, homeless people pick through trash cans, moms push strollers, old women in black pilgrim slowly to mass, and a certain subset of gay men duck into the gym, walk the dog, or scoot to the garage to pick up the car for a day out of the city. In the other dimension, certain other gay men who have been up all night—those with music still pulsing through their nervous systems—continue to hunt for cock and ass and drugs. They walk down the street, not so much shielding themselves from the sunlight and avoiding bustling morning activity as denying day itself, their undead eyes seeking other undead eyes. Within each dimension people are in tune with each other. Across the dimensions people hardly register.

For half an hour Emanuel has been sitting on the stoop of an apartment building between 17th and 18th Streets, next door to a deli. Young moms pass him. Residents dart past into and out of the building. Delivery men ignore him.

"Hey," says a passerby, a jazzed-looking guy in expensive Italian sunglasses, nylon track pants, and an unzipped nylon shirt.

Emanuel looks up.

"Wha'cha up to?" the man says.

"Nothing."

"Looking to party? I can hook you up if you wanna play a little."

"No, thanks. I'm just sitting here. But I could use a quarter though."

"No problem," the man says. He gives Emanuel a dollar.

"I'll be around for a while if you change your mind."

After the man leaves Emanuel buys a banana at the deli and calls Celia with the change.

"It's me again. I'm trying to get home. I don't have any money so I guess I'm going to start walking. If you were there I'd take a cab and ask you to meet me at the door. OK, I guess you're not there. See ya soon. Love you."

At the sink in the men's room at the Place a guy with a bulging belly and hairy chest, naked except for sneakers and a stained jockstrap down around his ankles, stands washing his short, thick, uncut cock. Good-looking Ethan, standing near the paper towel dispenser in boxer-briefs, snorts a bit of K without attempting to hide it. Water and piss puddle the floor.

This is the third bump of K that Ethan has done since arriving at the Place, half an hour ago. From the bottom of his mind has arisen an intention that becomes clear only when he does K at a place like this: to bottom out with anyone available, irrespective of looks.

With a gesture Ethan offers the naked guy a bump.

"Thanks," the guy says, taking a tiny bit onto a chewed fingernail and snorting it.

As Ethan puts away the K and the naked guy starts kneading his cock slowly Dwyer and John walk in, fully clothed, though John's fly is open. They have been exploring the club together, watching but so far not taking part in anything.

Ethan goes down on the naked guy and instantly, as if on a signal, the four of them turn into an orgy.

Ethan begins running his hands over the naked guy's belly, balls, and ass. Dwyer fondles Ethan's ears and the back of his head. Then Dwyer slips a finger into Ethan's mouth, along with the naked guy's cock. John pulls his cock out of his pants, and the naked guy notices and reaches for it. Ethan looks up to see John's face for the first time and registers him as the guy whose cock Ron was sucking in a stall at the Roxy. Ethan twists away from the naked guy and tries to get John's cock in his mouth but Dwyer beats him to it. Crouched next to Ethan, Dwyer does his best to suck John's eleven inches while Ethan goes back to servicing the naked guy.

"Mmmm," moans Dwyer, gobbling hungrily. *For once I'm really gonna go for it*, he thinks.

"Yeah," mumbles John.

The room is filled with the aroma of John's body.

"Mm-hm," Ethan is moaning, as the naked guy thrusts repeatedly forward.

Several men look into the men's room and don't enter. One happens to be Gil, but Ethan doesn't notice this. Another does enter to wash his hands, and this temporarily distracts Ethan.

"Yeowch!" whispers the naked guy, as Ethan's teeth get in the way of a thrust.

Downstairs at the building's main door Seb, who was leaving, runs into the overpreserved fashion designer, who has just gotten out of the waiting limousine with the gorgeous boys.

"Seb. Baby. "

"Hey. Hi."

"Anything going on inside?"

"Don't bother. Really."

"Really? We were going to stop in for a moment but—listen, finding you is extraordinary. You know we're on our way to my place in the D.R ...."

Seb didn't know that. The designer names a world-famous fashion photographer, a man, and a world-famous model, a woman, and explains that they are both meeting him today at his fabulous getaway on an exclusive bay in the Dominican Republic, for a shoot for the ad for his new fragrance. He has invited several friends, including a pop music star and a famous young movie actor to rendezvous there, to make it a big party for the stars and their people. The designer and the gorgeous boys are at this very moment on their way to the airport where he keeps his jet. Would Seb be interested in joining them and taking behind-the-scenes photos for a few days—party shots of him, the boys, and some of the others?

"You mean documentary style?" Seb says.

"You can call it that. But party pictures, Seb—sexy and truthful, like Andy used to take."

"Sex pictures?"

"Sure, I suppose some of that. I think we should go for something that's about the moment. Whatever happens."

"To be published?"

"Seb, they're for me, not *Women's Wear*. Come. It'll be fun. My instinct is that your work could grow in that direction. Do you need to stop by your place? I'll phone Phelan. Boys, back in the car."

7 to 8 A.M.

At Phelan's place a fisting scene is in progress—though "progress" is probably the wrong word to describe the directionless loop of sensation in which Phelan, Charlie, and five other naked men are lost.

Charlie is on his back at the edge of a deep, sheet-draped sofa in the living room, his rectum harboring the forearm of a short and very muscular man famous in certain circles for his exquisitely small, square hands. Charlie's legs are hooked over the man's shoulders and the coldish toes on his left foot are being sucked by a tattooed man standing at the fister's side, waiting for his chance to join or replace the muscular forearm. Charlie moans in response to little pressures or pushes within, as others position themselves to sink their soft cocks down his throat or feed him poppers and K. His electric smile has gone dim.

Phelan watches tranquilly from an armchair opposite. His legs are spread, his soft cock being worked on by a small, tight, hairy guy kneeling before him, clearly hungry for cum and probably resigned, because of the vast amounts of crystal everyone has ingested, to not getting any.

Lights are dim, movements slow. A New Age sound score with angelic voices shimmers quietly in the background. Words are few.

"Yup."

"There."

"Easy."

"See?"

"Right."

From the front door comes the sound of keys and the lock turning. Seb lets himself in and signals Phelan not to trouble himself to rise. Seb tiptoes around piles of discarded clothing to the bedroom hallway. Ten minutes later he tiptoes back, a small backpack slung over his shoulder, a camera bag in hand.

"Call me," Phelan mouths silently as Seb goes out the door. Phelan's cell phone sits on the glass-top table next to him, along with a tub of grease, a roll of paper towels, several cock-rings, and an Olympic-size butt plug.

The Place has practically emptied out. A few stragglers continue to circulate and things feel somewhere between desperate and calm. Navigation is easier and the human landmarks, fewer. The smell of stale poppers and lubricant hangs in the air.

In the back of the club Gil is bent over a sawhorse getting fucked, his head thrust into a corner near a window painted black, with a black drape hanging in front of it. He doesn't know who is fucking him and he doesn't care. He had been waiting there, his butt exposed, ready for anyone. It feels to Gil like the guy fucking him is short and heavy, and he does remember a guy of that description walking around the club—a very drunk guy with a shaved head.

Someone has opened the window a crack. A strip of sunlight and a fresh morning breeze filter in past the fluttering drape. Outside Gil can glimpse the tarred roof of a neighboring building and a large water tank supported on a framework of metal girders.

The men's room is empty. The orgy moment with Ethan and the

other three was over almost as quickly as it began. Ethan and
Dwyer both soon tired of being on their knees, and everyone wanted
to stand alongside John and feel the base of his cock while he was
getting sucked. John remained immobile, and a series of reposi-
tionings among the rest of them never yielded their previous sexual momentum, so everyone dispersed.

Ethan and Dwyer run into each other in the elevator, on the way
down.

"What happened to your buddy, the one with the giant dick?"
Ethan asks.

"I don't know. We weren't together."

"Oh."

"Had it for the night?" Dwyer asks. The acrid elevator light flat-
ters neither of them.

"Work." Ethan says. "I own a restaurant. Have to be there at
eight."

"Oh. Harsh."

Ethan names the restaurant.

"Oh, the place with the roof. I read about that. Didn't you
design it?"

"Just came up with the concept. Trained as an engineer before
discovering myself as a foodie."

"Hey, I'm an engineer," Dwyer says. "Structural. Cornell '67."

"Interesting. Cornell '88."

"*Really?*"

The elevator door opens. Both walk into the sun-filled lobby.

"Well, take care," Ethan says abruptly and pushes through a
glass door into the street.

On a whim, Ken decides to check out Mitchell's online profile before
he leaves for Mitchell's place.

Maybe he's got some new cock pictures, Ken thinks.

The profile is linked to a personal home page—home page-as-
shrine to wonderful self. Snapshots of Mitchell vacationing on a

beach, a snowy mountain, and what look like Mayan ruins. Snapshots of Mitchell in black tie, a wrestling singlet, and a plaid, button-down shirt. Snapshots of Mitchell's Jack Russell terriers, Hamilton and Henderson. A dramatic, black-and-white headshot of Mitchell obviously taken a few years ago. A baby picture taken in a suburban back yard. A bio, written in a breezy, narrative style, punctuated liberally with jokey asides and "clever" misspellings. Excerpts of Mitchell's favorite poems; references to a short-lived acting career; links to gay pride, recovery, and Jack Russell rescue sites.

Ken is appalled. The home page immediately kills any sexual feeling he'd had for the guy.

He IMs Mitchell.

Ken: Um, just got an emergency call. Can't come. Can we do it another time?

Mitchell: You got it. But am disappointed. Boo hoo.

Ken decides to run out for a few minutes to get some coffee for himself and Sperm Cow, who remains asleep.

Vince leaves King's Highway and drives three blocks to a popular neighborhood diner. Inside, breakfast business is brisk.

"Ginny, pick up!" shouts a voice from the kitchen.

An attractive, middle-aged woman behind the counter fetches the plate and delivers it to a customer. Then she comes over to Vince, standing at the take-out counter.

"Hey, little boy," she says. Ginny is slightly heavy, but she was once sexy and she still pays attention to her hair and makeup and the fit of her uniform.

"Hi, Gin," he says. "Can I get a sweet and light to go, please, hon?"

She leans over the counter and they share a peck. Ginny is Vince's wife. She has been working the diner's night shift.

"On your way home?" says Ginny, getting the coffee.

"A two-hour nap and I'll be all set."

"Big night?"

"Not big enough."

Ginny frowns tenderly. She knows everything. She can't explain it, but she accepts it.

"My mother is making manicotti," she says. "I told her we'd be there at one."

"No problem, Gin. Got it covered. The kids alone?"

"They're fine. Angela's alarm is set for ten and she'll get Joey up, feed him something. All you have to do is be nice to my mother and not pick a fight with her new boyfriend."

"He's a fucking bum. He needs a job."

"That he does," Ginny says. "Not like my baby boy."

She gives Vince's chin an affectionate squeeze.

The designer relaxes in the back of his limousine with Seb and the gorgeous boys. After stopping at several parties and after-hours scenes they are on their way to the airport. There is a tired though bubbly energy among them. Seb has already started taking pictures. Everyone is mugging, trying to be outrageous. As the car turns from 14th Street onto Eighth Avenue the designer phones Phelan.

"So, OK, I'm back on Thursday. I will or will not have Elton with me," the designer says. "Why don't we do a little dinner at Bottino that night? Do you wanna call Sigrid and Mandy?"

He is looking out the window as he speaks.

"Wait!" the designer shouts. "Stop the car!"

It's the Buddha, walking slowly up Eighth Avenue.

"What's that boy's name again?" the designer asks Phelan.

The designer lowers the mirrored window.

"Good morning ... Emanuel!" he says.

The designer identifies himself as the boy approaches the car. He is gratified to see that Emanuel knows who he is.

"Look," he says, "I know this is nuts but we're on our way to the airport and we'll be at my place in the Dominican Republic by lunch time. It's just a few days. You free to join us?"

Emanuel takes a moment to process this invitation.

"Um, actually I'm trying to get up to the East 90s," he says. "My girlfriend's place."

"Sure. Well, if you need to pick up some things we could swing by there real quick. But our schedule is getting tight. Come with us. It'll be fun."

"I better not, man. But thanks, OK?"

"It'll be shopping, dancing, swimming ... Elton, maybe Jennifer. And you know Mario ..."

"The photographer."

"Exactly."

"He's cool. But I can't, really. I'm sorry."

The designer thrusts a card at Emanuel.

"Here's my number," he says. "Call if you change your mind. I'll send my plane. Wouldn't that be fun? Bring your girlfriend."

The designer salutes and raises the window.

8 to 9 A.M.

"Ethan, it's Ron. Remember, gray hair? Antiques? Just wondering what happened with you. I couldn't find you when I got back from the men's room. Did you drift home? Anyway, find me. Let's talk. We hafta get together this week. What about dinner on Tuesday?"

Ken returns home with coffee and donuts. He has been gone less than half an hour and finds Sperm Cow awake, being done by an older man who's apparently just dropped over.

"Who the fuck are you?" Ken demands.

"Eddie," the older man says, not getting up. "'Desperm Me'? We chatted online."

"You said you wanted to get milked," Ken says. "What are you doing milking him?"

"I thought ..."

Sperm Cow interrupts. "C'mon, Ken, we were just ...."

Ken is livid.

"Out, both of you. Now. Please."

At Phelan's, it's break time. Men are lying around intermittently stroking their soft cocks, inserting and then removing butt plugs from each other's asses. It's leisurely—a parody of work, a caricature of sex. Tommy is reclined in a chair, tolerating oral service from the small, tight, hairy guy.

Phelan is sitting on the floor in front of Charlie, who is seated on the sofa, slumped back and to one side against a pile of pillows. He is between Charlie's legs with Charlie's small, soft cock in his mouth. This is the big bottom moment that Phelan has been looking forward to all evening and in fact has carefully choreographed. But something is wrong. Charlie seems somewhat more inert than he should.

"How ya doing, birthday boy?" Phelan asks, lifting Charlie's hand.

The hand is limp. Charlie is not sleeping, he is unconscious.

Some of the men come over to help Phelan examine Charlie's eyes and chest. They find a pulse, though it's very weak. They try to rouse Charlie.

"He'll be fine, he'll be fine," Phelan says. "Help me get his clothes on."

"I think you'd better call an ambulance," someone says.

"Uh, we can get him to St. Vincent's ourselves," Phelan says.

"Listen, I'd better get going," says Tommy. "Think you'll be able to manage?"

"Yeah, thanks for coming over."

"No problem," Tommy says. He drops two twenties on the glass table as he leaves.

In the end it's Phelan and one other guy who take Charlie to the St. Vincent's emergency room. The friend takes off the moment Charlie is placed on a gurney, on the sidewalk; Phelan oversees Charlie's admittance to the hospital. Luckily, Charlie's wallet contains all the necessary ID, including a medical insurance card. Phelan tells the admissions clerk that he doesn't have his own ID with him and gives the man completely false information.

The phone wakes Coby. It's his dad, the congressman, calling from Washington as he often does on Sunday mornings.

"Not catching you still in bed, son, am I?"

"Of course not, sir. You know I like to catch up on paperwork before church."

Coby sits up in bed.

"Very good. How are things going for you at the firm?"

"Very well, thank you," Coby says. "Very well."

"Splendid, son."

Coby looks around for his cigarettes, finds them on the night stand and lights one.

"Did I mention I'm working with Colonel Blount," Coby says. "The guy who wrote the book after leaving the army because he was gay?"

"The black guy."

"Yes. The book is being made into a TV movie. We're doing the contract. I'm leading the team."

"I met Blount at the White House," the congressman says. "Good man. Head on his shoulders. The kind of man, if …."

He stops. Then Coby continues for him.

"The kind of man, if your son is going to be gay, that I should …."

"You know what I mean," the congressman says.

"Blount already has a companion, by the way."

"Your mother and I only want you to be happy, son, though honestly we don't know what that means."

"And I think you know that I'm not necessarily into black guys."

There is silence on both ends of the line.

"Golly," Coby says. "That sounded so '50s. 'Daddy, I want a white boyfriend.'"

"And after church, son?"

"Golf. The club I told you about in Westchester. Me and some of the guys from the firm."

"Splendid. Enjoy yourself. Here, let me put your mother on."

"Dad, I... Sure. Have a great day, sir."

While Coby holds for his mother he grabs a pencil and makes a note to call Meeker and apologize for not showing up at the club.

9 to 10 A.M.

The Place is closing up for the night. One of the biker/porn producer owners emerges from a back office where he has been secluded throughout the night in private scenes with club patrons who have been specially selected and quietly approached. Everyone is gone now except the counter boy, who is locking up money and the popper inventory, and eleven-inch John, who is sitting in the reception area listlessly masturbating his half-hard monster.

"We're done here, champ," the owner says to John. "You don't have to go home but you can't stay here."

"OK."

"You OK?"

"Yeah."

"Hey, listen, I saw you getting blown earlier. I've seen you around."

"Yeah."

"Nice cock. What is that—nine? Ten?"

"Thanks. Eleven."

"Ever do porn?"

"Nope."

"Want to?"

"Maybe."

"I make videos. And you're certainly built for it. Only—do you ever get hard?"

"Yeah."

"Do you cum?"

"I can cum."

"I need energy."

"I have energy."

"OK, well how about you come back on Monday at noon and we'll audition you."

The owner gives John a card.

"Audition?"

"We'll set you up, have some boys work on you, and go for a cum shot. I mean, I can probably use you either way, but I'll pay you double if you can give me a good cum shot."

"Sounds like a plan."

Two policemen arrive at St. Vincent's, intending to interview Phelan. He's nowhere to be found. At the same time a nurse comes into the emergency waiting area looking for him, to tell him that Charlie will be all right. The nurse surveys the tired-looking throng gathered there—people sleeping upright in plastic chairs or absently staring at a talk show blaring from a TV that's attached to the wall—and she doesn't see Phelan.

A four-foot-high crucifix dominates the wall opposite the TV. The police check the men's room and don't find Phelan there, either. The nurse checks with the admissions clerk, who knows nothing.

TR wakes peacefully in a subway station in Queens. He is sitting on a bench, unharmed, his wallet safe. His appearance seems to cause no alarm among others on the platform. Five kids from the same family, dressed for church, share the bench with him, while their parents stand alongside.

He finds a pay phone and retrieves his messages. He hears Paolo's message and remembers that he gave Paolo his home number because he wasn't carrying his cell phone—not that he ever thought Paolo would really call him back.

He returns the call.

"There you are," says Paolo. "Yes. Thank you. Are you OK?"

"Yeah," TR says. "I got drunk. And I guess I got lost."

As he speaks TR notices a mysterious soiled patch on his chinos and finds a scrape on the back of his hand.

"Lost?"

"I'm in Queens. I don't know anyone in Queens. I live on the Upper West Side."

"Do you need help?"

"I think I'm fine."

"Good, good."

"I'm surprised you actually called me."

"My friend, my friend. Of course I call you. But tell me what are you eating later?"

"Eating?"

"Eat dinner with me. I am going to mass now but ... OK?"

"Oh. OK."

"At six o'clock."

"Yeah. Sure. I need a shower."

"Beautiful. So you ... like me?" Paolo says.

"Yeah, I like you," TR says. "Though I don't necessarily *understand* you...."

"The youth of our city are its greatest resource ...."

A small, private breakfast hosted by the Mayor is under way in the formal dining room at Gracie Mansion. Attending are several of the Mayor's longtime friends and financial supporters. Plates have been cleared and coffee cups refilled. From the podium the Mayor is describing a new cultural program he has created in public schools— a program of which Meeker's family foundation is the lead sponsor.

Meeker's head is pounding. He is almost blinded by the sunlight streaming in through tall, Palladian windows onto a table set with silver, crystal, white-and-gold china, and arrangements of peonies and yellow tulips.

"And we will help them develop their creative potential, which can ultimately result in careers that generate revenue for the city ...."

Meeker flags a waiter.

"I wonder if you have anything for a headache," Meeker asks, shielding his eyes from the sun.

"I'll see what I can do, sir."

"Did you have a good time last evening, John?" whispers the real estate developer sitting next to Meeker, whose family has been friends with Meeker's for generations.

"Last evening I ...," Meeker begins slowly.

"Nancy and I thought Maestro Ono and the orchestra did a first-class job."

"Of course they did. It was a lovely evening, wasn't it?"

Meeker finishes a glass of water and excuses himself. Suddenly, in a panic, he remembers inviting Mrs. Scovill over for tea this afternoon and wonders if he mentioned it to Ramon, who normally takes Sundays off.

Outside the men's room he phones home. The butler picks up.

"Sir. Was everything all right with the car?"

"Yes, yes, that's fine. I'm here now. But did I tell you about tea ...?"

"Mrs. Scovill at four. Beluga from Petrossian."

"I did tell you. Thank goodness. I couldn't have managed on my own. Not in my state."

"Well, you wouldn't quite be on your own, would you?"

"What do you mean?"

"You don't remember—again, sir?"

"Remember what?"

They are both silent.

"Ach. The dancer," Meeker finally says. "Lord, did I cum?"

"I'm afraid you didn't."

"Was I hugely inconvenient?"

"Of course not. You were charming. Gustavo laughed a lot."

"Gustavo."

"You don't remember making out with him?"

"No."

"Do you remember inviting him for tea this afternoon?"

"Oh, dear."

"Do you remember offering to pay for a hip-hop version of *Swan Lake* he wants to do in the Bronx?"

"Ugh! My head is killing me."

"Did you even check your suit pocket?" the butler says. "The right side. I knew you'd need your pills."

Jonathan is standing outside a magazine store reading headlines from the tops of stacks of Sunday papers. He is wearing the same clothes he was wearing at Seb and Phelan's party.

"Great T-shirt," says Coby. He is on his way to the gym—not to church—and has stopped in the magazine store for cigarettes.

"Wolf Trap," Jonathan says.

"I love that place. I used to go there every summer as a kid. I always thought the name sounded like a Canadian gay bar or something."

"Yeah, exactly."

"I'm Coby."

"Jonathan."

They shake hands, both smiling.

"Hi, Jonathan."

"Hi, Coby."

"Trying to decide whether or not to spring for a paper?" Coby says.

"I love the daily *Times* but Sunday is a train wreck, isn't it? Especially the cultural coverage."

"Must avoid. Farts and seizures."

"Well, that's two things we agree on. Now all you have to do is tell me you're a Sigourney Weaver fan and we can move in together."

Coby smiles.

"'I've indicated that I'm receptive to an offer,'" he says. "'I've cleared the month of June. And I am after all ... me.'"

"*Working Girl!*" Jonathan says.

Coby starts to light a cigarette, triumphantly.

"But Coby, I am going to be firm. Are you sure you want to sully the day, not to mention your beautiful lungs, with cigarette smoke? Nasty habit."

"You know what?" Coby says, "I am *not* sure I want to do that, thank you." He throws the cigarette onto the sidewalk and crushes it with his foot. Then, on second thought, he throws the whole new pack down and crushes it dramatically. "I'm not sure I like smoking at all. Though I sure could use a bite."

"Sure. Then you're free for breakfast? I promised a friend I would take a stranger to breakfast."

Coby mimes thinking.

"This could work," he says. "I can skip the gym."

Jonathan gives Coby's sleeve a friendly tug. They start walking together—but Coby remembers he has littered and runs back to retrieve the crushed cigarettes and toss them in a garbage can.

Jonathan watches, amused. Then, when Coby rejoins him, he claps Coby on the shoulder.

"I gather we have an issue with smoking?"

My Favorite Porn Star

I had sex with Vinny LoMaglio the other day—KJ and I did together. It was fun, though probably more so for me than for KJ, who did all the work. KJ was on suck detail. Vinnie likes a specific kind of blow job that requires a very circumscribed range of motion, degree of pressure, and pacing, let alone ancillary hand action—all of which can be difficult to coordinate and ultimately a little boring for the person doing the coordinating, except in the case of somebody like Vinny, who happens to be a porn star.

KJ has one of the most talented mouths on the planet. He thinks that hands are for amateurs, but he uses them with Vinny because Vinny likes it and he's hot: body by God and a big, friendly attitude. I got nipple detail. Vinny's needs there are as circumscribed as those of his cock, and though I am usually embarrassed for the kind of guy who gets off only on constant tit squeezing at this or that angle, somehow I didn't mind in this case, because it allowed me to cradle Vinny in my arms as KJ worked and to speak quietly into Vinny's ear what all top guys wanna hear about: bottoming out.

Vinny lives in my neighborhood. Last Sunday morning at the gym where Vinny, KJ, and I all work out, I had spotted Vinny bench pressing and I mentioned that fact to KJ when I called him afterward. "Come over and we'll sit on my stoop for a few minutes," I suggested. "He always walks by on his way home." I was still horny from the night before, when KJ and I had gone to a sex club. I had watched KJ suck off two or three really hot guys while I served as narrator/coach—meaning that while KJ worked I stood next to the suck-ees, felt up their pecs, lats, and delts, and periodically said things like "Yeahhhh." I told KJ in the cab on the way home that I could have used some cock myself, and he smiled exasperatedly,

"Then why didn't you drop that daddy-top thing you do," he said, "and get down on your knees and shove me out of the way? Have you ever thought about how much fun it would be to suck cock together?"

When KJ arrived that morning, we decided to get some coffee from a shop located between my house and the gym. As we were about to enter, there was Vinny coming up the sidewalk right on schedule, strutting amiably, open denim jacket barely covering his popped-out shelf of tank-topped pecs, striped stretch leggings straining to contain his snaking-to-one-side cock, looking massive though soft. I'd never seen any of Vinny's movies. He and KJ have hooked up a few times at the gym in a "secret" bathroom off a back stairway that I still can't find. To tell the truth, it took me a few weeks to finally figure out from KJ's spooge-laced descriptions exactly which "big, tattooed, muscled porn star on the workout floor" he was talking about—and once I knew, I never said hello to Vinny myself, because there's something about a gym that still, decades after high school, makes me shy.

KJ said hi, and there the three of us stood outside the coffee shop conversing genially about the movie Vinny's currently working on, which KJ had asked about. Vinny beamed and said, "It's goin' good. I'm gettin' a lotta great head." As he described (and partially mimed) a one-on-one scene he'd just shot—"I was holding this guy's skull like a melon, using his mouth like a fuck toy!"—I noticed that Vinny's cock had begun to bulge outward a bit more. Yet it was his large, intelligent-looking hands that kept my attention. How would it feel to have those clamping my head to his crotch? Through the coffee shop windows, we could see all these nice folks enjoying their after-church breakfasts, probably with no idea of what devotions we three faithful were cooking up. Finally KJ said something like, "So what are you up to, man?" Pause. "Well, I don't know," Vinny said. "Guess I'm headin' home." Another pause. Trying not to smile, though clearly knowing what all of us had already agreed to do next, KJ said, "You wanna ... fool around? My buddy lives just down the block." "Yeah," Vinny smiled. "Always up for a BJ."

Now I know you've never heard of Vinny LoMaglio. That's because I made up the name. Even though Vinny has sex for a living, I don't want to use his real name, since he has boyfriend—a well-known furniture designer, whom I met once at an art opening—and I don't know what kind of agreement they have about seeing other people. My agreement with KJ obviously does include the possibility of threesomes. I knew that the moment we got to my apartment—as I slipped into the bedroom to find the right music—KJ would go straight for Vinny's cock and start chowing, sperm hound that he is. And I felt a little silly when I rejoined them moments later and realized how completely nonessential music is (even DJ Cam's *Mad Blunted Jazz*) to a Sunday morning hook-up.

Vinny was spread out naked, on his back, propped up with pillows on the daybed, moaning. KJ was kneeling between his legs, throating him hungrily. Like in a movie comedy, I bumbled quickly out of my sneakers and sweatpants and hopped around to the side of the daybed. Perching next to Vinny, I put an arm around his shoulders. Somehow, until that point, I hadn't really noticed how incredibly tattooed he is—with dragons, angels, flowers, scimitars, a bar code, and a motto (in Latin) teeming over that naturally smooth musclescape. And it was only when KJ paused for a sec that I got my first close look at Vinny's cock, which is so beautifully shaped that I want to describe it with a word that straight men use when they talk about a sexy woman with a really fantastic body: stacked.

Vinny pulled my free arm up to his chest so I could work his nipples. Each time I let it wander over his bumpy-defined abs down to the pubic area, which he keeps shaved except for a neatly trimmed, 1 x 3-inch "mustache," he pulled it back up. It took KJ about eleven minutes to get Vinny's load out—time I spent not just doing the nipple thing and whispering secrets about my favorite muscle bottom boy, but figuring out whether there was any way to reposition the three of us gracefully so that I could get my tongue around

Vinny's cock or meaty nut sac, or into his pretty, shower-fresh butt. There wasn't. Suddenly, Vinny was pulling out and shooting his load onto his abs, while KJ's face hovered close.

KJ thinks that wasting loads is for amateurs, too. But Vinny wants his money shot.

The sight of a big cock gone soft after a blow job always turns me on. So when Vinny came back from cleaning up in the bathroom I was hoping I might get it—dangling so friendly!—in my face as KJ went to work on me. But Vinny pulled his gym stuff back on, chatting, and KJ and I stood up to act the good hosts. Good-byes at the door were warm. I suppose it shouldn't surprise me that Vinny is such a nice guy. After all, I've fucked around with enough porn stars since coming to New York, and they have all been princes: "Big Max," whose real name was Sam, the first really huge body-builder I ever had sex with (and a writer who did an article for me about being a sex object, when I edited a gay magazine); "Frank Vickers," whom I knew as Roger, whom I found in a straight sex club one summer night begging a straight couple to pee on him (I watched them pee on him, then got him to pee on me); "Bruno," a.k.a. Herman, who used to live a few blocks away from me and patronized the same dry cleaner; "Peter" a.k.a. Armand; "Eric" a.k.a. Craig. There were others. What impressed me about them all was this porn-specific quality of their stardom: a generosity of spirit that translated in nonsexual circumstances as, well, something really decent, like camaraderie.

"So, don't be a stranger in the gym, OK?" Vinny said to me as he left, winking. He kissed KJ.

Of course, since then I haven't seen him at the gym at all. And I am so ready to transcend my shyness and slap him on the back like an old friend, maybe even ask how things are going, in audible—no, booming!—tones, just like the straight guys do with each other. Maybe Vinny will even show me where that secret bathroom is. 'Cause now I'm fixated on having that cock in my mouth, and I kinda got the impression that he wants mine in his.

Easter Sunday, St. Francis Xavier

My grandfather's funeral took place on a cold January day in 1972. But it wasn't so cold as to require a coat, and that secretly delighted me, despite the sadness of the occasion. I was twenty-one and had come back from college for the day to my small, upstate New York hometown. Since I didn't own anything black I was wearing a suit I'd borrowed from a school friend: a black, Carnaby Street number so highly styled it could have been a costume for a Beatles movie—a long, Edwardian jacket with pinched waist, stand-up collar, and flared cuffs, plus bell-bottom pants, worn with a white turtleneck. I didn't want a coat to cover up all this drama, and sure enough, when I walked down the aisle of the hundred-year-old, white clapboard church of my childhood, St. Mary's and St. Andrew's, I could tell that people were noticing.

Is that Stephen—the one who used to be an altar boy?

Among the family members and friends in church that day were many of the people who had overseen my religious education: Father Gilbert, our beloved parish priest during the '50s, when I was a kid; Father Fitzpatrick, who had the same job during the '60s and was not as well liked; Sister Dorothy and Sister Mary Virginia, from our local order of nuns, the Daughters of Mary, who taught in our church's program of religious education; and my bachelor uncle John, who helped run the parish as a lay volunteer and was also my godfather. My mother had told me that I didn't necessarily need to wear black, but the funeral was too good an opportunity to borrow my friend's suit, which said everything about where I wanted to be in my life now that I had broken free of small town ties.

"Sad day," said Mrs. Rutledge afterwards, greeting me, with Mr.

Rutledge, on the steps of the church where I stood with my family.
The Rutledges were the parents of my high school girlfriend, Mary,
who was away at school.

"Stop by and see us, if you have time," said Mr. Rutledge. Then
he added dryly, "Looking sharp, Steve," which made me wonder if
he had figured out why my relationship with his daughter had
remained atypically chaste for seven years. I was out at school and
had told my family, but I still hadn't made much of an effort to let
old friends in on the news.

In the parking lot, my sister and I were getting into a limousine
that would take us to the cemetery, when we saw Father Gilbert.

"Good to see you, Stephen," he said, smiling.

"How are you, Father?" I said. "Thanks for coming."

Though long since reassigned to a parish in another county,
Father Gilbert had remained close to our family. People liked him
because he was funny, smart, and warm. He was also quite handsome, with flashing black eyes and dark, wavy hair. During our
childhood Father Gilbert had been tireless in helping the nuns
teach religious classes to those of us kids who attended public
school. And because he was a friend of the family Father Gilbert
took particular interest in my sister and me, frequently calling or
visiting our house on Sunday afternoon, to see if we had any
questions about that morning's Gospel or the sermon he had
preached.

I hadn't seen Father Gilbert in years. He had to be fifty, but he
still retained a youthful vitality.

"Attending mass regularly, I hope?" he asked.

"I don't know that the Church wants me, Father," I said. I
almost said "... people like me," but decided not to burden this old
friend with an angry comment about the Church's attitude toward
homosexuality.

He made a sad, amused face, as if I had made a joke in bad taste.

"Of course the Church wants you," he said. "It welcomes
everyone."

"We'll see," I said.

He blessed my sister and me, then said good-bye.

I had walked away from the Church six or seven years before that, in the mid-'60s, just after entering high school. A visiting priest I encountered in the confessional one day told me that because I had admitted to masturbating I needed special counseling.

"I do not," I said. "Besides, I don't think masturbation is really a sin."

The priest seemed stunned for a second.

"It most definitely is a sin and you need to talk to someone about it," he said.

"Yeah?" I said, jerking up from my knees. "I don't think so." I tore out of the confessional and never went back.

The breach had been coming for some time. It was fueled by new attitudes that were then sweeping through the church, which were best represented in our little town by the Daughters of Mary, who were open-hearted and open-minded—anything but the black-and-white terrorist-nuns of Catholic lore. They taught my friends and me catechism but they also lent us books on philosophy and theology. They encouraged us to ask questions about the historical Jesus and study the origins of Christian doctrine. They were big fans of Vatican II, the historic council on modernizing the church that began in Rome in 1962 and ended in 1965—which dates happened to bracket the onset of my puberty. When the nuns encouraged me to develop a personal, exclusive relationship with God I took them seriously, and I framed my relationship in accordance with an instinct that the body is good, that it is connected profoundly to the spirit, and that the connection can illuminate a path toward the divine. If there is anything in my life that I would call a blessing from above, it is this instinct. My prayers questioning the virtue of my sexual feelings—most of which I'd had for as long as I could remember—were answered by a heavenly Thumbs Up.

Soon after bolting out of the confessional I said good-bye to the

Easter Sunday, St. Francis Xavier

plaster statues of St. Mary's and St. Andrew's and stopped attending mass regularly. I embarked on my own course of spiritual study and practice that flowered in college and continues to this day. I know there are many Catholics who, despite their objections and anger, continue to work inside the Church on issues relating to the body, but years after my breach I am satisfied with my choice—even proud that it's in line with the kind of unmediated communion with the divine that early Church authorities attacked as heretical.

I had been as pious as any child could be in chrome-plated, split-level, postwar America. I learned my prayers, said them faithfully, was always up for a mass or Novena. Like most boys with Italian immigrant grandparents I had a crucifix on my bedroom wall, as well as a framed illustration entitled *Christ Our Pilot*, in which Jesus stood behind an athletic young sailor in a tight T-shirt at the wheel of a boat, during a storm—Our Lord steadying the sailor's shoulder with one hand and pointing the way with the other. My room also featured an architectural niche that I modeled for a while as a shrine, with cardboard-tube columns, a cigar box tabernacle, and two antique candlesticks I brought up from the dining room. I "said mass" there, complete with handmade wafers of pressed Wonder Bread, for a congregation consisting of my sister, my maiden Aunt Mary, and my grandmother, who sewed me up some vestments out of white dish towels. People said I might become a priest and this pleased me, since I liked the idea of doing good works and going around in a floor-length cassock.

My parents, though, weren't especially religious. During my childhood they'd made some effort to attend mass regularly with my sister and me, but by the mid-'60s family-style Sunday mass was a memory. My father often attended mass in the prison where he worked as a guard, which was fine with me since he had a temper I didn't understand and often provoked, and preparations for church excursions—any excursions!—regularly turned into horrible scenes. My mother, who read a lot and had her own questions about the earthly imperfections of the Church, grew into a classic, post-Catholic agnostic. She provided me with quite a beneficial example of thoughtful skepticism—she made sure, for example, that I knew what the discovery of the Dead Sea scrolls might mean for the future of Christian faith.

Nominally, it was the job of my Uncle John, as my godfather, to see to my spiritual development. Dear to all, overweight for most of his life, and devoted to collecting Waterford crystal, Uncle John was active in the parish. He counted the weekly collection, planned social events for the church hall, and organized trips for the parish priests. Unmarried but with a lucrative position as a bookkeeper for a nearby resort hotel, he lived with my grandfather and my Aunt Mary—his and my father's sister—in my grandfather's house, which boasted a document of papal blessing on the dining room wall. In his bedroom Uncle John had *his* crucifix and *his* illustration of Christ, plus a framed, black-and-white photograph of a handsome priest named Father Flynn, who had been a friend of the family during the '40s. Posed and lit as dramatically as a Hollywood star, Father Flynn always seemed quite glamorous to me—his having been "called to a parish in the city," as I was told, sounding like a secret, papal mission. In addition to the gifts Uncle John regularly showered on both my sister and me, he brought back rosaries, prayer books, and other devotional items especially for me from New York, where he sometimes went for dinner and a show, with Father Gilbert, Father Fitzpatrick, or a mild, blond, young priest who arrived in our parish in the '70s, after I had moved away, Father Healey.

Uncle John seems to have had a special attraction to priests, though I can't imagine this ever encompassed physical relations. I believe he was celibate all of his life, and my family didn't talk about why he never married (even when, at his wake, in 1990, an adorable young Puerto Rican employee of the hotel where he worked, whom none of us knew, showed up grieving). In the years before I stopped going to confession Uncle John would let me come with him on occasional Saturday afternoon drives to nearby towns, where he would go to confession in other parishes. Why my uncle did this, I didn't know. My parents were mute on the subject and I assumed it had something to do with the modern architecture and pretty landscaping of newer churches than ours. I was happy to ride along in his Buick convertible and have the opportunity to tell a strange priest about *my* heinous sins, which at the time included wishing my parents dead because they insisted I keep my hair shorter than my friends', wishing my sister dead because she interrupted my friends and I when we were secretly masturbating, and wishing certain of my schoolmates dead because they made fun of me on the playing field.

Between the ages of nine and twelve I was an altar boy. I was great at it and enjoyed it. I showed up for mass on time and knew my Latin perfectly. I outfitted myself sharply from the jumble of odd cassocks and surplices in the large closet where altar boy vestments were kept, and on the altar I was punctilious—hands crisply folded when not deftly lighting candles, pouring wine, or folding linens. I liked embodying the standard to which Father Fitzpatrick, who oversaw us, always said he wanted the other altar boys to rise.

There were fifteen or so of us. We all met on Saturdays in the sacristy, the room behind the altar, to practice Latin and receive our weekly assignments. I looked forward to being with this bunch of boys, because it was more diverse than the narrow stratum of classmates I normally hung around with. Composed of boys from different grades, even from different schools, our bunch was free of the habitual relationships that had gelled among my classmates, who had been together as an intact social entity more or less since the first grade—endlessly playing the same roles, choosing the same teams, courting the same girlfriends and boyfriends. I think this is why a certain preadolescent, homoerotic friskiness could bubble up so freely among us.

It bubbled up whenever Terry was around. Terry joined our group when I was eleven. Only eleven himself but as large as a teenager and almost as physically mature, Terry went to school in a neighboring district and was said to excel at all sports. This would have intimidated me except that Terry was friendly and outgoing, and treated me like an equal. I was not too young to have my first, deeply erotic thoughts about holding Terry's strong-looking body in my arms and spending the rest of my life with him. Terry's younger brother, Billy, was an altar boy too, and always willing to follow his lead—as all the altar boys were when Terry introduced us to several crotch-grabbing games that were clearly favorites of the brothers in private. We all used to run around and play these games in the sacristy on Saturdays, while waiting for Father Fitzpatrick to arrive for our meeting. If Father was late, as he often was, he found the lot of us rolling around in a heap at the bottom of our vestment closet, squealing with laughter, our boners melting instantly at the sound of his stern but tolerant voice.

"Gentlemen, shall we begin?"

If the priest ever found anything wrong with our horseplay he never mentioned it.

One day during a week when I was serving daily morning mass with Terry I arrived early and found him already in the sacristy, standing with his back to the door, his hands in front of him, doing something I couldn't see.

"Greco!" he said, startled but apparently relieved it was me.

"Hey, you're early," I said. We were the only people in the building. The caretaker, who unlocked the doors, had come and gone. Not even the regulars had begun to appear out front, in the pews. "What are you doing?"

"Fooling around," Terry said. He turned slightly so I could see that his hard cock was in his right hand. He was masturbating. His left hand held open the fly of his corduroy pants.

"Oh," I said.

"Had to," he said. "Ever wake up and just have to?"

"I guess," I said.

I had been masturbating for three years—either alone in my bedroom at night, or in secret places around the neighborhood with the kid next door, Bobby, who was younger than me and fairly immature. With Bobby, it was just play—as it was with my classmate Glenn, the first guy whose cock I ever touched, on a dare (in a school bathroom in the fourth grade—a moment that led to guilty tears that night after supper, and confession to my mother and forgiveness). I had not seen any other cocks except in locker rooms, where the presence of other guys prevented my acting on the curiosity that always struck me like a blow.

Glenn's, Bobby's, and those other cocks were like toys, though. Terry's was something else.

"Let's see it," Terry said, pointing with his chin. He knew I wanted to.

I took out my cock, and Terry and I stood facing each other. His stroke style was a little faster than mine, more mechanical. For a while I tried matching his pace but found it painful, so I went back to my own. We alternated between stroking and just holding our cocks, or letting them just stick out in the air hard, showing them to each other.

Terry's cock was larger than mine. It was also darker and curved to the right even when he wasn't touching it.

Is that what jerking off does to your cock? I thought.

Then Terry invited me to take hold of his, and as my palm wrapped around the shaft I knew the moment would not be historical for him, as it would for me. It was as though a current much stronger than electricity began to flow into my body from that little appendage—a shock caused not simply by touching something normally hidden or forbidden but by the unforeseen recognition that human flesh compounds power with inestimable preciousness.

I knew it wasn't Terry's soul I had touched, yet everything I had been taught about how the soul epitomizes a person's existence applied more to this human contact than any other I'd ever had. The moment was amplified, I admit, by the fact that Terry hadn't showered that day. Daily morning mass was at seven, and he had probably gotten up twenty minutes ago and biked furiously over to the church, as I had done. He was only eleven, but he smelled like a man. Smells like that would always guide me to sacred things.

"Now what?" I said.

"I know!" Terry walked over to the closet where the priests' vestments were kept and pulled open the double doors. There were mirrors on the inside of the doors and he positioned us so we could see both each other and our reflections.

"There," he said. "I figured this out in my mind during one of those boring meetings. Do you think Father Fitzpatrick does it like this?"

We knew we had only a few minutes to finish our business. We meant to shoot our loads into cupped hands but Terry's positioning was off and half his load flew onto the lace sleeve of a priest's surplice. The milky glob hung there opaque and glistening, like a moonstone. We laughed as we zipped up and used some paper towels to minimize the damage.

Father Fitzpatrick donned that very surplice ten minutes later. On the altar, Terry and I stifled giggles right through to the final benediction, when the sleeve waved as Father Fitzpatrick's hand made the sign of the cross.

I did wonder sometimes how Father Fitzpatrick "did it," or whether he did anything sexual at all. I had been taught that priests kept those feelings under the control of their vows, yet I had heard Father Fitzpatrick joke crudely about busty women and could easily imagine him, unlike the other priests I knew, married, with real kids and a real job, like selling cars. Years later my sister told me that Father Fitzpatrick once came into the restaurant where she was working as a waitress and, drunk, cornered her in a phone booth and started sputtering about what he would do if he weren't a priest. No priest ever came on to me—and I was never attracted to a priest *that way* until I met a sort of celebrity priest, also a friend of the family.

A year after jerking off with Terry—who soon moved out-of-state—I was asked to accompany the choir on the organ at weekly services at St. Jude's "Within the Walls," which had just been built inside the prison where both my father and my other uncle, Frank, worked. I was one of my school's star music students and Father Madsen, the prison's Catholic chaplain, was a frequent dinner guest at my Uncle Frank and Aunt Fanny's house, which was just across the street from mine. Father Madsen—young, tall, and charismatically streetwise—had built St. Jude's by way of a well-publicized national campaign he created involving trading stamps. Ladies from all around the country, instead of trading the stamps that came with their supermarket purchases for gold-toned, starburst wall clocks and matching sconces, sent them to Father Madsen, who, with the cooperation of the Trading Stamp Institute of America, turned them into cash and commissioned an in-the-round church of soaring, parabolic arches. The priest and the arches appeared in lots of national magazines that year.

Father Madsen—Mike—was always a hit at dinner. He showed up in polo shirts and sneakers, joked around over beers with my aunt and uncle. I loved the effortless way he could swing from solemn, leading us in grace before dinner, to jolly, telling stories about dim prison guards versus wily inmates, to sentimental, describing repentant inmates who had built the benches and the baptismal font at St. Jude's with their own hands. I loved the way he made us see that condemned souls nonetheless deserved our love. Father Madsen's tales of growing up as a scrappy kid in the big city and playing basketball in public playgrounds made me see that he was pretty regular guy and not likely to fall in love with me, but I liked being around him anyway.

The idea of my playing the organ at St. Jude's came up on a summer night when we were all sitting on my uncle and aunt's back porch, after a barbecue.

"I can't pay you anything, Steve, but I'm sure this will accrue to your account," Father Madsen laughed, pointing heavenward.

"That's OK," I said.

"Is it safe?" Aunt Fanny asked.

"Sure," he said. "It's a great bunch of men. They'll love him."

Father Madsen winked at me.

"You'll love these guys—honestly."

"Alright," I said.

My father often came home with dreadful tales of violent men behind bars, so I was a little afraid of what Father Madsen's inmates might be like, but I didn't say anything about this, because after years of hearing about these mythical men I wanted to see for myself what they looked like. I had heard hushed references to "prison sex" and though I didn't know exactly what this entailed I knew it was between men and that excited me.

Father Madsen called my parents and arrangements were made. It was a hot Saturday afternoon when my mother dropped me at the prison gate. I was in shorts and a T-shirt. A buddy of my father's showed me across the yard to the church. Inside, Father Madsen was conferring with the choral director, a music teacher from a nearby school. They greeted me and sat me down at the organ, then Father Madsen began the rehearsal by introducing me to the twelve men who were already sitting there in two pews, on my left.

"This is Steve, guys. He's going to be playing the organ. Let's make him feel welcome."

The men responded warmly, with shouts of "hi," "hey," and "how ya doin'?" I saw that they were under the surveillance of two guards who stood nearby, chatting with each other.

So many of them are handsome, I thought. *Such big, bright smiles. They seem nice enough.*

They were all probably less than ten years older than me, wearing short-sleeved prison shirts that revealed veiny, muscular arms, some of which were tattooed. The population of that prison at the time consisted mostly of young black and latino men from New York City. All had committed serious crimes, but any fears I might have had melted away instantly. Even at the age of twelve I found these men completely sexy in a way I couldn't define but knew was different from the attraction I felt for, say, certain members of my school's football team, who were mostly white and now seemed irremediably callow.

We rehearsed for an hour and a half. The church had no air conditioning. My pants were so short that I had to unstick the back of my legs periodically from the organ bench's plastic upholstery. I saw some of the men notice this; some kept trying to catch my eye. I could hardly stay focused on my musical scores because, well, I'd never seen so much brown muscle or felt so much masculine energy. A guy named Willie was the most appealing. An angelic-looking Puerto Rican just out of his teens, he had curly black hair, green eyes, chunky arms, and a terrific voice. There were several cues for a solo Willie sang that required special timing of my organ entrances. The choral director took us through them carefully, and after each one Willie smiled boyishly, in relief.

After the rehearsal, as Father Madsen conferred with the choral director and the guards continued chatting together, the men stood up and started joking with each other, waiting for their instructions to move. Willie wandered away from the group and came over to say hello to me—probably a minor infraction.

"You play real good," he said. "You study music?" The smiley way he enunciated the "pl" sound in "play" was music itself.

"Yes," I said, flushing. Talking this close gave me a chance to look at his hands, which were immense and square and tattooed with a cross between the thumb and forefinger. "Are you?"

"Am I studying music?" Willie asked.

Suddenly I understood what I was asking, given how different circumstances were for him and me.

"I mean, do you get to study ...," I said.

At that moment a guard came over for Willie.

"See you next week, Steve," Willie said, with a click from the side of his mouth. I was surprised he remembered my name.

Father Madsen strode over and tousled my hair.

"Good work, buddy," he said, "Same time, next Saturday?"

I nodded yes, eagerly. Then Father Madsen put his arm around my shoulder and lowered his voice.

"Only, no shorts next time, huh? It's the rules."

The priest winked. He didn't explain why I shouldn't wear shorts but at that moment I understood something—was blessed with something—that made everything in the seventh grade seem paltry. I got a huge erection which I then desperately tried to lose as I was escorted back to the gate, where my mother waited in the car.

That night I masturbated thinking about wearing shorts with Willie, having boners with him, masturbating together. Somehow it didn't matter to me that, as Father Madsen had mentioned, Willie had killed his best friend and was in prison for life.

Willie wasn't in the choir when I went back to St. Jude's the following week, and I only played at the church for a few more weeks. By then, Sunday mass was attracting so many guest dignitaries that a professional organist was deemed necessary.

I realize it's odd that I should credit the Church with helping nurture the happily sexual creature I have become—especially today, when so many stories of priestly pedophilia are coming to light. All I can say is that perhaps I fell through the cracks of coercion and repression. Or perhaps a fuller exploration of sex and the Church would reveal as many good stories as bad ones. I take heart in the reports of good relationships between priests and other men (even boys!) that I read in Boyd McDonald's *Straight to Hell* anthologies and elsewhere.

How far away my grandfather's funeral seems now! My aunts and uncles are all dead. So are Fathers Gilbert and Fitzpatrick, Sisters Dorothy and Mary Virginia. After visits to prehistoric caves in Basque country and the ancient ruins of the Bolivian altiplano I feel more in sync, in my gut, with sun worship than with the Roman rites. Still, I attend mass every now and then, as an opportunity to meditate on my relationship with the Church, which I suppose will endure in some form until I die. For the last few years I have been making it a point to attend Easter morning mass at St. Francis Xavier, on West 16th Street in New York—because Easter is my favorite Christian holiday and St. Francis draws a fairly liberal crowd, including a lot of openly gay people. I don't feel as much like an interloper at St. Francis as I do in other churches. Even though I don't assent to most of the tenets of Catholic faith or want to take part in the Eucharist, I feel as though I can sit there in good faith among people who have their own, individual formulas for assent and express a communal persuasion in Christianity.

Sometimes, however, in spite of my heresy, an episode of altar boy decorum will recur, as it did last Easter Sunday as I sat in a pew toward the back of St. Francis, waiting for mass to begin. I was obsessing over whether I smelled like sex.

It was a warm day and the church was packed. I was freshly showered and shaved, and had put on a blazer in an attempt to show respect for the occasion, which I had planned for weeks to take part in. I was there by myself—my boyfriend was away for the weekend, with his family. The lady and gentleman seated to my left, at the end of the pew, were both dressed in suits and looked like the kind of people who might have attended a sedate dinner-dance at a country club, the night before—or so I couldn't help thinking because four hours earlier, at seven o'clock, *I* had been playing in a sweaty, all-night sex club.

The club had been filled with hot, horny men, and after two hours there my body had been anointed with several applications of piss, cum, beer, sweat, lube, saliva, and poppers, which produced a bouquet I found intoxicating but inappropriate for Easter morning in church. I had forced myself to go home, clean up, and nap for a few hours, particularly regretting that I hadn't gotten a second chance to play with the adorably punkish, pungent-smelling stranger in a tank top and Keds who arrived around six and, on his way inside, spent several minutes piggishly forcing his tongue down my throat.

It was heaven. The guy was short and compact, shaped like a gymnast, with smooth, untanned skin. He promised to come back after a look around, but we never found each other. I didn't get his name. I could swear the guy's saliva and sweat lingered in my nostrils.

Could that smell have survived a shower? I wondered as I sat watching final preparations on the altar, also aware of the scent of my geranium soap, the herbal shampoo that the young woman with long, curly hair in front of me had used, and whatever makes well-worn wooden pews smell the same in every church in the world.

All seats were taken. The organ was playing Bach. The aisles near me had become choked with standees.

I'll bet that club stays open all day, I thought. *Maybe that guy is still there.*

But I didn't have to think long about going back after mass. I was craning to the left to see how many standees were jammed into the aisle at the end of my pew when I saw him—the guy from the club, standing not five feet away, dressed in the same tank top and a pair of jeans.

Jesus, he's come straight from the club, I thought. *Good for him—I guess.*

The guy looked out of it—propped against a stone pillar, eyes narrowed to slits, swaying occasionally. But there was something angelic about him, innocent—the light from a blue and red stained glass window falling onto his bare, white shoulders, bathing his body in celestial radiance.

The smell was not lingering in my nostrils. It was coming from the man himself, and my pew-mates noticed this, too. The lady in the suit whispered something to the man. He looked over at my friend and smirked, then whispered something back. The two huddled a little closer together.

In that moment they became slightly less Christian in my eyes. I waved toward the pillar.

"Hey," I said in a hush that I hoped would be loud enough to carry.

My friend looked like he was in some kind of trance, though it could have been prayer. He was having a hard time standing. I felt oddly selfconscious about relishing the contractions of his deltoids and lats as I watched him try to brace himself with one arm.

I caught the eye of someone next to him and indicated I was trying to get his attention.

When he looked over I waved again.

"You made it! I'm so relieved," I said in a church-hush. "Come sit—I've done my best to save your seat."

At first he didn't recognize me. Then he understood.

I stood and asked the lady, who was sitting next to me, to excuse our new arrival. There was probably no room for everyone in the pew, but I was determined to squeeze my friend in close to me.

The lady and gentlemen both stood up as he shuffled past them in a parody of grace. The gentleman actually stepped out of the pew to admit my friend.

"Hey, funny meeting you here," the guy said, as he slumped next to me. "What happened to you?"

He still seemed a bit unsteady, so I put my arm around his shoulders. His body was tighter and harder than I remembered. He didn't really smell that bad. It was just a very masculine funk.

"I left to take a shower," I whispered. "I had to come here. It's so great to see you here."

He grinned beatifically.

"I had to come, too. I always do," he said dreamily. "Good for the soul. I think about my soul even when I'm fucked up. *Especially* when I'm fucked up—right?"

The suits decided to leave the pew, which was tight. Another person took their place.

My friend looked upward and bumped his shoulder gently into my chest.

"*Love* the windows. By the way, what are you doing afterward?"

I wasn't doing anything.

"We can go to my place and get holy," I said.

My friend giggled.

The nuns taught us that any of us might be saints. My cock stiffened as the organ processional cranked up, horn and trumpet pipes blaring, and mass began.

The Sperm Engine

I don't fetishize cum, but I do take my responsibilities for load production seriously. I like to have enough for all the guys who wanna feed on it, and since I am a real blow job addict, that means a lot of guys. I also want my load to taste good and have a nice consistency. So I eat well, work out, get plenty of rest, and take lots of vitamins. If somebody told me that taking castor oil would improve my cum production, I'd be taking castor oil every day.

Same goes for load manipulation. I like to be able to put on a good show, even if only for myself, whenever I shoot somewhere other than down a throat or into a rubber. That requires controlled aim and thrust, so I practice a lot. Seeing cum is very special to me, a pleasure that has intensified as I have gotten older. When I masturbate, alone or with one of the sensitive JO freaks I know, I get to experience my load as a very particular substance or event, rather than a blind injection into a hidden place that, no matter how well I feel it, I cannot really know. Recently I met a guy I call "the best cocksucker on the planet." His technique is flawless—from breath control to popper bottle manipulation—and though there's nothing like depositing a cumload deep in his esophagus at the end of a session of quiet but intense massage of my cock by his pharyngeal muscles, I love that he knows how we both sometimes want to watch as my sperm emerges from the inner world into the outer one.

Which often means sperming up his face. I love having him sit on the floor, nestled between my legs as I recline in my favorite armchair. There's a point when he slides up off the shaft and starts making love to the underside of my cock head like it was the neck of a new boyfriend. I sit up a bit then and bow over him protectively. "That's right, show me my load," I whisper, as he lovingly turns a blow job into a scum show.

His name is John. When I say that he's the best cocksucker on the planet, I am taking into account that I say the same thing about two other guys I see regularly, one of whom is my boyfriend. The other guys worship cock; John worships cum. He works from a very deep love of the substance that allows him, like an opera star, to coordinate all the consequences of talent into a performance that goes beyond any rational accounting. When John has me in his mouth, building my third or fourth orgasm, his cheek resting on my thigh, breathing contentedly through his nose, he positively whimpers when I narrate the progress of my cum toward his tongue.

Actually, I don't like the word *cum*. It sounds too *Penthouse* to me, too cheesily heterosexual in its origins. But since the word clearly has become useful in gay male erotic writing, I don't avoid it entirely. I just try to use it compounded with other words, to give it some spin: *cum addict*, *cum freak*, *cum dump*. Forget *come*. As a verb, it reads weakly; as a noun, it's a disaster. I like *sperm* for the substance itself, though obviously I know the difference between sperm and semen; and I like *load* for the substance in action, the idea of semen as a bi-product of recreation. *Seed* is OK, though I wonder if its resonance can be adequately felt by those who have never taken the Bible literally. I love to use *sperm* as a verb, both transitive and intransitive; I also like the verbs *dump*, *lose*, *waste*, *produce*, *trade*, *leak*, and *feed* in connection with sperm. In fact, I like all talk about eating and feeding on sperm: It sounds so sacrilegious, yet of course it describes only a healthy, gratifying practice that should probably be taught in elementary school. *Creamy* and *thick* and *sweet* and *salty* are OK adjectives to describe sperm, though as in all written and verbal expression, it's best to avoid clichés. If you're lucky enough to be free of the kind of sexual ick that can lock your imagination into clichés, you might agree that *chunky* and *fragrant* and *weighty* are interesting for describing certain kinds of loads.

Some cum words find their power in the smart side of adolescence—the anti-status-quo, bad-boy side. Some, of course, reflect the dumb side of adolescence. Like *wad*, which I've always thought silly. Or *jizz*, ditto. (Though, inexplicably, *jizzwad* is fine, as is either *jizz* or *wad* used to describe something spermy other than sperm, as in, "Waiter, what's up with this jizz on my string beans?") As a teenager, I was weirded out by guys who were too focused on sperm. Back then, I was repelled by all that talk about producing it and cleaning it up, eating it and freezing it, defrosting it and putting it in omelettes and such. It was AIDS, I guess, that pushed sperm mechanics beyond adolescent fixation into the realm of adult manners, as the sexual negotiation surrounding the once demonized stuff gelled into etiquette.

"I'll take your first load before people get here," John once said to me, before a group scene I had set up for him at my house, when I asked how he wanted to cum. "Then I'll drain everyone else's load, one at a time. Repeats welcome, of course. I'll cum once at the end by jerking myself off as I take my last load, which should be yours again. And I'd like your cock to be coated with at least one other load at that point, so if you could get someone to jerk off on you ...."

These days, I often find myself thinking about my body and its busy sexual life in terms of scum husbandry, the biggest result of which is that after years of bonering out power-blast after power-blast, I really love cumming soft. I'm grinning as I write this too, because I'm kinda pleased with myself for learning how to pee a rope of warm cum out of my big, floppy soft-on. Heightening the sheer body-enveloping pleasure of this practice is a nice transgressive feeling, since my ability to cum soft is both the result and the cause of my rethinking the function of the orgasm and the purpose of pleasure—a process I first began during day-long group sex scenes in which no one could stay hard because of drugs, yet everyone kept ... trying.

I don't do drugs anymore, but I brought a lot of sexual understanding away from those scenes. The reason I continue to pursue the soft orgasm is that it's more like the sex I want than any sex

I've ever had. It feels like truly making love—conjuring love out of nothing—as opposed to that pounding, invasive thing that feels to me more like work in sexual form.

My number-one imperative now is this: play with sperm. Sperm play is where we start getting into divine territory—which is, for me, the goal of sex. A vision of John's has burned its way into my mind: men walking around invisibly, except for sacs of semen floating a yard above the pavement. It sounds funny, but there's something in this vision surprisingly consistent with the orthodox understanding of men's bodies as precious reserves of fuel for the ancient engine of human reproduction. Only I see this engine as giving more to our species than plentiful offspring. As a big scum cow, I can tell you that dumping load after load, day after day, somehow makes me the beneficiary of an evolutionary system designed to protect men whose sperm is obviously in demand. Nature seems to bless champion scum-bringers with health and youthfulness, and if they happen to write books, arrange flowers, mentor the young, and enrich life in other ways as well as reproduce it, well, then let the textbooks be revised.

Sometimes when I am sperming up John's lips, I find myself deeply moved. It's more than affection, more than respect. I think it's the feeling that we are close to life's font. It's a holy feeling that I think was often there for me during sex but lost among coarser, porno-consistent sentiments that gay pop culture tells us we're supposed to feel. John believes in this holy/sexy thing as much as I do—and I sense that we're right on the edge of some new, freaky-good, pseudo-religious scum-prayer territory that could really get us beyond ...

On second thought, I do fetishize cum.

A former senior editor of *Interview* magazine and *The Advocate*, Stephen Greco has contributed to *Afterwords: Real Sex from Gay Men's Erotic Diaries*, *The Penguin Book of Gay Short Stories*, *Obsessed: A Flesh and the Word Collection of Gay Erotic Memoirs*, and, anonymously, to Boyd McDonald's *Straight to Hell* series. Currently editor-at-large of the international style magazine *Trace*, Greco lives in New York.